A Virtuous Ruby

A Virtuous Ruby

Piper Huguley

SAMHAIN PUBLISHING

Samhain Publishing, Ltd.
11821 Mason Montgomery Road, 4B
Cincinnati, OH 45249
www.samhainpublishing.com

Editing by Latoya Smith
Cover by Kanaxa

First Samhain Publishing, Ltd. electronic publication: July 2015
First Samhain Publishing, Ltd. print publication: July 2015

Dedication

Everything came together in my life, work and writing when I realized that I had to tell my Great Migration stories. After all, I had made that promise to my great aunts so long ago and at the time, I struggled to tell them how much I admired their sacrifices.

I dedicate this story to those Great Migrators in my life: my mother-in-law, grandmother and great aunts who numbered among the six million in the United States who knew there had to be a better way of life. Thank you, thank you so very, very much.

Acknowledgements

I thank and appreciate all of those critique groups who had a hand in shaping Ruby, especially Julie Hilton Steele and Elaine Manders, who both took a great leap of faith in believing in this story. I thank you so much for your belief in this most unusual story. The comments that you made, for good and bad, helped to shape me for the better.

Thomas Hardy's novel, *Tess of the D'Urbervilles* is Ruby's foremother in that they were both young women who had great strength, courage and fortitude, but were wronged. I always felt Tess deserved a happy ending and I endeavor to give her one by way of my Ruby. For you and all of the young woman who have been attacked, you all deserve a happy ever after.

Chapter One

1915-Winslow, Georgia

"You got to keep things quiet, Ruby, or they be lynching you next."

Ruby Bledsoe ignored her younger sister, Margaret, and picked up her pink hat as she readied to leave the house for the first time in a year. Margaret dubbed Mags—much browner than she with a nice maple color—didn't need to wear a hat to protect her skin. She thinned her lips as she adjusted the hat on her head. Brown Mags could choose. Pale Ruby had no choice.

"You can't keep stirring up trouble," Mags admonished her.

Her envy vanished. Mags always followed the rules, just like their mother. *I'm eighteen. And light skinned. I can do what I want.*

But all of that wasn't true because the outside loomed—large, hot and unfriendly.

Staring out through the window onto the porch and the red-dirt road beyond, she clamped down on the fear threatening to consume her. It went down hard, like a dried-out biscuit. The outside. Where the attack happened. Fifteen months ago.

Be quiet about the lynchings.

She'd stayed inside so long, old Paul Winslow probably thought he had succeeded.

But he hadn't. Not today.

She turned on her high-heeled boot toward the corner of the room where all of her sisters slept and her gaze rested lovingly on the cradle where the result of the attack napped.

Solomon.

For him, she must speak. She would not be quiet. She would leave the house, starting now. Ruby stepped out onto the porch, trying to feel brave, but felt the contents of her breakfast stirring in her stomach instead.

"Coming, Mags?" Ruby held the screen door open. Two years younger, Mags was the one of her four sisters who would not deny her. Besides, everyone else in the house told her no. Good old Mags came through the door, just for her.

"What about Solomon?" Mags asked.

She adjusted her large, wide-brimmed hat in response to her sister's question. The pink in the hat matched the embroidered roses on the white shirtwaist and matching skirt she wore. Wearing white would help her look respectable. The wide brim would protect her too pale skin from the June heat.

"He's the reason I have to do this. The company store is first." A pain in her heart surged with a fierce love for her child. *Thank you, God.* Solomon was the only light in her life. And nothing would happen to him. "I have to make things better for him. Especially since Uncle Arlo…" She shook away the horrible picture. The lynching. She had seen things about his mutilated body no niece should ever see.

"Just so long as you don't end up like him." Mags kept up a nervous chatter with another reprimand as they strolled along the country road into town. Ruby hated the town because Paul Winslow had not cared to make it beautiful. Town was a bunch of knocked together, thoughtless buildings: the square red brick cotton mill, the tan pinewood general store, a gray clapboard hotel and a drinking establishment, painted a dingy brown with red dust at the fringes of everything. Silence was the order of the day, since they reached the edge of Winslow just before lunchtime.

She stepped up to the wooden sidewalk and kept on walking and talking. "Is it right Paul Winslow can hire more Negroes and pay them less 'cause of some old war in Europe? What about Travis? He can make more money after we help the men protest Paul Winslow for more money. Then you can get married sooner."

"That's why I come with you." Mags's maple skin could show a red blush in its dusky undertone and did.

"Came. Speak proper, like Miss Mary." She directed her younger sister.

"Now you see why we got to say something. Time for things to change. Specially for Uncle Arlo." She had to make things right. His blood was on her hands.

Her nose wrinkled as they got closer. She hated the smell of town, especially the stink of the mill. Linseed, Uncle Arlo had told her. It burned on the wheels of the machine and filled the air with a sharp tang. More like burned pecans. In the wintertime whenever her family wanted a snack, they would toast pecans and sometimes, the edges turned black. The smell from the mill was stronger than ever now.

The scream of a whistle split the air.

They stopped.

Something was wrong. The emergency whistle sounded from the mill.

She arranged her own features into calm, not reflecting the fear on her sister's face. People spilled out of the small buildings and stood around on the wooden sidewalks. No one seemed to know what to do. With a quick glance, she could see Dr. Morgan, the white doctor, was not in his office next to the general store.

"I'm going to go to see if I can help." She started toward the mill.

"What can you do? You just help with baby birthing." Mags shouted after her.

"I've seen blood before." She put more certainty in her voice than was in her heart as she yelled over her shoulder. "I can help. You stay here."

No need to reinforce the warning with Mags. She did not like blood and she never moved.

The whistle of the afternoon train sounded as Ruby rushed on to the mill. Normally, the arrival of the train was something to note in little Winslow, but the screams of a man coming from the edges of the mill yard, distracted her. Four men, including Mags's suitor Travis, carried out another Negro man. Jacob. Blood trickled from his hand. *Thank God, Travis wasn't the injured one.*

"What happened?" She asked him.

Travis showed no surprise at her question. Apparently a midwife, even a disgraced one, was better than nothing. Even one who hadn't left her house in a long time. They were clearly going to try to take this man to Dr. Morgan, but it didn't mean he would treat him.

"Hand got caught in the machine."

She swallowed. The flesh had been cut deeply across his palm, but luckily, all of his fingers were there. Moving. Underneath his dark brown skin, the man had colored to an unhealthy gray. "Set him down on the sidewalk."

The men did as she directed and almost immediately, Jacob's co-workers stepped away from him in fright. "No Dr. Morgan?" He managed to grit out in pain.

"He's not there. You'll have to do with me, I'm afraid." She tried to ignore the alarm on his face. Jacob had a family of four young girls and a baby boy. She struggled to keep her hands steady. She prayed for guidance.

Inhaling the familiar metal-rich tang of blood, Ruby touched the stripped-apart flesh. "Does anyone have a clean cloth?"

The men stared. They had just come from the machines and they were dirty. One by one, they peeled away. All of the onlookers who had been there moments before had also vanished. "I go find something, Ruby," Travis said, and he left Jacob to her, rushing off.

No time to lose. Looking quickly from side to side, she reached up under her white dress and, with a sharp quick tug, pulled at her slip and ripped way some of the white cotton. Tearing the slip into strips, she startled.

A man had pushed her to the side and began to probe at Jacob's hand.

"What are you doing?" An unfamiliar deep male voice spoke sharply to her and with the push to the side, red scuffs marred her best high-topped shoes.

Back before her shame, she would have been completely humiliated in front of a strange man. Now, pushed aside, she stopped. The man had large, beautiful grey eyes edged with long, black fringe lashes, which would have looked female if his cream-colored features were not so chiseled.

"I'm trying to fix his hand."

She fixed him with a hard glance, and spoke again, demanding, "Who are you?"

His angular, handsome face reflected scorn and disapproval.

Then, she immediately regretted her quick words.

Was this man white or a Negro?

His color sure gave her pause. Even now, as she took her glance away from his disapproving gaze and to his lips, there was a hint of fullness to them.

She blew out a sigh of relief. She had not been wrong. He was a Negro, just as light as her. They were the same.

"Don't use those dirty bandages on his hand. What's wrong with you?" The man sat next to Jacob and probed Jacob's hand with sure fingers. Jacob calmed. Her pride prickled and she clenched her teeth at the stranger yelling at her now. Everyone was after her today.

"And who are you?" Ruby repeated the question. Her mother always told her she was too forward, but she couldn't help it.

"I'm a doctor."

"Praise God," Jacob said with clear relief. "See Ruby. This man here a doctor. He can fix me up good."

"How do we know he's a doctor?" Ruby pursed her lips together and applied pressure to keep them shut.

"Fetch my bag over there on the train platform, there are sanitary bandages in it. Hurry."

Who was he to tell her what to do? Directing her! Ruby tossed him a quick look of distain, but she raced back on fast feet. Jacob's situation required speed, even if this strange man treated him. When he got the bag, as if he were a magic man, he began to take out bandages and other things from it.

He handed her a needle and a spool of thread. "Please thread this. Try not to get it dirty."

The nerve! She knew how to thread a needle! Well, enough she supposed. Sometimes after a delivery, a woman needed to be sewn up some, but sewing wasn't her strong point. Did this man know about her poor sewing skills just by looking at her? Maybe he did, just as she knew his secret by looking at him.

Jacob's voice was too polite even as he enthused. No, he didn't suspect the man was as much Negro as them. "Wait 'til May hear about this. God was sure looking out. I got some real doctoring."

"I'm glad for you." Ruby handed the threaded needle to the doctor. "This sewing up part can't be no fun now. Calm down, Jacob."

"It's all right. Long as my hand can get fixed."

"It will take some time." The doctor splashed some smelly stuff on the gash. Jacob jumped but the doctor held him firm. He applied neat stitches to the gash in Jacob's hand, which had stopped bleeding, "But it will be as good as new in a few weeks time. You will need to keep it clean so infection does not set in."

"Infection?" Ruby asked.

What did I just say? She knew what infection was. This stranger moved her and made her act like she knew nothing.

The handsome stranger stared at her as if she had taken off her slip right there in the middle of the street. "Yes. Infection can be worse. Please be still, Mr. Jacob."

That confirmed it. A white man would not have addressed Jacob so respectfully.

Now she'd talk to him any way she liked. Still, she continued watching in fascination to see the competent way the man sewed up Jacob's wound and bandaged it with the clean bandages from his bag. And all Ruby had was a ripped-up slip.

No loss. A torn slip was an easy fix for Em, one of her sisters who sewed the best.

With the proper bandages, the metal tang of blood cleared from the air and the mill stench reasserted itself again. Jacob struggled to right himself, but stood up, holding his bandaged hand in the other. "Take it easy, Jacob." Ruby patted his good arm.

The man waved off her concern and her eyes smarted at his bravery. He had to go back to work. No time off for his injury. It just wasn't fair.

Jacob said in a shaky voice, "I don't have much to pay you, Doctor, but thank you kindly."

"You're welcome. Try to keep it clean. The dressings have to be changed in two days time." He wiped his glasses with the edge of a clean bandage. He was all business wasn't he?

"He heard you the first time. Jacob works here at the mill." Ruby inserted herself into the conversation. "I'll come back here in two days time at lunch. I can change your bandage for you."

His color was a bit better as they watched him go back to the mill. The doctor repacked his medical bag and picked up a valise from the train platform before making his way back to her. "Thank you for your help, Miss. Could you kindly direct me to a hotel?" His voice was deep and brusque.

"The only hotel is the Bouganse. It's on the left side of the street, right over there." Ruby pointed to a grey clapboard building down the street, the tallest building, three stories high. "But, I…"

"Thank you." He tipped his bowler and carried his bags, making his way to the hotel. Where did the doctor think he was going? Did he know Negroes couldn't stay at the Bouganse?

She guessed not. He strutted down the street with a defiant, proud carriage. He was being white. What a fool he was. Did he know passing could get him lynched? It would be mighty sad to see a handsome stranger be lynched, no matter how rude he was, pushing her to the side and putting scuff marks on her shoes. No more. For Solomon's sake. She would save him.

Ruby's short legs had a harder time keeping up with the handsome man. He had to be almost a foot taller than her, but she caught up with him. Breathless, head lowered and body slumped, she was now in proper posture to speak to a white man first and not be seen as a prostitute. Be lower than him, willing to step into the mud and scattered horse offal. *Great. More marks on her shoes.*

What a foolish man. Even if he were nice to look at. She would do her good deed today and be on her merry way to remind the workers about her organizing meeting. Ruby kept her eyes downcast as she approached him.

"Sir, how you doing this fine day?" She addressed him to keep up his charade, since he insisted on it.

"Yes, Miss?"

Ruby kept her head down, even though she wanted to look up. She had never been addressed that way and it was very startling. "Good. Sir, I wondered if you knew this hotel house establishment is not one of the best places in town to stay."

"It isn't? But they told me…" Ruby did glance up at him then, and those gray eyes were on her. The beauty and clarity of them made her heart skip a beat. "This was the place to come if you wanted to stay in Winslow and not leave it."

"There are other places." Ruby kept her voice particularly low and stared down at his shiny black shoes. "This one for whites only. Sir."

What if she were wrong?

He looked Negro—to her.

But then, his shoes and clothes were almost too nice.

She could be wrong.

The June heat intensified in the form of sweat under her armpits and began to soak through the white dress. If he were white, he would be fully justified to beat her up, right here or worse. And she had already endured worse.

The stranger had hesitated too long. No, she wasn't wrong. Ruby's heartbeat slowed and she relaxed.

"Where can I stay then?"

"Down the road, about three miles, past the end of the big house, turn down the road and go another mile east. The Bledsoe farm. You would be more comfortable there."

"This hotel is for whites." His voice was gravelly and low, but insistent. Slight alarm traced across his chiseled features as well.

Ruby's pink hat bobbed up and down.

"I see. Thank you for letting me know." He was about to turn away but stopped and regarded her. "My name is Adam Morson."

"What will you do now, sir?" She addressed him to keep up the charade, just in case anyone was watching. His uncertainty showed and she wished she could remove it.

"I'll go where I'm wanted."

"It's down the road about three miles. To the right. A nice place. You'll be comfortable there." She pointed in the direction she and Mags had come from.

"Okay then, Miss…"

"Ruby. Thank you. We'll see you soon, Mr. Adam."

"Dr. Morson."

Ruby's gaze went upward to see the sight for herself, once again. Male beauty, foolishness and smarts all in one body. And a doctor. She had never seen a Negro doctor before in all of her life.

"I see. Is the Bledsoe farm anywhere near the Winslow house?" He pushed his glasses up on his nose. The heat was getting to him, and the warmth spread in her belly a little that even a Negro doctor had to endure the heat. Just like her.

"It's the big house you'd pass on the way to the farm. Our farm."

The sharp angle of his jaw intensified. "Well, it's providential then. I had to go there anyway."

"You know the Winslows, Doctor?" Ruby knew her prodding of this stranger was rude, but she had never met someone who was the same as she, and she wanted to know all she could about him.

"Let's just say we have a long standing relationship." Gray eyes faced the distance as he spoke.

What did this Negro have to do with the most prominent family in town? Did he know David? Despite the June heat, she shivered.

"I thank you, Miss Bledsoe."

She appreciated the view as he retreated down the road, carrying his bags as if they were nothing. How did he move like that? The human anatomy was a wondrous thing, especially in this doctor man. She sure could not breathe at the sight of him. Amazing.

Mags came and stood next to her. "Who's he?"

She answered her sister and Mags shook her head. "Why would he risk doing such a thing?" The lunch whistle at the mill sounded in the distance. Good. They weren't too late to tell the men about the next organizing meeting.

"He wanted to go to a clean place where he could stay. It's what anyone wants." She had passed a few times. Just to see what it was like on the other side. And she had learned her lesson not to do it again, sure enough. "It's not what we all get, though." Ruby marveled at the beautiful foolish man. A chill went up her arms thinking about his eyes. Why did they haunt her?

"Let's go." Ruby shoved the sleeves of her dress up on her arms. There was enough work to do without having to save the doctor's precious hide. She turned to go to the company store, so the clerk could give word about her next organizing meeting. She wouldn't risk getting too close to the mill. What if Paul Winslow saw her? Fear knotted again in her belly, but she squashed it down like a chigger bug.

God had made it the work of her life to save Negro men, and she had to keep on doing her work—no matter what the cost.

Chapter Two

Adam ambled down the dirt road, but he refrained from drawing out his colloid collar in reaction to the heat. He coughed from the iron-tinged red dust kicking up at his feet and landing on his pants' legs as he continued on. Would he run into the Pink Hat lady again? Ruby. It had been a long time since he had been intrigued with the mystery of a woman—a very long time since he allowed himself to be intrigued. Dr. Adam Morson had no time for women. He wanted to be sure—no he made sure, he was dedicated to his studies.

The white woman who had fallen and twisted her ankle last month did not see color when he approached her. She needed medical attention and he gave it to her. The same thing had just happened to Jacob. Adam's color and the confusion he always caused ceased to matter. It was a good feeling, just to be a human being.

But now what he wanted was his father's respect. And to belong.

All of those nights he had stayed up late. All of the studying, and being the virtuous and best student. No courtships. No friends. How would his father regard him when he saw him for the first time? Would he be proud? He must be, because Paul Winslow had asked him to come. It was not a request, but a directive in the form of a telegram on his graduation day. *Come to Winslow. I have a few ideas about your future.* His heartbeat had raced, the first joy that stirred in him for so long. He was wanted somewhere in the world. The chance to meet his father was worth postponing his other offers to get to know Paul Winslow. He had never met his own father before.

Now, he was here in this rough little town, to learn what his father had in mind. He wished he had spoken to Ruby better, but they had been in a medical emergency. Maybe he would have a chance to apologize and thank her. He hoped so. And he had not been away from being Negro for so long that he didn't understand what she had done, in Pocahontas-like fashion. Lynchings, chain gangs and other ways to torture Negro men existed when he was growing up in Tennessee.

And she had saved him.

A shiver went through him. He had moved in the white world for so long, he had erased from his mind what was at stake for a Negro man in the south. And Ruby, this young woman, younger than his twenty-five years, risked herself to stop him from making a grave mistake. A small woman, much slighter of stature than he, only about five feet to his six feet, but in her defense of him, she loomed tall and proud. And certainly older than her young years.

He'd better keep an eye out for the house. But Ruby's comforting figure, draped in a very simple but tasteful white dress, rose before him again, and stirred him in a pleasant, yet unfamiliar way. She was trim with just enough roundness in the front and in the back. Roundness? He was a doctor, for goodness sake. What had provoked such a thought? Seeing Ruby again?

There it was. A large white clapboard house loomed up on his right and he turned down the pathway leading to it. The design was simple but large and open with a huge wraparound porch in the front. The house appeared to befit the rich mill owner of a small town like Winslow. Paul Winslow lived very well.

He clenched and unclenched his sweaty palms as he continued down the long walk to the house. Why was there never suffering for the rich? Couldn't Paul Winslow have suffered somehow in his life as his mother did in having him, dying young as she did? Why did the Mattie Morsons of the world have to pay?

No time for resentment. Whenever he thought of his mother in this way, he lost his logical center and he couldn't afford to lose himself in emotion. Adam shook his head, unclenched his teeth, and pulled out his handkerchief. He wiped his hands and the sweat pooling his forehead. Even in this heat, the Winslow home was surrounded by beautifully manicured shrubbery. Who kept up all of this? Certainly not Paul Winslow himself. And he probably never gave a thought for who did. This man had not suffered, from all appearances of his home. Adam shook his hands to release the tension in them. Calm down. If his father had suffered financially, Adam would not have been able to attain his education. He wouldn't be a doctor, worthy of earning the respect of a rich man.

Adam went to the front door, raised his hand and gave it three rapid knocks. A surge of regret swelled in his chest. Was he going too far? Given Ruby's cautions about the hotel—perhaps he should have gone around the back. Goodness, he had been in the white world for so long, he had forgotten how to be Negro.

There was a stirring inside. Too late. He straightened out the lapels of his suit and waited.

An older white lady with grey hair opened the door. "Yes?"

He could tell instantly from her manner and slight smile she believed him to be white. If she thought him Negro, she would not be smiling at him at her front door. Dreading the shift in her manner that would surely come once he revealed himself, he mused. Should he continue to play what he used to call, "the game?" Just pretend, for as long as he could, what it was like to be a white man? As he had all through med school?

He cleared his throat and readied himself. "I'm here to see Paul Winslow. I'm Adam Morson."

And there it was. The woman turned pale, and she nearly backed away, almost as if she believed him to have a dreaded disease. The doctor in him wanted to offer her a tonic—something to brace her up.

"I see. I am Mrs. Mary Winslow. Come in."

Poor lady. It wasn't everyday a woman was faced with the results of her husband's youthful indiscretions with a household maid. "Thank you." He followed the motion of her arm into the house. Then, Mrs. Winslow gestured to a maid as a queen might and told her to retrieve her master, fixing her royal, frozen stare upon him again.

The house had a grand foyer, and there was a lemony scent in the air. And it was pleasingly cool inside on this hot June day. He followed her back toward the kitchen, but on his way he could see he nearly passed the company parlor. There. He belonged there. Adam stopped his tread and went in. Sitting down on a chair in the parlor before Mrs. Winslow invited him to was probably rude, but Adam was the son of the man of this house. Recalling the ramrod-straight pride of Ruby, he sat up a little straighter.

A rotund man with thinning brown hair dressed in a gray suit made his way toward Adam. Mrs. Winslow stood behind him.

He stood to meet the man. Paul Winslow. His father.

"There he is," Mrs. Winslow said. Adam guessed she had left off the words "in my front parlor." But the affront was just the same. Adam had been through those insults enough times to know when he was not welcome or wanted. Still, her tone stung. So hard to get adjusted to the old way again.

"Well, Dr. Morson." Paul Winslow situated himself on an overlarge stuffed chair opposite Adam's smaller chair, not coming close enough to touch the flesh of his first-born son. Mrs. Winslow sat on a small settee in the corner, clearly wanting to observe all of the proceedings. "Welcome. Welcome indeed."

"Thank you." Not even a handshake. He sat back down, thinking it was good to sit or he would be reeling at this rejection of his humanity. From his father.

"You have the Winslow eyes," Paul Winslow said, even though Adam could see he clearly didn't mean to speak those words aloud.

He continued on, "You'll see, in David, your younger…"

His father would not finish the sentence. And Adam wanted him to. Who was David to him? Why couldn't he say David was his brother? *Say it.*

But there was quiet.

This meeting was not going as he hoped. *Breathe. Stay calm.* The house was cool, but he was not and he didn't want to pull on his collar. No discomfort. Thank goodness for his training. He called upon it to help him deal with this strange encounter. "I was about to check in the hotel in town, but I couldn't."

Confusion reigned in Paul Winslow's face for a second. "I set up accommodations there for you."

"I was stopped by a woman on the street who told me the hotel was not for people like myself."

"Who was it?" Mrs. Winslow asked.

Adam started a bit at her sharp tone. "She wore a pink hat and told me not to go in. So I didn't."

"Ruby," Mrs. Winslow hissed, as if her name were a curse.

"Yes. Ruby." Adam let the jewel name linger on the tip of his tongue. A precious, fiery stone. It suited her well.

Paul Winslow waved a hand as he took up a cigarette. "She's just a colored gal from around here who likes to cause trouble. You shouldn't have listened to her. I set up the room for you. You can go back over there and check in once you are finished here."

"She implied it was a matter of my life."

"She knows!" Mrs. Winslow gasped. Paul Winslow paid her no attention.

"Well, we'll figure something out. You look like one of us. Seems to me you could just go in there—couldn't you?"

"I guess I could. If I wanted to." Adam shifted in his seat at his father's clear implication. Wrong choice. His heart sank a little. If he had just gone along with it and played "the game," he would be more acceptable to his father. So why did the notion of ignoring Ruby's advice make his stomach clench? "She had very compelling reasons not to."

"I'm so tired of her," Mrs. Winslow said.

Paul Winslow raised a hand.

What was going on? What had Ruby done to provoke Mrs. Winslow?

"If you don't want to go back there, you can stay here." Paul Winslow's statement caused them both to stare at him.

"He cannot stay in this house." Mrs. Winslow's eyes seemed to nearly roll back into her head. Adam shifted forward. Maybe he should recommend a tonic. Was she near fainting? But her reaction was only because of the thought of her husband's indiscretions.

"He can. He will. Because I say so," his father spoke with pointed accuracy and calm.

"Very well. He can stay in the sewing room." Mrs. Winslow flounced out of the parlor as regally as Queen Victoria.

"That'll do fine, Mary. Thank you," Paul Winslow said to her retreating form. He turned to Adam. "I apologize. She always has been sensitive to the fact I was with Matilda first. Mattie was such a fine woman."

"A woman?" Mattie Morson had been eighteen when she died.

"Yes." Paul Winslow gave a little laugh. "So sunny, and as sweet as sugar."

A slightly sour taste entered his mouth. How dare his mother's name come from this man's lips? His father. His mother had died when he was young, and she was barely a woman. He had known so little of her. His father should explain more, and not just talk about her as if she were a slice of cake. His heart panged. Who was Mattie Morson? How to ask this of a stranger who was also his father?

Still, it rankled him that Paul Winslow dared to say her name. Adam's countenance grew warm with rising blood. Did he even know what he was saying? Maybe he should remind him of a few things. "She died without proper medical care. At the hands of a dirty Negro midwife."

"I know. That's why…you're here. To help these colored here in Winslow."

"Winslow." Adam repeated the name of the town again.

"Yes. They insisted on naming the town after me about ten years ago when I built the mill. It keeps a good many people employed and the n—" Paul Winslow stopped short, seemingly checking himself. "The colored workers are always getting sick and costing me money at the mill. They need their own doctor. You could come here and work and make a fine living."

"There's a doctor here?"

"Of course," his father explained, "for the whites. But I am willing to provide a doctor for the colored here."

"Why?" He fixed his Winslow gaze on his father.

"What?"

"I wonder why. They've been sick all this time. Why not let them die off?

You can always get more." He pulled at his collar, loosening it now.

"Well, that's not the attitude I expected a doctor to have." Paul Winslow reached over and took a cigar from a box next to his chair.

Adam stood. The slickness of sweat on his palm stopped him from clenching his fist. So he kept his hand loose and let the cool air blow over it. "Well, if I don't get an answer, I'm not going to do it. I've had other offers for my services. I was at the top of my class." The words just slipped out. He did not intend to brag to his father. He shouldn't have to.

"I'm sure you have. But you would be paid handsomely here. You could stay nearby."

Ruby came to his mind and the prospect of getting to know her was pleasant. A doctor needed to make connections in a community, but something was holding him back.

Maybe it was the pleading look in Paul Winslow's eyes. His stomach turned. Why plead to him? "I need to think about it. I'm tired from my travel and I had to treat a man in town. One of your workers, I suppose. He cut his hand."

"Ah, yes. See how you are needed here?" His father waved his cigar in the air and a maid appeared quickly. "Please show Dr. Morson to the room Miss Mary wants for him."

The young Negro maid's eyes grew wide. "She say, let him have the sewing room."

"Well, take him—Dr. Morson—there. He's tired." Paul Winslow's voice floated out to him. "We can talk further later."

He didn't care. As he went up the grand Winslow staircase, he counted himself in full rebellion mode. Paul Winslow didn't want to be a father to him. He just wanted Adam to do his bidding. Could he avoid doing what his father wanted and still interact with the intriguing Ruby? He certainly hoped so.

Chapter Three

"Solomon sick." Her mother spit out the words as soon as she returned to the house from town.

Was this her punishment for venturing outside? Her heart pounded in her throat. Everyone could probably hear it.

Please, God. No. She swallowed her heart down.

"What you mean? I was only gone for a little bit." Her voice echoed small in the front room. She rushed over to the cradle and Solomon lay there, blue and struggling for breath.

She picked him up and cradled him to her, kissing the silky skin pulled taut over his little skull.

"Babies get sick quick sometimes. He's puny and small, Ruby." Her mother shook her head at the baby and seemed not to care at all about Ruby's trouble. "Always has been. There ain't a whole lot can be done."

"Who says?"

"God's will."

Even in her present distress, her heart went out to her mother. Her mother's repeated attempts to have a boy, the very thing shameful she managed to succeed at with her first child, combined to make her mother resent her. She understood, and did not love her mother any less. But ever since Solomon's birth, she thought of her mother as her equal. Not Mama but Lona.

"I have to try. He's suffering so." She laid him back down as he gave her half a smile. She kept her hand on him touching his pale milk-white forehead, the skin so transparent she could see a blue vein throbbing there. Her six-month old boy smiled in his sleep, but it was the distinct small caving in his little chest that made her throat go tight and dry.

"Sometimes, babies don't make it, honey." Her mother spoke in hushed low tones. Unfortunately, she knew this to be true from bringing babies herself. "We jus' let 'em go."

She focused on Solomon. His sweet features rearranged themselves in repose. He already looked like an angel to her. But that didn't mean she wanted him to be one. "You want me to let him go."

"God's fixing it this way. Let it be."

She lifted her head with her crown of long jet-black hair feeling heavy on her head and neck all of a sudden. Her hair. How much lighter her head would be if she just cut it all off. Her hands itched to find a scissors or a knife. But she had other, more important, things to do at the moment. "Solomon was the only thing that fixed it right, Mama, what David did to me. God wants me to fight for his life. I'm going to get help. Please watch Solomon. I'll be back soon." Things could change so fast in a day. The fear now was for Solomon, not about going outside.

Following her, her mother grabbed onto her arm with determined, hard fingers and a strength she didn't realize she had. "Don't do it. Please."

Standing in the setting sun, she asked the old favor once more. *Make me brown, please.* The little prayer popped into her head unbidden, whenever she stood in the sunshine. The sun never obeyed. A failure. She had been trying to be browner for years now, and she could never change colors. To be less obvious. "Making things difficult is the reason this has happened to me, Mama. Why should I stop now? I can go there and ask him for help, can't I?"

Her mother shrank back, horrified. "It's too much, Ruby. What about us, your family? Your sisters?"

"I do it for them. Do you want each one of them to go through the shame I have endured? It is time for it to end. The Winslows have to help. It is the only way."

"We can pray, daughter." Her mother grabbed her arm again and tried to pull her to her knees, but Ruby refused to lower herself this time.

"I have prayed. I prayed all the time David got me in the cotton field and

I begged him to stop. I begged him, Mama, and David didn't care. And now, he owes me. I have to ask for help."

"Take care, girl." Tears shone in Lona's eyes like bright diamonds.

"I am." This time she was not afraid. She wrenched free of Lona's strong hold. Her midwifing knowledge helped newborn babies, not six-month-olds. She had to get help for Solomon.

She stepped off of the porch into the red dusty land bordering the Bledsoe property and made her way down the road to the big Winslow house, tugging on the shawl covering her head. She had changed into her heavy work shoes and her feet dragged in the dust, as she rushed by the blossoming fields, feeling stiffness in her knees. Sharp and painful in her lungs, her breath came shallow as she risked the dusk alone. Her activity in town today made her vulnerable to another attack. She didn't care. She had to get help for her child. He was all that mattered.

The Winslow house stood in the distance with its impossible whiteness glowing in the near dark. It was not weatherbeaten like the Bledsoe house, no matter how many times John Bledsoe whitewashed it. The difference was money. David's family had plenty of it. They were going to give her some to make everything better for Solomon. Today, she was not going to the side door, the servants' door, where she entered with her mother whenever the Winslows needed help for countless entertainments and dinner parties. Today, she knocked on the front door, relishing the feel of the hard wood scraping against her knuckles.

The maid had gone home by now. As she lowered the shawl from her head, she imagined Paul Winslow stirring his bulk, acting as if he would answer the door. His wife would hold him back, compelling him not to do it because it wouldn't be proper. It would be David who would answer the door to make this request easier for her. Or harder. Did she have the strength to face her attacker again? *Please, God. Give me strength.*

Sure enough, David appeared before her, tall and confused. "Ruby? What are you doing here?"

Instead of fear, she bristled. Certainly, he meant to question why she had come to the front door, instead of to the back for work, as she always had?

But nothing was going to stop her from getting help for Solomon. Not even having to face him again. David's tall, rangy body meant that she could step easily into the front foyer underneath his arm. So she did.

Smelling the lemon of the pinewood polish, she tried to ignore the grandeur of the Winslow home, knowing intimately the hard work it took to keep it looking so beautiful. She was surprised, however, to see Paul Winslow in the front parlor with the handsome doctor from earlier today, in there with him. He had not been in her imaginings. Not those ones. She turned to David, and her ears pricked at the sound of Miss Mary approaching them both, her dress bustling quietly behind her. She had worked here long enough to know the sound when she heard it.

Her gaze met David's confused eyes. David had the same gray eyes as the handsome doctor in the parlor. Goodness. The shock threatened to take her down, but she could not let it. "I need help." She spoke in a firm but low whisper. "I need money for a real doctor."

Miss Mary came and stood between David and Ruby, making her elegantly garbed body a shield between her only son and disaster. "Ruby, why are you here? Go on home."

Despite the shock, she did not move her gaze from David's face. "He knows why I am here. I need a real doctor to help my baby."

Now Mr. Paul came and stood in the hallway. "This is all very irregular. Any appeals you people make, you know to come back, and you know to come before dinner, not after. You're lucky Dr. Morson is here. I've brought him down from Tennessee to help treat your people."

"I need the best care for my child, Mr. Paul, sir." The honorific sound for the town's lead man came from her and sounded disrespectful. "This is to save my baby. I need a real doctor. Mr. David knows why."

"I'm sure he doesn't."

She moved her gaze from David and met Miss Mary's eyes. Miss Mary knew. She was supposed to keep her eyes downcast, to look away, to be ashamed. But she didn't. She met a Winslow's gaze, and she did not feel the least bit of fear for the first time in her life. She was not ashamed of Solomon. She could be ashamed of how he got in the world, but his start was not her fault, not one bit of it and she knew it now, despite hiding away from the world for all of those months wondering if God had abandoned her. He had not. He had given her courage.

She turned to David. "Are you going to help our baby?"

"Now, wait just a minute, girl," Mr. Paul blustered. "You cannot come into our home before the Lord's day and do this kind of thing. It just isn't done."

"What does your mother have to say about this kind of behavior, Ruby? This is most astonishing." Miss Mary twisted a handkerchief back and forth in her hands.

"She can't stop me from trying to save her only grandchild." Ruby willed David to make a move, to help, to do something. What happened to all of the brute strength he had used against her in the cotton field? Now it was her turn to have brute strength. "Your only grandchild."

"Leave at once, Ruby." Miss Mary slumped back into the chair. "You're nothing but trouble—making up organizations and carrying on, causing trouble around here. If it weren't for your mother working here for so long, well, you can tell her she needn't come ever again." Miss Mary pointed her long arm toward the door.

Dr. Morson stepped forward, "Miss Ruby, is that you?"

Miss Mary huffed. "I just want her out of here now."

Ruby had been thrown out of places before and steeled her body for any physical attack. She would not be cowed. Still, Ruby had to work hard to address David because of the magnetic pull of the very handsome Negro doctor, who had not taken his gaze off of her. No man had ever looked at her like that before. She wasn't sure that she liked it.

Paul Winslow said, "Dr. Morson here will take fine care of the child."

"I'll get my bag." Dr. Morson slipped up the staircase in a quiet, and unassuming way.

"Let him take the car," David addressed Miss Mary.

"What? We cannot have colored people driving around aimlessly in our cars."

"If you won't, then I'll drive." David was speaking to his mother, but he put his Winslow gray gaze on Ruby.

Was he sorry now? Too late.

"David, you cannot be a part of this." Mary Winslow insisted.

"I already am."

She followed the doctor through the dark garage past all kinds of cars and the horses in the Winslow stables. David followed.

"Thank you." She steadied herself, leaning on one of the cars.

"I hope it'll be okay." David touched her arm and his touch burned her, threatening to carry her back to when she was frightened and alone in the field with him. *Stay calm.* She willed her arm to stay in place, so that her fear did not show.

"Yes." She climbed into the car with the handsome doctor. David cranked the car and they drove down the driveway. She glanced backward and the curtains were parted, with the faint outline of Mary Winslow showing through the window seeing them off.

And Ruby was in the car with a man she barely knew.

Normally, she might have cared about this impropriety, especially after the attack, but she couldn't now. She had to get help for Solomon.

But she needed to know something first.

"How you get to be a doctor?"

"I went to the University of Michigan medical school and graduated last month. I was paying the Winslows a visit." Then a pause. "He paid for my education."

"Paul Winslow?" She couldn't help but let out a laugh despite the seriousness of the situation. "He ain't even helped to build a high school down here to keep the Negroes in the mill on his dime. How in the world is he paying for a Negro man's college education? Pull up over there."

Dr. Morson pulled up in the Bledsoe yard. "He was compelled to do me a kindness."

"Why?"

His gray eyes held Ruby's gaze, once again, without blinking. "I'm his son."

A fist of fear clenched in Adam's stomach as he climbed out of the car. Ruby had a baby? And that baby was his…nephew?

Whenever he had gone to the houses of his Negro patients, their places were always dark. He expected to see something downcast and downtrodden, like the homes he had grown up in.

The Bledsoe home was not like that. The home was well-lit inside and from a wide front porch he stepped into a comfortably furnished large front room with beautifully appointed pine furniture, davenport chairs and colorful quilts. Brightness and light, not the dark.

He nodded his acknowledgement to the people gathered in the room, a man, surrounded by four attractive young ladies dressed in white nightgowns—a verifiable rainbow of brown, all with worried looks on their faces. They stood around a cradle, again, made of pine and beautifully appointed as well.

"How you get this doctor to come?" the smallest girl asked, whose beautiful skin matched the furniture. "He white."

"Delie, hush your mouth." An older woman approached from another room. "Didn't I tell you not to speak unless you are spoken to by an adult?"

"I was surprised to see a white doctor come in here." The little girl pouted.

Ruby stepped to the child and put an arm around her. "I went and got Solomon the best help I could find. Now, we all need to pray for him, okay?"

"I been praying, Ruby. I been praying real hard." Delie shook her black plaits back and forth. "I love him so. He's the little brother I never had."

Touched by the child's simple and plaintive plea, he gulped. Ruby was affected as well. In the lighted room, silent tears slipped down her creamy colored skin across her light brown freckles. When he laid eyes on Ruby's baby, he shook his head, nearly voicing a denial.

It couldn't be.

It wasn't the fact the child's chest caved in and went out, back and forth. He laid his hand on the child.

Goodness.

This child, this precious baby was an exact copy of him . He had one childhood picture of him at about the same young age and it was true. As he touched Solomon, a tingling went up his arm and he connected with another human being. All of his professional distance as a doctor evaporated and he understood, in a way he never had before, why he was a doctor. To bring his knowledge to this little Georgia town and to take care of this baby.

Where had David been? Why didn't he take care of his son? What kind of man was he?

No kind. Clearly. Adam reached down into his bag for his Franklin-Bell and listened to the baby's chest. He turned Solomon's small body with loving care and gentleness.

Solomon's tense little body relaxed, and the baby's breathing eased almost right away. Some of the other young women in the room took in a sharp gasp of breath.

"Praise him," someone said.

Was that Ruby?

Solomon had asthma. Adam moved his Franklin-Bell over the thin child.

Did he have enough to eat?

Something in the home, as well kept as it was, made it difficult for him to breathe. The beautiful quilts in shades of bright red, green, blue, and orange might have something to do with it. He put the Franklin-Bell down and used his hands to inspect the baby again. "Come here, little fellow."

He had been so angry at God for years, yet his mind scrambled in amazement as he examined the child further. Had he been brought here to care for this baby? He slipped one hand under Solomon's tiny head and one under his bottom and lifted him up into his arms, holding him close. As he shifted the baby in his arms, Solomon opened his eyes and stared at Adam with a knowing stare, a gray stare. Adam's skin tingled.

Solomon had Winslow eyes too.

He smoothed down the little shirt that had been lovingly embroidered by someone and the child was clean, even though he was small.

"Will he be all right?" Ruby's freckles stood out on her pale, creamy skin, and her brown eyes brimmed with fear and anxiety. He would do what he could to calm her fear, since he didn't want to see her beautiful countenance disturbed in such a fashion.

"Yes." He couldn't say more. It was as if healing the baby was healing himself, and a sharp pain he didn't know he had inside of him began to scar over.

"But you came in and made him sleep again."

"I would like to believe I have a magic touch with babies, and my mere arrival could put them to sleep." He chuckled as he took Solomon away from the little room back through the kitchen. Continuing to the large front living room where the Bledsoes sat, he cradled the baby as the family stopped chattering and stared at him, striding through their home. He took the baby out into the June night air and Ruby followed him.

"But, there is something more going on here, isn't there?" Adam smoothed down the baby's brow. Sweet little fella.

"I don't understand."

"He seems small and light. He's what, four months old?" He shifted him in his arms. The baby didn't seem to weigh enough.

"No, five almost six."

He shook his head, icy alarm running through his veins. This was his nephew…was he being well cared for? Keeping his voice calm he asked, "What are you giving him to eat?"

"I—I nurse him." Ruby retreated back from him, folding her arms over her chest.

"He needs more to eat. If he were a little bit bigger, he might be able to ward off this asthma better."

"What should he eat?"

Ruby's intelligence showed earlier. He had to make sure she understood though, for her baby's sake. "He needs food, not just milk. Do you have enough to eat here? If not, then David should be providing it."

Ruby folded her arms and shifted her stance.

No. A tight feeling suffused his body. He'd offended her. It was the last thing he wanted to do even as he appreciated her well-made chin in her heart-shaped face. The sweet touch belied the steel set of her jaw.

"We take care of our own." Her jaw became more defined in the darkness. "Solomon is my cross to bear—my shame," she told him, "or at least that is what people think. But I am not ashamed of him."

He nodded, not judging her in anyway. One thing doctors learned, babies happened. "I have a syrup he can take whenever he has a breathing issue, but he should stay away from the kitchen. It's not a good place for him. And you need to give him some finely ground up food, purees, protein. Something solid. Mashed up peaches, strained fine."

"You telling me how to feed my baby?" Her brow furrowed. Clearly she wasn't used to taking direction.

"He needs to be built up more to be able to ward off the asthma. It'll take some time, but I'm sure your mother can help you."

"She don't want to help. She'd rather God take him." Something sharp pierced his chest at the thought. Babies died too, but not this one.

"I can say something to the Winslows if you can't provide for him."

"I can provide for my baby. He will be fine. I just thought nursing him was good."

"That's fine. He needs more than that. I can stay and watch him, but as I said, he needs more."

Ruby stared out into the night and the rigid set to her shoulders eased a bit. There was clear relief in her at his words and a sudden gladness in his heart. Gratitude washed through him, happy to have helped her. "We can take care of him. I didn't want to believe it, but he's a gift from God."

Why did she have to keep mentioning God? Was it because of the strange connection to Solomon he had just experienced? He didn't know, but he wanted to reassure her, "I can tell he's a well-made child."

"Who looks just like you," Ruby faced him in a defiant stance. "It's very strange isn't it?"

The sleeping child stirred in his arms. "Incredibly."

"He's a Winslow, you know."

"Yes. I guess he's related to me." He had a nephew. Not the family he had come to find, but family, nonetheless. And with Solomon as family, Adam would ensure the baby was sustained properly. Not that he looked forward to going back to the Winslows tonight anyway. His stomach plummeted at the thought. It would be better to stay here to help them.

Ruby stared back out into the night. "They thought if they had David attack me, I'd stop asking for better from Mr. Paul. Solomon's what happened. They can point and stare at us all they want." She looked at him, questioning. "You did good things with your life, being a doctor and all. Why can't my son? Why does he have to be talked about?"

He didn't flinch from her question. The way she spoke made such common, quiet sense, but she was angry and somehow, she had to talk out her anger. "He's a beautiful baby. He's just small."

"They ought to be ashamed thinking they could keep me quiet." Ruby set her jaw again. "But Solomon's coming only convinced me even more to speak out against Negro men being lynched in this town for no reason at all."

Adam swallowed a deep gulp. "Lynching?"

"Yes. That's how the Winslows keep Negroes in their place 'round here. 'Cause I said something about the lynchings, I was attacked. And then Uncle Arlo got his lynching."

Who was Uncle Arlo? Her allegations had his head swimming. Paul Winslow was responsible for these things? His father?

He swallowed. "What do you mean said something?"

Ruby's eyes blazed in the darkness. "The Winslows used their precious son to try to keep me quiet. It didn't work. I'm going to do more than ever to keep the life of my Negro son safe in this terrible place. They won't get to him. God will make Solomon a great warrior in this battle. I'll see to that."

"Fine. But he needs to eat more, and keep him from the cookstove." A sense of doom collected through his fingertips and gathered in his stomach. Given the way she had voiced it, he had no doubt what Ruby said bore truth. "Try to keep him calm and quiet as well. He doesn't need extra anxiety in his life."

She turned to face him, "Anxiety? What do you mean?"

"Don't give him any cause to worry. What would Solomon have to worry about as a baby except his mother is causing trouble in the town by speaking up against lynching? You should be here, taking care of him, feeding him food. He needs his mother here."

"I take care of my child. How dare you say I don't?" She reached for her baby and with great tenderness, took the child away.

"I'm sure you do. But you ought to stay at home and see to his needs instead of going out and stirring up trouble. I hope that's not why you were in town today. It won't help him. What if something happened to you?"

"It's what will help him, Dr. Morson. It's people like you who don't seek to help the cause who are part of the problem."

"People like me?" He crossed his arms. What did this fiery woman mean?

"Do you know Mrs. Barnett? Do you know about the NAACP and the work they are doing?"

He opened his mouth, ready to respond, but Ruby continued to speak, cradling her son.

"Of course you don't. You just keep silent, 'cause if you speak, you open yourself to being seen as one of us, instead of one of them."

She lifted the baby to her shoulder and moved away from Adam, into the house, leaving him in the dark.

How could this beautiful stranger have such intense and direct access to the heart of who he was? Or who he wanted to be? Bolstered by the connection with the baby when he doctored him, he stared into the abyss of confrontation. He put a hand to his temple and rubbed it to get some relief. Confrontation involved heated emotions, a place he didn't like at all. It was best to avoid her at all costs.

If only she, and her small son, had not already claimed some small portion of his heart.

Chapter Four

The meeting would take place in just three more days. Ruby didn't have enough contact with the men to tell them about the meeting. Would they know? Would they come? Jacob's hand injury and Dr. Morson's attempt to cause trouble in Winslow had interfered with her plans to let the men know about her starting the NAACP chapter, her Uncle Arlo's dream.

She harbored no ill feeling toward Jacob. He couldn't help his injured hand. But she had to go back to town. And she couldn't.

She couldn't go anywhere. It was all the doctor's fault.

On the big wraparound courting porch, she sat with Solomon in the fresh air, as Dr. Morson had recommended. The nerve of him, suggesting that her family didn't have enough food to eat, or they did not give Solomon enough.

Her father was one of the most prosperous Negro farmers in the surrounding county area.

He had plenty to feed his grandson, if he wanted. But everyone knew that babies needed to stay on their mother's milk for as long as possible.

How dare he?

As she reviewed some papers sent by the Chicago chapter of the NAACP about starting a chapter, the earth shook with the clip-clop of horses' hooves. Or was it a mule? Yes, it was a mule, being pushed as fast as it could go, coming toward their place, but not slowing down, maybe headed to town. She set Solomon to the side, and stood to brush off her skirt. She recognized Nessie the mule and her owner, Bob Turnman riding hard toward the Winslow place.

Where was he going? To work? He couldn't be in such a hurry to drive Paul Winslow anywhere.

Agnes's time must have come.

Should she go?

Would he ask her to come to see to his wife? He better stop now. This was Agnes's third baby and might not take that long to come.

However, the hooves did not slow down, seemingly fully prepared to go past the Bledsoe farm, if she hadn't opened the gate and hurled herself out into the road. "Bob, Bob! What's going on?"

Seeing Ruby, Bob pulled up on Nessie and stopped, the open concern etched on his face. "I-I-Agnes sent me to fetch help for herself. Baby's coming."

She clapped her hands on her apron. "I knew it. Let me get my kit. I can ride behind you."

Alarm further etched on Bob's brown features. "Ah, before the Almighty, Ruby, I wasn't coming to get you. I, uh, was going to fetch the doctor up to the Winslows."

Had she just been slapped? "He ain't up there. He's inside cause my baby took sick yesterday. But it don't matter, I do all the grannying around here."

Bob pulled up Nessie and turned around in the Bledsoe's front yard. "You, well, Mr. Winslow said, you wasn't doing it no more and if Agnes needed help to get the doctor up to his place."

"I brought your own Sadie and Edie into the world."

"And I blesses you for that. But, this here, well, its different. Mr. Paul says he fires me from my driving job if I get you. I'm sorry, Ruby. I've got to go."

"Well he ain't up there. He's here. He stayed seeing after Solomon last night."

"He okay?"

"He's fine. I go and get him."

She retreated into the house. Well, then, she had been slapped down. Paul Winslow was determined to cut off her access to her people in this way too. Agnes had been kind of an older sister all of her life. She wouldn't want some strange man touching her.

Mags stood on the porch holding Solomon, and she knew her sister had seen the whole thing. "He don't want you to come?"

"No. That doesn't mean I'm not going though. I'm getting my kit."

She opened the door and was faced with the sight of the uppity doctor sitting at the big center table with her family wolfing down her mother's food. He ate to his heart's content of bacon and biscuits and her mother's famous peach jam. Guess he was eating plenty big today.

"Agnes's time has come. She's having her baby."

Dr. Morson stood instantly and adjusted his shirtsleeves. "I appreciate your hospitality, Mrs. Bledsoe. I'm going to help this woman."

"Bob tied Nessie up in the barn to start up the Winslow car."

"That's enough time to get ready." Dr. Morson ducked out of the room and her entire family turned to her.

"You afraid to go and help Agnes, daughter?" Her mother asked.

"No. Bob told me he don't want me going."

Silence.

"Well, maybe that is for the better now, since they's a doctor now." Lona determined and bent over her piecework again.

Ruby stood and spread her arms out. "So we just going to turn Agnes over to this here strange man, all because he say he have a fancy degree from a school. I say this. Negro doctors don't go to no Michigan school."

"Michigan?" John Bledsoe looked confused.

"That's right."

Dr. Morson stepped back into the room, fully dressed, gripping his black bag. "I went to the best medical school I could find."

She whirled on him. "Did you go as a white man or a Negro one?"

"Ruby Jean! That's enough," Lona snapped

"She's going to get it now," Delie said in a loud stage whisper to Em, almost provoking Ruby to smile.

"Well, which is it?"

"I went to the best medical school I could find."

"And as a white man." She folded her arms. "How shameful."

"If people choose to believe what they believe, it's not for me to say."

"And you won't bother to tell them." The metal clanging chug of the

Winslow car came around the corner. "There's Bob now."

Dr. Morson fixed her with a strange look and went out to the car. Mags came and they watched the men retreat with the car.

"I can't let no fake-telling liar doctor bring on Agnes's baby," she said, clenching her fist.

"You going to have to walk, if you going. Unless you take Nessie."

Quivers hit her in the stomach. "I'm not riding on no old mule." If she had been able to ride, David might not have gotten to her. Still.

"I've got to get to Agnes. She won't want some strange man helping her."

She untied her apron in the back and ducked into the house to retrieve her kit. She hadn't used it in a while. Her mother had used it to help her have Solomon, so she had to make sure that everything was in its proper place. It was. All those months in the house, she checked it and rechecked it, wondering what she would do if a birthing happened. Would she be able to go out to help the mother? Now, Paul Winslow beat her to the punch and brought in some doctor to start bringing babies in this small town.

Since when was he concerned with how Negro babies were born?

She had to go.

She put all of her tools down in a clean blue floral-printed flour sack and went outside where Mags stood with a worried look on her face. "Bob probably already there."

"Agnes still might want a woman there in her present time of trouble."

"Be careful, Ruby."

"I will, Mags." She pressed her hand to Mags's shoulder, so much higher up than hers and turned out of the Bledsoe gate toward the forested area where a number of the Negro families lived on the other side of First Water Christian Church.

Instead of fear at passing those same cotton fields where the attack had happened, a happy laugh bubbled inside her throat and came spilling out. Men. Bob's taking the doctor in the Winslow's car was a nice idea, but there was no way they would be able to get to Bob's house in it. The woods were thick and forested. A swift-footed, purposeful midwife would advance better. Paul

Winslow had not thought of everything in his deep desire to improve the lives of the Negroes of Winslow.

The sight of the car parked before the thick forest where the road died out kept her smiling. Bob and Dr. Morson emerged from the car and she kept up her stride. Those men may be better than her, but they couldn't best her spirit. Still, neither one of them looked happy to see her.

She didn't care.

"Good morning, gentlemen."

Ruby kept moving past them, even as Bob tried to grab at her arm to stop her. He was not fast enough. "I got the doctor here, Ruby."

"Fine. I'm just going to see Agnes."

"What're you carrying in that rag bag?" The doctor's deep voice resonated throughout the forest. The tone had been enough to stop her and look at those gray eyes again, shining this time through sparkling gold-rimmed spectacles.

"This's not no rag bag." Her resolve to remain happy went away. He wasn't anybody to insult her things. "This's my kit."

"A kit."

"Midwifing kit."

"You don't need to bother. I have the latest implements right here in my leather doctor's bag. You can return home to tend to your son. He needs his mother with him. Feeding him."

"As I said, Doctor, I'm making a friendly call to Agnes. Excuse me, but she doesn't know you from Adam." She smiled at her little joke. "Bye."

She pushed on through the thick piney woods and the carpets of kudzu. There might be snakes under the thick green leaves, but she couldn't think of that. She had to get to Agnes before that citified, passing for white, very handsome, but shameful doctor got to Bob's house. She relied on the age-old signs of the forest. There they were: moss on the trees, peeled pine bark, the fork in the road, and the bare space Bob and the other families kept for the children to play in. Thankfully, she could move fast because of her years acting more like a boy than a girl, running around Winslow, playing with David in the piney woods.

It was not cold but the remembrance of her carefree childhood made the chill rustle up her body.

She might wish to be alone, but that intense gray gaze burned through her thin cotton housedress. So, the citified doctor could keep up? She would have never thought it possible. Wonder where he had come from? She had no time to ponder it, but instead, realized that Dr. Morson's hot breath was at her back and his large hand had encircled her wrist. The last man to lay a hand on her was David and she wasn't going to let that happen to her ever again. So when he touched her, her workboot-encased foot reacted by lashing out at the doctor right in the shin.

He bent over, in pain, but he kept going through the clearing. Bob stopped to help him and Ruby heard him behind her say, "You okay, Doctor? Ruby, you ought not to have done that."

"I'll be okay. From what I hear, your wife is in worse pain."

"Ruby, you're just like a she-cat," Bob fretted.

"Don't nobody lay a hand on me," Ruby shouted out in the woods, free of town talk.

And she meant what she said.

Adam closed his open hand on her arm and she seemed stunned to see him standing next to her. He wanted to speak clearly, but her kick had marked him. "I'm trying to get you to return to your son."

"My mother and sisters will take care of him." She struggled to be free of him, but kept walking on, dragging him with her.

"A boy needs his mother."

"You need to watch your own business, white man, sir."

"Enough." He stilled her accusations with a firm hand and Bob's house emerged in the clearing. This house looked more familiar to him. The property was well-kept but the peeling paint and the crooked nature of the front door told a different story. A slight shiver went over him despite the heat of the June day. Did they have enough to eat here?

Bob's wife shouted from within. He had only delivered about five babies, but the circumstances they were born into always gave him pause. Just as his had. It looked to him like Bob's next child was to be born with no advantages. And this was the house of the man who worked for the Winslows? Did Paul Winslow pay this man fairly?

Bob held up a thick branch of the rich green kudzu foliage and beckoned Adam through. "Please, sir."

He went up the unstable porch steps, made of wood. Darkness. His eyes adjusted enough to make out the poor bed in the front of the room and two small girls in the corner, arms wrapped about one another. The metal smell of blood resonated throughout the one-room house. No, this place was nothing like the Bledsoe's.

Agnes thrashed about on the bed and before he knew it, Ruby was there next to her, and she almost growled in a low-pitched voice. Amazing. She sure could be loud when she wanted to be. "Aggie. Calm on down. You know the more sound you make, the worse it will be."

"Ruby, what are you doing here? Thought you didn't come out no more."

"You come to see me when I had Solomon. I couldn't leave you alone. You going to be alright."

"Help bring my baby."

"I brung the doctor, like Mr. Paul said." Bob stepped forward and the doctor stepped forward with him.

"Mr. Paul ain't told you to bring no white doctor up here." Agnes's voice carried a hint of wariness in it. Did he have some kind of marking as if he were a murderer?

"Aggie, this man is as colored as us. And he's a sure enough doctor, I suppose, but I didn't want you to be alone with him." She patted her arm.

"Ma'am, I can help you bring forth your child with the most recent medical knowledge. Do you have a basin of some kind?" He made his voice loud and full of confidence.

"Of course she does, what kind of question is that?" Ruby shoved him to the side and reached through a faded and greasy curtain tacked onto the galvanized tin sink. "Sadie, go pump this full of water."

A small brown girl with many braids on her head went outside to do Ruby's bidding. The other little girl squatted in the corner and he smiled at her, never thinking that he had a fearsome presence, but he did for this child.

Ruby had donned an apron, a clean looking one, he was relieved to note, but she kept reaching into that disturbing looking flowered rag bag full of clanking tools. "I'll need another basin for my tools. I need to wash them."

"This ain't no time to wash dishes, it's time to bring this baby." Ruby placed herself squarely between Agnes's bent knees and began to touch the woman with her unwashed, unsanitized hands. He could have acted much faster if the ache on his leg hadn't reminded him of what he had gotten the last time he had dared to touch her small, cool wrist. He spoke instead.

"Aren't you going to wash—?"

A loud moan, long and anxious escaped from Bob's wife. "Be still." Ruby held Agnes's brown legs apart with her elbows. The cream-colored petite woman looked as if she had enough strength to hold off a battalion of men.

Still, she did not have the proper tools. He stepped forward and Agnes began to thrash about, but Ruby stayed with her and held her firm. "Agnes, you done this two times before. You know better! You want to break the child's neck?"

Agnes stilled, but her jet black eyes fixed on his every move. For the second time in two days, a strange twinge traveled down his arms. There was something so large at work here he had to bow to it. Was this how his mother had looked at the end of her time? In pain, suffering and wild? The small dark cabin seemed close all of a sudden.

"Breathe with me. Breathe." Ruby's brown eyes trained on Agnes, compelling her, willing her to calm down, and Agnes did.

"I have something to put her to sleep."

"Sleep?" Ruby crowed at him. "Ain't no time for her to sleep. Time to bring the baby." She turned her body and focus back to Agnes.

"If you give her something to calm her down, she won't put her child's life in harm's way," he said. Saying it was by rote from a textbook. But Ruby's sure hands and manipulation of Agnes was a sight to behold. This was someone who knew what she was doing. It always amazed him to watch a person in perfect control of their situation.

"I don't want nothing to hurt my baby." Agnes called over her husband who was sitting at their eating table, hands folded and watching the whole scene. "What you call yourself doing bringing this whiter than white Negro up in here? What kind of father are you?"

"Agnes," Ruby's voice came low and firm. "Bob loves you and wanted the best for you. This old doctor here has a lot of book learning that could be of some help."

Old? He was only twenty-five. How old was Ruby? She called herself a granny, but she was barely more than a baby herself.

"I don't want him looking at my woman parts." Agnes slid down in bed and he bristled.

"Oh for heaven's sake. I'm a doctor, I've seen plenty of parts."

Ruby's eyes flashed bright, almost as bright as the stone of her name. "That's nice for you to say, you ain't laying up here having a baby. Who do you think you are talking to her like that? Go sit on down with Bob over there and stay out of my way. If I need you, I'll let you know."

Agnes moaned again.

Well, Ruby had the situation well in hand, as Agnes rejected science out of hand. Agnes's left leg was propped up on Ruby's shoulder and the intimacy of the gesture startled him.

"I'll be right here if I am needed."

"Thank you." Ruby turned back to face Agnes and he heard her whisper, almost chanting to Agnes, soothing her.

Solomon was her affair, even though she was right. Still though, her hands were unwashed. From where the table was with Bob, he sat and watched Ruby rub a lightly-scented oil all over her hands and place her hands over Agnes's lower body. What was she doing?

"Come on, Agnes." Ruby's gentle voice accompanied her sure touch. "You doing fine now."

"I want it over."

"It'll be over soon." Ruby crooned and he marveled at the care she showed Agnes. Being a doctor could be such a distancing profession. The distance came in handy sometimes. He didn't have to be close to anyone being a doctor.

Sitting at the table with Bob, he peered over at the action in the far corner of the room and took the cup that Bob offered him, then pushed it away. "No spirits." He murmured. "I'm temperance."

"Just my wife's ginger water. Help yourself. Nothing spirited in there."

He sipped at the delicious ginger water and tried not to think about the cleanliness of the tin cup. Bob took a jack knife and cut at the fragrant peaches in a bowl on the table and the shy little girls stepped forward to take slices from their father. "Want some?"

"No, thank you." That jackknife had not been cleaned, he knew.

"Wanting a boy this time." Bob wiped the fragrant peach juice off of the knife and handle and pocketed it again. He pitted a peach and took a half into his mouth. "See what I get."

He never understood this propensity to deciding what a child should be. What should it matter if the baby were a girl who came healthy? "We'll see here soon." He kept an eye on Ruby who stood now with Agnes's leg still thrown over her shoulder.

More agonized yelling came from Agnes. Maybe he would do better getting to know these people before he started practicing. They had to be comfortable with him, as Ruby seemed to be. "I'll make sure they are both safe and healthy when she's done. I'll do my part."

"That's fine. I just want Mr. Winslow to know I didn't want her in here. I didn't invite her here."

"Why?" Adam sipped some more of the ginger water, honestly wanting to know this perspective of his father.

"She'll start talking about what we deserve as employees. Mr. Paul don't like it."

"Did he have her attacked?"

"That's what she say. She been shaking herself around Mr. David for years. Then here she come saying he attacked her. How can that be?"

Had David forced her? "Did people think they were courting?" The ginger water made him warm to the topic.

"She always running around saying he going to marry her. Folk tried to tell her about herself and who she was, but she didn't want to have none of it. Then the attack happened and they had nothing to do with each other again."

He couldn't help it. A surge of anger went up in him at David. Why didn't David protect her? "Then she had a baby, as quiet as it's kept. Ain't nobody seen it. I only seen it today. White as snow."

"Like his father," he said. Solomon resembled him more, but he didn't want to get into the incredible coincidence.

"Come on, Agnes. Here it come!" Ruby stood and Agnes's white-soled brown foot dangled in the air. "I got him. Oh, yes, my. He a big boy. Praise God."

He stood too and clapped Bob on the shoulder. "Congratulations, Bob. I'll go take a look at him if that is okay."

The wet shone in Bob's eyes. "Please, Doctor."

Ruby rubbed the baby with an unclean towel, and the baby gave a lusty cry as she put him into the tin tub. He stood over her and threw out his shadow. "I'll take over from here, Ruby. Go on home to Solomon now."

Ruby seemed reluctant to give quarter, but did. "I'll see to Agnes, then, before I go." She stopped. "Take care you don't hurt him."

He lifted the baby from the tin tub, cradling him, cherishing the silky feel of his newborn skin, newly emerged from its protein cocoon. Ruby had done a wondrous work, bringing this boy into the world, but he kept an eye on her every move as she treated Agnes. This beautiful boy with reddish-brown colored skin should not have to grow up without his mother. No boy should have to grow up that way.

Chapter Five

Three days after the birth of Bob's son, Willie, the tips of Ruby's ears still burned about how that doctor tried to bring Agnes's baby.

She had nothing against him. A wonderful doctor, maybe, but not a wonderful man. Adam Morson was a hypocrite and she wanted nothing to do with him. And he was part Winslow. That made everything worse. Ruby put Solomon into his cradle and patted his bony back and her mind raced. Solomon was getting better, but maybe he needed more care.

Dr. Carson, a white doctor in the next town over, didn't mind treating Negroes for a very high fee. Her little savings came from doing laundry, not births. She would give the money to the other doctor and pray it would be enough. Adam Morson's deep voice floated out from the big front room and she did not like the way the maleness of it stirred her. "Good night, Miss Bledsoe."

He kept saying that as he left to go on back to the Winslows, every night. *Stop calling me that.* Why had her feelings changed in such a short time? At first it made her feel like a lady. Now the address was a raw wound, pointing up her unmarried, shameful status. What of it? That was not a disadvantage, was it?

"Goodbye."

She kept her voice curt. Would he pick up the clue and leave? She certainly didn't want to wake Solomon.

The front door slammed and she strained her ears for the time it would take for him to start up his car and counted until the engine sound faded away. Good. She took a deep breath. A free breath. The very air had changed since he left. Things were better, weren't they? She turned from the window back to the bed and faced her sisters who crowded in the doorway, staring at her. What were they looking at? She did not give them a second glance. "He said Solomon shouldn't sleep in the back room, so we'll have to sleep in the front with you all. I hope it's okay."

"Ruby, you know we want to protect our little man," Mags said.

"If you want to take the back room, do. I'll sleep out here with him."

"I'll collect my things right now." Mags responded a little too eagerly to suit Ruby and she wished she could take the offer back. Travis could come slip in through the back door and...why would she think that about Mags? Mags just wanted privacy, that was it. Ruby was sixteen once too.

"She shouldn't have the back room." Nettie folded her arms and pouted. Things were so touchy for Nettie at fourteen. The middle child, Nettie always wanted those little extra special attentions. Because Nettie had been a sickly child, she usually got them, but not this time. "I should. I have a lot more to think about."

"Stop being so selfish," Ten-year-old Em chided her older sister. "This is our little man here. We have to make sure he's well."

Ruby put a finger to her lips, hushing them. "Thanks. Sorry, Net. You know Mags is the next oldest. It is only fair. I hope you don't mind me being in here."

"We don't mind," Delie piped up in her five-year-old treble, "but what about Mama?"

Well. Her mother was something else. Ever since she had found out she was going to have a baby, Lona harped on her about her shameful conduct. Told her that she was the one with low moral standards, even though her mother was the one who had first seen her, dazed, rumpled up and clothes ripped up from the attack. Lona had drawn the bath in the kitchen for her right after, even though it wasn't the weekend, and begged her to forget all about it. *Don't tell anybody. Let them think you and David went too far one time since you had known one another since you was young.*

So she buried the pain at her mother's request. If she talked about it, it would happen to her sisters. And Ruby didn't want her sisters going through what she had gone through. Ruby's silence could protect them. Now her job was to reassure little Delie. "It'll work out."

"What about the doctor?" Em asked. "Is he coming back?"

"I like a handsome doctor." Delie clasped her hands together. That child was a mess.

"He saved Solomon," always sensible Mags put in. "That was what was most important. And the way he kept looking at Ruby." Well thank you, Mags.

The sisters started laughing and Ruby glared at Mags. Why had she ever thought her sensible? Or trustworthy? "Do you deny he was looking at you?" Mags spread her hands out from her skinny frame that never got fat, no matter how much peach cobbler she ate. Time to set her straight.

"He was looking at me because he was talking to Solomon's mama."

"He was looking at you as more than Solomon's mama," the five-year-old, boy-crazy Delie said. "Even I can see it."

Her sisters all hooted. "It's time for bed, girls." Ruby lay down on Mags's bed. "I'm tired. I need to rest if Solomon wakes up. I can get my things in the morning, Mags. 'Night."

Mags waggled her fingers at them and it did not escape Ruby's notice she kept elbowing her sisters as she left to go back to her private sanctuary in the back of the house. Oh yes, she better keep an ear out for that back door. The rest of her sisters fanned out and went to the other beds in the room. They blew out the light and Ruby did not respond to their giggles and hoots that resounded through the darkness. She closed her eyes and tried to forget the intensity of those grey eyes. A prayer of thanksgiving was appropriate, before she fell asleep. *Thank you, God, for taking care of my baby.* Better not to think of the agent of the care. Or his gray eyes.

The large, white Winslow house stood enrobed in darkness when Adam returned that night. Everyone must have gone to bed. But he was wrong. As he went in the front door, he could see David sat in the front parlor, looking anxious. What could he say to this young man, some stranger who had committed one of the vilest and heinous acts a man could commit on a young woman? He went past the parlor and started up the steps to the sewing-turned-guest room the maid had shown him. "Ummm. Hello?" David called to him softly. "Dr. Morson?" The way he said it sounded as if the whole idea of a Negro doctor was a foreign concept and he was deciding how well he liked it in his mouth.

Well, Adam didn't like his name in David's mouth, either. *Go see what he wants and get to bed.* Being an only child was a blessing. He had wanted a sibling, someone to belong with his whole life long, but now, hearing David call him, his only child status in the world transformed into a blessing. He didn't like having a brother and certainly not this one.

"Yes?" Adam brought the full weight of his position into one word.

David tip-toed to him, where Adam was trying to go upstairs. "How is it doing? Is it okay? Ruby's baby? He got better?"

David's heavy whispering to him, loud as his regular voice, confirmed David's thoughtlessness. Paul and Mary did not deserve disruption by what he wanted to say to David. So, as tired as he was, Adam came back down the few stairs he had climbed and into the front parlor. David followed him, like a puppy dog.

"*It*," Adam put across in measured tones, "is a beautiful child named Solomon—a name his mother probably gave him on purpose to remind anyone who would care to know his father's name is David, correct?"

David ran a hand over his little moustache, over and over. His thin developing mustache reminded Adam, David was very young himself at just nineteen years old. Just home for the summer from the University of Georgia, David seemed overwhelmed that his reprehensible actions the previous year had resulted in fatherhood. Adam almost felt sorry for him—almost. He remembered the defiant set of Ruby's stance. His attack of Ruby meant to ruin her. Despite all his best efforts, the resentment Adam believed submerged, welled up as he glared at his brother. David's face grew warm and flushed in the June heat. Doctors were supposed to sustain life, but Adam wanted to choke David with his bare hands. "I guess."

"I don't know you very well, David. I'm sure my presence is a jolt to you. But, let me tell you, people like you make me feel ill. You can acknowledge the boy is yours. Why don't you?"

David bristled. Good. He didn't want him to like him. The developing dislike for David comforted him. "Look, I just did what Father told me to do. That's all. I have to go on and finish school, and make sure I know how to run the mill and our business interests. That's what Mother says."

"And clearly, you aren't man enough to do what you should do," Adam bit out between clenched teeth, "since you are so concerned with what your parents tell you to do." His mind reeled at what David said, "What were your father's instructions?" Adam stood there and met David's gaze—matching Winslow grey eyes.

"We had a break from school. He said he had a special job for me because someone had to teach Ruby a lesson. We had grown up together and I could get her to go with me easier. He thought it was a great chance to let me have some experience, and get it all over with on a colored girl—he had done it, and so, I did what he told me. I didn't think a baby would come."

"Neither did your father, apparently." Adam could barely speak, stunned at the arrogance in David's statement as well as his choice of words. "Yet, here I am, proof."

"I know, and now I have to provide for," David gulped and spoke, "Solomon. Just as Father did for you."

"And let me tell you about my childhood, David. My mother died young and I was handed around to various relatives of hers who pretended to want me, but really didn't. They only wanted those handsome monthly checks Paul Winslow would send to provide for me. They would keep the money and give me as little as possible in anything I needed. I wore rags for the first seven years of my life. I was always hungry. So when he offered me an education somewhere up north, I jumped at the chance. I thought it meant he was ready to claim me. But all he wanted was to claim someone he didn't have to feel ashamed of, since I reflect a time when he was less than prudent."

"And you came out fine."

"Sure. I've lived alone all my life, one foot in the Negro world, where I was too light to fit in and then a white world where no one knows who I really am."

"Well, at least you look like one of us. You should be glad." David wheeled away from him. Little coward. "At least you can choose your own path. Father has it all mapped out for me."

"So you did what he told you to do by attacking Ruby."

Ah! A hit. Good. David faced him again, having the nerve to look upset. "Look." David ran a hand through his parted hair, "I've always been half in love with her. I wanted her to think, *believe*, I had the right intentions."

"Except your intentions were not right, nor good."

"She's colored." David lowered his head, embarrassed enough to remember who he was talking to. "She'll be all right, they always are."

"Yes, they always are." Making fists of his hands, he put them inside his jacket pocket, afraid of what he might do with them if he did not put them away in some fashion. Doctors sustained life, not compromised it. *Breathe.*

"And the baby?"

Sick of looking at him, and feeling sick that David looked so very similar to himself and to Solomon, Adam moved away and went back to the stairs. "You just said it yourself. They're always all right. Good night, David."

Adam walked past him and went up the stairs slowly to the small corner room where his trunk was. A small garret room and the smallest room on the second floor Mary Winslow could give him. He might as well be last year's furniture, stuck in the attic.

He lay out on the bed, not bothering to undress, and reflected on the past few days. This situation just continued the vagabond way he had been brought up. No, he certainly was not a guest in this house, this terrible house of hypocrisy. He remembered Lona's offer to stay at the Bledsoe farm. Yes, that was the answer. Better to be in that house than this one.

The beautiful face of Ruby came into his mind. Ruby had a resolve and an inner strength his own young mother did not have. The heaviness in his heart lifted. Still, he had to help her somehow, regardless of whether or not she wanted help. However, the first thing he would have to do would be to get out of this house, and this small suffocating room. He wanted nothing to do with the Winslows anymore and decided, as sleep came to him, to pay Paul Winslow back every cent of the money that he spent on "providing" for him. The provision money, tainted with the blood and labor of his mother, corrupted him and he wanted nothing to do with it, or Paul Winslow, anymore.

The next Monday, she and Mags were back in front of the mill at lunchtime, talking with the men as they ate in the dusty courtyard outside. Ruby spoke to each man individually. "There will be a meeting in our backyard tonight at six. Anyone who is not working second shift should be able to come. We need to figure out how to get you to vote this fall and get equal pay here at the mill."

"Will Miss Mags be there?" Travis shouted out.

"Of course she will," Ruby answered, despite Mags poking at her with her bony elbow. Served her sister right. Give her a little taste of her own medicine.

"Then I be there." Travis waved his cap as he went by after eating his lunch and heading back inside to work.

Mags lowered her head, and everyone laughed. One of the men hovered nearby Ruby's left elbow. "You be careful now, Miss Ruby."

"I am, Jonesy. Mags is with me. I always come protected now."

"The baby at home?"

"Yes. He's still recovering and I don't bring him out much. I'll wait until he's a little older."

"He's precious, I'm sure, if he looks like his mama."

Ruby smiled and just moved on. Jonesy, along with other people who had not seen Solomon, were trying to get her to admit Solomon looked like a Winslow. But she was not going to bite. Everyone knew who Solomon's father was. She didn't need to say it out loud. It would be wrong to.

The men would come. She even got Mags into the spirit of the thing as they headed back home. However, when she and Mags arrived, the same car that had brought her back to her parents' home on Saturday was parked in front. One of the Winslows or Dr. Morson was there. Which one? Ruby's heart beat fast at the prospect of the latter. What was worse, facing one of the Winslows or that fake Dr. Morson? When she and Mags opened the door, her heart leapt. Dr. Morson sat in her father's chair, bouncing a drooling Solomon on his lap.

Ruby removed her big pink hat and stuck the hat pin in the back of it as if it were Dr. Morson. She would be mean so he'd know he wasn't welcome, so she did not address him directly but spoke to her mother. "What's he doing here?" Ruby swallowed a lump in her throat, angry they had eaten dinner without them. She also wanted this tall, muscular and undesired presence gone from her home.

How could the entrance of a person matter so much to him within a few short days? Adam's heart lightened as he watched her put up her pretty pink hat and ignore him.

He got to her. A warmth spread through him at the thought.

Maybe not in a good way, though. Her fair skin, like his, reddened as she directed the question to her mother. Adam gave the baby a pat. She couldn't keep ignoring him as long as he had this capital little fellow with him. What a great baby he was. Solomon was improving, getting better, thank goodness and he readied himself to face her.

"He's here checking on the baby. He going to be staying in the back room. I got to thinking about it. He need someplace to stay and Mags don't need to be back there by herself."

She did not like his appearance in her space.

Ruby donned a crisp white apron and tied the strings a little tighter than needed as her mother made her revelation. Adam enjoyed watching her squirm as she kept ignoring him. "Meeting is here out back, so as long as he don't interfere."

"I thought you had stopped having them meetings, Ruby Jean," Lona addressed her daughter as they stood in the kitchen. Adam overheard their rising voices as he played with Solomon in the corner of the big front room.

Then it occurred to him.

This was a home.

The wonderful hospitality of the Bledsoe family was enjoyable. They laughed and chattered as they had eaten dinner and had their fill of the delicious dinner of side bacon, fresh pole beans and potatoes, sliced tomatoes, and split hot biscuits with sugared Georgia peaches. It was basic fare, but at least they had enough.

He had a good time when Delie took him out to their orchards and showed him the well-kept farmland that made up the Bledsoe lands. Clearly, John Bledsoe had the magic touch with farming, something Adam lacked despite working on the farms of the various relatives he grew up with. Farming was not easy, but John and Lona Bledsoe were onto something with their farm.

And they had their priorities. As Adam played with the baby, in the time after dinner, books came out. Clearly, there was a great deal of emphasis on academic work even though school had dismissed for the summer. When she came in, Ruby started to direct Delie, Nettie and Em with their work and made sure they had plenty to do to keep up their skills. Mags read a book while they worked. But what about Ruby's skills? Struck by Ruby's intelligence and quick mind, he marveled at her. How had she gotten so smart? What was her training?

John came up to him and took the baby, smiling down at Solomon, but then taking on a solemn look when he sat down on a pine chair next to Adam, dandling his grandson on his knee.. "My girls are going to be somebody."

Adam nodded his head. He didn't know what to say to the man, so it was best to keep silent. "They jewels. Each one of them."

Mags came by and kissed her father on the cheek as she took some dirty napkins out to the kitchen. "He means it literally, Dr. Morson. Ruby, Garnet, Emerald, Cordelia and Margaret."

Adam puzzled. "Margaret?"

"It means Pearl, Dr. Morson. Mama didn't like the name, so Margaret had to do instead."

John nodded. "She didn't like Pearl at all. Had a friend named that a long time ago and wasn't going to name our second born that, 'cause of her."

"Nice names."

"They are jewels. Especially Ruby. She don't have anything to be ashamed of with this here fine boy. She going to be something and so is he." The proud man gripped onto his grandson a little tighter and adjusted him on his lap. "You have something to say?"

"No, sir." Adam blinked his eyes fast.

"Hmm." John lifted Solomon up and made the baby laugh. The bond between the man and the child was good for the baby. And the man. Some close contact with this wonderful child might do Paul Winslow a world of good, but it would never happen. Adam enjoyed sitting in the bosom of this family. Had he been brought there to ensure Solomon's life would be different than his? "You know, but you got to find it out for yourself."

John got up with the baby in his arms and walked into the parents' bedroom, leaving Adam puzzled at their encounter. Now, Lona and Ruby fought in loud voices, with Ruby coming out of the room, the victor in the whole affair. "We're meeting in the orchard."

"You know she don't want them meetings near us and the house." John came back in, toting Solomon on his hip. He had diapered his grandson and the baby's face was wreathed in smiles. How had John done the woman's chore so quickly? "And you know why."

"That's why we're meeting in the orchard. Goodness, I can't believe you all don't want to help." He could see Ruby's brown eyes examining the room, purposefully not settling on him. Adam wanted to laugh at the measures she took to evade him, but he didn't. He couldn't. Ruby was right in some way. He had to figure out what way.

"That's enough, girl. You got your way. Don't rub it in—your mama has enough to deal with."

"Yes, sir." Ruby stepped over to her father and took the baby. "Let me try to get him to go down so no one sees him."

"Go on into the front room." John directed her as he took the baby out on the porch. Suddenly, Adam was aware his presence changed the dynamic in the household. Ruby had to get Solomon calmed down by feeding him, by giving him her breast and Adam didn't need to see it even though he was a doctor. No. He shifted a little in the chair he was sitting on. Delie's reverent gaze stayed on him the whole time.

"She'll be back soon, Dr. Morson. She just don't want Solomon at the meeting with the workers."

"Why not?"

"He ain't no one's business. He's our baby. He hasn't done anything wrong, just because he came out of the cotton field." Delie turned to him. "Maybe you could be his daddy. Solomon likes you. Remember how he was on your lap and how you calmed him down and all? You're good for him."

"Delie, hush," Em told her younger sister as she worked on a piece of mending.

"Can't I just say what I think?"

"No, ladies don't do that."

"I don't want to be no lady. I want to be like Ruby."

Lona appeared in the doorway and coughed. The two young girls scattered out through the back door and the kitchen where Mags had disappeared. Lona sat down opposite him in the chair John vacated. "It's mighty hard keeping track of these girls. Now here's Mags, she sixteen and Travis already got something for her. She see Ruby and no one ain't giving her a hard time. Everything fine, even better since Solomon come. None of them, not Mags, Em, Net or Delie know what is wrong with how Solomon come. They all be up in here with their own babies soon enough, and I'll have no peace."

"They seem like sensible young women," Adam spoke in their defense.

"Humph."

"Especially Ruby."

"Really?"

"Yes, ma'am."

"Why?"

Adam cleared his throat. "She's strong, she's defiant, and...very strong." *And beautiful.* There the words were, unspoken by him, but in his mind, loud and clear. He might as well have said them. His words brought her out of the kitchen and he appreciated the smooth neatness of the apron over her dress, and the braided black hair surrounding her head like a crown. The freckles across her nose brought a sweetness to her dignified countenance. Very beautiful.

"She need more than strength." Lona fixed her gaze on him. "She need support because she is too hardheaded to see what trouble she can get in. You got to let her know and even better, take her far away from here. I'm afraid of what will happen for her here."

"What do you mean?"

"She can go somewhere and learn more than what Miss Annie taught midwifing. John and I put aside some for school, but she needs to go somewhere and learn a skill so she can be ready for the world."

"It seems as if the world isn't ready for her, ma'am. What does she want to do?"

"She midwifing, but she always want to be a nurse. Don't you need a nurse?"

Adam cleared his throat. He did. His visit in Winslow was a prolonged stop on his way to a new position as chief doctor for the Negroes in the steel mills in Pittsburgh. Some of the steel barons had looked for doctors to care for the Negroes because they couldn't get anyone else who wanted to do it. The barons agreed he needed a nurse and provided funds for it. But it wasn't easy finding trained Negro nurses.

Adam's mind clicked apace. The money Paul Winslow had given him was ample enough to get Ruby into a program and help him part time. Then when she was done, he could pay her a salary. The salary could help Ruby, as well as Solomon and her sisters to gain a foothold somewhere away from this place, where they didn't have to live in fear of being attacked. If Adam believed in divine providence, or what some called God, he would have thanked the being. However, as it was, God had taken his mother from him, and ever since he was a little boy, he was enraged at him. So he let God go his way and he went his.

"I might."

"Well, then," Lona huffed. "You got a church?"

"No, ma'am."

"We got our church here. Hard to go these days though, since Ruby's shame, so we read our Bible here and worship in the mornings on Sundays. That's what happens when you got a daughter who makes trouble."

"Enough, Mama." Ruby smoothed her tapered fingers over her apron as she came back in the room, and walked past Dr. Morson to the back porch. "I'm ready for the meeting."

Lona shook her head. "She thinks these white people are playing around here. They ain't playing."

"I guess not, ma'am."

Lona fixed him with a stare. "I don't know you. I know the Winslows."

"I don't know them either." Adam began.

Lona held up a hand and he was silent. "They're good people and paid good money no trading. David and Ruby grew up friends and she went shaking herself around him and he couldn't help himself. He just a boy, trying to find his way."

No. Adam could not agree with her assessment, knowing what he knew. David was a spoiled young man and always got his way. Ruby's resistance to his seduction didn't change his desires. No. Her resistance might have made him even more determined. Adam's stomach turned over thinking about it. However, he didn't want to take Lona on after she and Ruby had fussed at each other. He frowned.

"She makes trouble around here with these ideas and meetings and such. Think she doing what my brother wanted her to do. If Arlo were still living, he tell her the same thing. Get a home she can settle down in. You got a wife?"

"No, ma'am."

Lona clasped her hands. "You're what I been praying for. You got to take her on away from here. She won't listen to nobody, she so bossy and all."

"Lona, come on." John slipped an arm around his wife's shoulders. "She a good girl, but she just stubborn."

"She think she know everything. She don't. She has to find out what she don't know, and then she can set back in life."

Ruby's strong insistent voice sounded out on the back porch. Through the open door in the scrubbed and clean kitchen, he viewed Ruby and Mags sitting on wooden peach boxes out in the orchard and about five men sitting on boxes as well. Ruby stood up and waved her arms around and spoke. Words like "pay" and "equality" and "justice" were in the air and the men were nodding their heads, dazed. Most of them were infatuated. The meeting seemed nothing more than an opportunity to court either Ruby or Mags, an audition for future husbands. Ruby didn't see that, however. Lona came and stood in the doorway next to him.

"Any one of the men in the mill would marry her. They seem quite taken with her." Adam pointed out and a sharp pang entered his heart as he spoke the words.

"Who would beat her every Saturday night when he got paid. The mill ain't no good for nobody. John ain't a part of it. And I kept my girls out so far." Lona folded her arms and regarded him again. "What's wrong with you?"

There she was, brave and beautiful Ruby, talking to the men about their rights, refusing to be silenced by the powers in Winslow. "Everything, ma'am. I'm not worthy of such a virtuous prize."

"You know your Bible." Lona seemed pleased and Adam swallowed. "It's where we got her name. 'Who can find a virtuous woman? For her price is far above rubies.'" Lona quoted then fixed him with a frown of her own. "What you mean worthy?"

"She's unafraid, even when they tried to keep her down, tried to humiliate her."

"And?"

"I live in fear of who I am." Adam turned on his heel and went into the little back room they had given him to stay in, Ruby's former room, feeling the need to be alone for a while.

He must have fallen asleep there, fully clothed on the bed, for he startled awake when he heard a lot of noise and commotion in the front part of the house. He stood and brushed himself off then opened the door to the room. The nightgown-outfitted Bledsoes hovered in the doorway and a scream came from one of the girls. "Get the doctor, get the doctor!" John called out over and over again. Shining in the dark living room was a familiar bloody pulp which only slightly resembled a man's face.

My bag is in the car. "In the car." And the bag was there at his side as he mentioned it and so was Ruby who carried it. "I need light." Lona lit multiple lamps in their big front room.

"Travis," Mags held onto his arm, "what happened?"

"Someone at the meeting told. They came and got me and want me to tell."

"Tell what?"

"Ruby," blood frothed from Travis's lips as he spoke. An internal injury. A hard-to-heal injury. Adam's heart sank at the sight.

A basin of warmed water appeared at his elbow even though he had not requested it. Ruby spoke in calm tones, steadying his hand. His body jolted into action. He would do what he could to help Travis. Her presence made his job healing easy somehow, lighter. She gave him strength and resolution he didn't know he had. With some effort, Adam cleansed the man's wounds on his face and chest then got some old strips of cloth from Lona to bind up his broken ribs. "I'm to give Ruby a message."

Adam shook his head. "You don't need to speak, Mr. Travis. You need to remain calm or you will reinjure yourself."

"Ruby, they don't want you to do what you do. They keep me alive to tell you. Stop."

"Take this." Adam poured a sedative down his throat. The liquid made the man quiet down and fall asleep. Travis needed to rest so he could heal. Travis's voice, coupled with what Lona and John said earlier, made him even more resolute. He had never been so sure of anything in his life. Ruby had to get out of that small horse town.

As soon as possible.

And he had to help her.

Somehow.

Chapter Six

When Adam and John helped Travis to the back room, he used his sterilized instruments to work over Travis, but the blood continued to froth and foam from the corner of his mouth. At first, Mags stayed in the small back room with him and Ruby, wiping the blood up, but each time Mags did so, her eyebrows met in the middle of her brown forehead, which wrinkled in worry and consternation.

"Mags, you might be more comfortable in the big room." Adam adjusted the stiffened ragchest cast that he made for Travis to try to bring his cracked ribs together for them to heal.

"I want to stay. If- if-if something happens."

Without him even uttering a word, Ruby, so much shorter than her younger sister, guided her from the room with authority and care.

Having Ruby with him was like having another pair of hands. He could accomplish so much more with such assistance. So just what did he want to accomplish in his practice? He hadn't given it much thought before because his efforts had been so focused on his education. Strange, but he didn't realize until he came to Winslow that he could actually help people.

How could this simple country woman have such poise? She was just a midwife who didn't know proper procedure.

But she could be taught.

Adam turned his attention back to Travis and he could see that Travis had slipped into sleep. He was not in pain, which was good because he would not live very long. Travis would be his first death in this community and he didn't want to be blamed for it. Maybe it would be better if he left for the steel mills opportunity he had been putting off in Pittsburgh, tending to the Negro workers there.

Ruby tip-toed into the room. "He not long for this world is he?"

"I'm afraid not."

Big round tears slipped down her brown freckles. "It's all my fault. That's what people will say."

"You didn't attack him."

"I had the meeting again. After I had been attacked before."

"What do you think that your meetings will achieve?"

Her large brown eyes fixed on him. "My mother's little brother, Arlo, he came here to live a few years ago. He needed a job and Daddy thought he could help on the farm. But he wasn't too good with farm work."

"Not everyone is." Adam could well sympathize.

Her eyes grew pointed and pieced him. "There aren't a lot of choices for a Negro man down here. So Uncle Arlo went to the mill. He could see how things were there. He said things weren't right. Said if the men stood up and asked for more, Paul Winslow could make things better. That's when the lynchings started. People didn't know at first that Paul Winslow was behind it. Then…"

He went and stood next to her. "Yes?"

"I was attacked. By David after I was coming home from a delivery. He acted as if he was my friend, like always, but then he got mean and said things. I didn't know him. I think he had some liquor or something."

Adam touched her arm and a surge of feeling shot through him. "You don't have to continue, Ruby, if you don't want to."

She took a deep calming breath and he pulled his arm away. He shouldn't have touched her, but she seemed so upset. He wanted to take that upset away, just as when she thought something bad would happen to her son. "The attack, Uncle Arlo knew, was 'cause they were trying to come for him by getting me since I was helping him spread the word about organizing and making a NAACP chapter down here. He dared to go to Paul Winslow and say something to him. He was shot in the woods after he was coming home from working at the mill one day. I found his body."

"That had to be hard."

"It was hard that he never got the chance to say goodbye. He kept saying to us that the mill wasn't right. It wasn't fair." She turned her eyes to the bed where Travis lay. "He and Travis were friends. They were about the same age and Travis wanted to pay court to Mags, the first one of us somebody wanted the right way."

A realization seemed to shadow across her pretty features and reshape them into pure sorrow. Her hands covered her face and she began to sob.

There was something in a doctor's training about remaining calm. Stay apart from the situation. But the sight of her pretty face and rearranged freckles hurt him to his core and he slipped an arm around her shoulders. "I'm sorry. I've tried to make him as comfortable as possible in these last hours. He shouldn't linger long or be in pain."

"What kind of place is this where a man can't even come to a friend's house to hear about improving himself?"

That was the question wasn't it? "Ruby, I haven't been here very long, but it seems to me that you have some choices. You don't have to stay here. You can go somewhere else. There can be other places where Solomon might have a better chance in life, better educational opportunities. These terrible murders, and your circumstance, it's a way to control you so you don't disrupt things."

Ruby took her hands from her face. "What other place? We were born here. Our Daddy has farmed this land. It's his. He's one of the most prosperous Negro farmers in Becker County. Where we going to go that's better than that?"

He had no answer for her.

"Something has to be done here. Change got to happen. Paul Winslow is your daddy. Maybe you can do something to help."

"I don't know him that well. And frankly, after some of the things I've seen and heard, I don't know if I want to."

She stiffened and he slipped his hold off of her shoulder.

"God brought you here to help us. We need help and you, his Negro son, you can talk to him, make him see."

"I'm a doctor, Ruby. I treat people's bodily injuries, not their work circumstances."

She lowered her hands to her sides and went to the other side of the bed. "I thought you would say that." She moved to her knees next to Travis and grasped his hand. "Trav. I'm sorry. I didn't think they would go for you. They should have gone for me, and they didn't. I'm sorry."

His presence was a sudden interruption into a conversation that he had no part of, but then she clasped her hands together and prayed in a firm, sure voice: "Dear God. Please help us. You give me this boy to raise. Help me to raise him right in your ways. Help me to provide for him, so he could get a good education. Help me to make this a better world for him here in Winslow. Please. And help bring Travis into your arms. Peacefully."

She lowered her head onto Travis's arm and cried some more. As uncomfortable as her outburst made him, Adam's job was to stay and tend to Travis. The man's breath began to slow. It seemed as if Ruby was going to get her wish. Even though Travis had been sleeping very peacefully, suddenly his body jerked and went limp. Adam went to him and pressed the points of his body where his pulse should have been, checking for signs of life. Nothing. "I'm sorry, Ruby. He's gone."

"I'll go get Mags." Ruby sprang up and wiped at her face.

As she left, Adam pulled one of the bedsheets up onto Travis's body. Ruby and Mags came into the already cramped back room crying, leaning on one another and Adam stepped back. His function here as a doctor was done, but seeing the death of this Negro man was sobering. How could someone be gone on the basis of what someone else had said? Too much time had passed, too many things had happened. Something had to change.

And then the idea came to him. Ruby could change. She could be educated and learn how to be clean and come away from midwifery.

He needed a nurse. She could help him.

If she wanted to.

She and her sister were so distraught now, they probably wouldn't even know or understand what he proposed. Still, he was a light, literally and had to be that for her. Again, a shadow passed in his mind. He had been so distant from God for so long, but was his hand in this? Was this why he had come to Winslow? To make his father understand?

Travis had no family. He had worked to get one, though. The poor man had been paying such hard court to her sister in the past year, when he thought Mags might marry him. Would Mags have married him? Ruby looked over at Mags being surrounded by family, as she sobbed.

Mags was too young to get married, she had insisted. She needed to finish high school by correspondence, just like she was trying to do.

But had she any right to interfere in Mags's life? She made her come with her to tell the mill workers about the meetings, just so Mags would get a glimpse of Travis, or was it the other way around?

A cold feeling came over Ruby.

Had she engineered Travis's death so he wouldn't or couldn't marry Mags?

Since no one was ever going to marry her. Ever.

Ruby folded her hands and went down on her knees in front of Travis's freshly washed body. The heavy blows of her father's hammer rang out as he constructed a quick casket for poor Travis, after Lona had washed him. In Winslow, these tasks fell to certain ones in the Negro community, since the undertaker in town was for the whites. They would hold a small funeral for him tomorrow as the sun set, with wake and funeral all in one day. A body wouldn't hold long in hot, humid June Georgia weather.

The doctor was out with her father, helping him to build the casket. What kind of purpose would he be able to serve? Did he know anything about carpentry? As Ruby shifted from Travis, she looked out the back door to the barn. She could see that Adam was helping. Amazing.

Who was this man who knew so much about doctoring and didn't want to help out his fellow Negroes? A Moses and didn't know it.

Moses had his own troubles too. Maybe it was the same for the doctor.

Soon, her father came out of the barn carrying the casket and the men laid Travis in the hastily-constructed casket with care. Lona had put a white cloth on the dining room table and they lifted the casket onto some sawhorses. People started to come and lay their food offerings on the table, which had been pushed into another corner with the davenport and the chairs.

And the moment came that Ruby dreaded the most.

She had no reason to encounter the pastor of First Water Christian Church ever since it had become known in the community that she was going to have a baby. She had not been to church. Now he was going to have to come here.

And here he was. Reverend Charles Dodge big as well as tall, but not as tall as the doctor. Where had that come from? He used his imposing figure to make it known and understood that he was a very important somebody in this small community. Ruby wouldn't have minded that so much if only he didn't use his power to make her feel worse.

Her mother was all too keen to help the minister in. She had not been able to see to her duties as the church superintendent because of Ruby's shame. "Come on in, Reverend. Some folks brought a parson bird and I know you're fond of chicken."

Ruby stood next to the door where Solomon slept in her parents' room so that no one should disturb him. He wasn't anyone's business anyway.

"Thank you, Sister Bledsoe. It was a shame to hear from Bob about poor Travis." He stood next to where Mags sat in a chair, staring off into space with hot tears streaming down, leaving white tracks of salt on her brown face. "He was a good man."

"He was. Good to the church, the community and for God."

"A shame." Reverend Dodge intoned, so that the family and the arriving families could hear, "If he would have been in the mind to stay at home and not cause trouble here in the town, he would still be alive with us today."

The room fell silent.

Was everyone looking at her?

Yes.

Where was the doctor?

She would look for him. Solomon would be fine.

Keeping her eyes and countenance downcast, she walked out of the front door around the side of the house and stood under the window to hear Solomon if he cried. Maybe it would be better to hide from people as they arrived to give their condolences. Maybe that was what Mags would want. Where would she go to give her sister some peace?

She felt a familiar hand on her shoulder, urging her back to the edge of the porch. Mags slid her long, graceful body next to Ruby's. Ruby's short legs swung, but Mags's narrow feet were firmly placed on the ground. Naturally, Ruby slid an arm around Mags's shoulder and hugged her hard. "I'm so sorry, Mags. Please forgive me."

Mags laid her head on top of Ruby's. "What for?"

"Like Reverend Dodge said. If he hadn't been trying to make things better in the mill with me, he wouldn't be dead. He would be alive and you could get married."

A tear fell on her face from above. "That's the problem. I did poor Travis wrong."

"What you mean?"

"He was older than me, and I just…well, I didn't want to be married yet."

Ruby gripped her sister's hand as she looked at her. "You what?"

"I'm only sixteen. I want to go to high school. Like you. Travis wouldn't have wanted that for me and I…well, I liked him well enough."

Ruby embraced her sister. "I thought you was mad at me. For killing him. With all of my activities."

"That's what Uncle Arlo was trying to do. Him and Trav were friends and they was going to make things better. Now they both dead."

"Hard to believe isn't it."

"They both dead and you, you got hurt. Ruby, please, don't do nothing no more, okay?"

"Mags, what you saying?"

"I'm saying, you got to stop this. Things won't change in that mill. Paul Winslow going to have things there the way they going to be."

"And then what?"

"I don't know. I'm going down in the morning and take up Travis's job."

"No. Please, Mags. Don't do that." Ruby's heart thudded hard.

"Someone will be applying for that job after the funeral. I'll go in the morning, so Paul Winslow will see I'm serious."

"I don't want any of you down in that mill."

Mags' smile crawled across her face, but her eyes were sad. "One of us was bound to be in there after a time, Ruby. There's too many of us. Might as well be me."

"What about high school?"

"You keep studying and share with me what you know at night. I'll get there. Just like you been doing. And with both of us doing, then maybe Net and Em and Delie won't have to go in that mill. But now, somebody got to. I'ma do it. For Travis."

Ruby bowed her head and covered her face in her hands. "I've failed. I meant to save you all."

"You can't do everything alone, Ruby. You got Solomon now. What about him? He got to be taken care of. You got to get him out of the mill."

Ruby's head snapped up at Mags's words. She had not even thought of that. In a few years' time, Solomon could end up in his grandfather's cotton mill, dodging between the machines to pick up bobbins.

Unless she did something but what?

She would figure it out. It would take some time.

And that doctor better stay out of her way. Or she would kick him again. The warm blood rose high in her veins at recalling her earlier behavior to him. She hoped to become a better person.

When Adam came around the corner, the sight of Ruby murmuring words of comfort to Mags and wiping her sister's salty tears away with her bare hand struck a deep chord in him. He was a full-fledged intruder and turned away to the corner. Then, Ruby opened her eyes and glared at him. Her gaze made him want to shrink away, but then he stopped himself. He had come upon an intimate moment between sisters for sure, but he had done nothing wrong.

"I'm sorry," he offered by way of apology.

"Thank you," Mags took up a sodden handkerchief. "I know you done what you could, Doctor."

"Did." Ruby corrected.

"Did. Travis was just a soldier in this cruel world. I tell—told—Ruby I'm going to that mill to start working and then Travis would be proud of me."

"I'm not sure that's the right thing to do." Adam didn't attempt to stop the frown from crossing his face, making his brow crease.

"Well, that's one thing we can agree on." Ruby sat up a little straighter next to her taller sister and squeezed her sister's hands.

Mags held her head high and stared at both of them. "I need to get inside to the guests. Make sure Mama has help." She drew her long legs up under her from the edge of the porch and stood, steadying herself before going into the house to the embrace of the community.

Ruby shook her head. "Mags can be mighty quiet, but stubborn when she wants."

Adam ventured closer and the very faint traces of some of the salt on Ruby's face came into view. His heart thudded at the sight of her pain, and he wanted to reach out and wipe them away for her. "But I appreciate you coming in and saying that to her. Maybe, you being an educated doctor man, you can get her to see that mill isn't for her."

"I can do my best."

"I need to finish high school. If I can get to finish, I can help my sisters."

"It must be nice to have sisters. A family. People you can count on."

"You don't have any?" Ruby lowered her head. "I'm sorry. I forgot."

"It's fine. I sometimes don't remember that I have a brother either."

"He hasn't tried to be your brother."

"Certainly not." Adam stood next to one of the strong beams that held up the house and the solid nature of the wood that John Bledsoe used to protect his family struck him. What a good man he was, and still, despite his protections of building this big porch for his daughters, they were still terribly vulnerable.

"That's something. David always wanted a brother growing up."

"Really?"

Ruby nodded. "Yes. So I told him I would be his younger brother."

"You look far away from being a brother." Adam tried to keep the admiration from his voice, but he couldn't help it. Her rounded womanly figure with her white dress and tiny roses was very pleasant to watch in the cooling heat of the summer day.

Ruby laughed. "Not when I was younger. I wanted to be a boy. David played along with me for a good long while, and let me believe it. My family helped too. Always letting me do boy stuff in helping Daddy with the farm work, until Mama forced me to help her with her laundry work. I can push a plow better than any of my sisters."

Was that anything to brag about? "Can't push a plow forever."

"Truly. Can't be a boy forever too, especially when you are a girl. Things started happening, changing when I was about fourteen. Life ain't never been the same since."

"Ruby, those changes are a natural part of life," Adam cleared his throat and hesitated. How to comfort her? "They make us who we are."

He had upset her. And he didn't mean to. His fingers tingled with uncertainty. He had never known how to talk to women. Or maybe it was this one. This one very singular woman who was different from anyone he had ever known.

"It was me changing that set everything off. I changed up to a woman and then David changed and he wasn't my friend anymore." She held her neck high and proud. "I talk to my sisters all the time. And we're close. But David. I told him all my dreams. And he took everything I said, and used it for himself. I can't ever forgive him."

How could he blame her? But standing there in the twilight of the day, watching the sun go down and the people of the town make their way into the Bledsoe home to pay their respects to poor dead Travis, he palmed his chin with a thoughtful hand. Somehow, someway, all of that shouldn't have to matter for Ruby. There was a whole world out there and he had to introduce her to it.

Chapter Seven

At breakfast a few days later, Adam used his most convincing words and his logical arguments to appeal to Ruby to forward his proposition for her future.

"No," she said. Immediately.

"Excuse me?" He swallowed some of the good strong coffee to wash down the remnants of his biscuit, covered with some of Lona's excellent peach jam. He'd get corpulent on Lona's food if he ended up staying in Georgia for any length of time, perhaps another reason to keep going. But those deep brown eyes of Ruby's and the wonderful, independent toss of her head compelled him like a siren's call, telling him to convince her, even though she didn't like him and this was the first time in days they had spoken.

"I don't want to go up north. I have my work to do here. I have my family here. Why would I go up north to some cold place?"

"So you can stay alive." Lona slapped a plate of fried salt pork on the table. "And I ain't taking Solomon on. I'm done raising babies."

Ruby glared at her mother. Adam was glad that her glare wasn't at him— this time. "Of course I won't. Why would I have gone to all this trouble to have him then? To keep him alive?"

"I don't know, child. Tell us. Here this man. He got an opportunity for you so you don't end up shot like a deer like my baby brother. Go on and go to nursing school."

"I can't believe you are willing to sell me off to the highest bidder, Mama. Just some man who comes into your door, says he's a doctor so you let him carry off your first born. I would never do that to Solomon."

Delie swung her bare feet as she sat next to Adam and her short braids stuck out on her head. "I think Ruby's afraid to go up north. She don't talk right. None of us do. You talk nice."

Delie gazed at him with all the love a five-year-old heart could muster. The sparks in her eyes made him want to chuckle, if he weren't so concerned about Ruby's welfare. Life could turn around so fast. He had no ties last week and was all alone in the world, an outcast. Now, he was surrounded by this wonderful family, whose prized jewel, the oldest daughter, refused him because she had work to do in this town. And she didn't like him.

Ruby had different sparks in her eyes, looking at her little sister, as if she wanted to kill her. "I'm not afraid of anything."

"Then you a fool, as we always knew you were," Lona called in from the kitchen. "Everybody got to be afraid of something."

"Is it true, Ruby?" Adam swallowed the last bite of delicious biscuit, savoring the tang of the bright peach sweetness.

"I'm a southern woman. I belong here." She shifted and her bare feet peeped out from under her day dress, and the sight made him uncomfortable. Why? He was a doctor. Why did it matter, and why now? The sight of her bare feet made something in his heart surge and he clenched his fists. The sight was so intimate it was as if he were seeing her naked somehow. "I don't belong with fancy talkers there."

Adam wanted to encourage her away from Winslow. "You could do more raising money for your anti-lynching crusade there. Ida Wells-Barnett lives up north."

Ruby's eyes lit up. "In Chicago."

"And she assists her husband in his legal work. She works within the law to see about helping people from the threats of being lynched."

"I thought you didn't know about Mrs. Barnett's work."

Adam spread his hands wide. "You never let me say what I knew. You just presumed. You could go on to nursing school and help that way as well."

"They have nursing schools for Negroes up there?" Ruby's eyes were wide with wonder. The rest of the table was very interested in his answer.

"Yes, of course. They have them everywhere, and in Pittsburgh where I'm going. Where else would they train?"

"I don't know. I never even thought about it before." Solomon gurgled with appreciation, but Ruby tossed her head again. "I don't have a high school diploma."

"You been trying," Lona said, in defense of her daughter. "It ain't your fault there aren't any high schools around here. All my children, once they leave the eighth grade school down in the Bottoms that ain't worth anything, they all study and read and talk."

Their hunger to educate themselves was admirable, surely. "You do need a high school diploma to get into nursing school, although some programs have it combined. You could go to nursing school and high school at the same time. The need for Negro nurses, as well as doctors, is very great."

"Is this school in Pittsburgh one of them?" John pulled Solomon in a little closer to him.

Adam's face fell, knowing he had to tell this wonderful family the truth. "I am afraid not. Ruby would have to get that some other way." Then Adam remembered something in his schooling. "Where I went to school at Michigan, they had a correspondence program where bright people would be able to take exams for their high school diploma by mail. I could proctor these things for Ruby so she could meet the standards. She could also get some beginnings to her nursing school education by working with me."

"It sounds like a lot of money."

Lona might not have been educated, but she understood a few things.

"They do cost money, ma'am." Adam addressed her, respectfully. "But there's such a shortage of nurses, it may be possible to have some fees waived. I would like to help however I can." He could even say to Paul Winslow he needed help training a nurse and get money for it from him. His father didn't need to know who the nurse was.

"And I can stay here?" Ruby spoke up.

"For now. The correspondence part means writing in and submitting something regularly, but you would be here, or anywhere."

"That might be the answer, John." Lona's eyes shone bright. "Ruby could get a high school diploma. It would help the others."

"I always wanted a high school diploma too." Mags put in.

"Baby birthing isn't regular enough. Being a nurse would give me the perfect excuse to see people in their homes, stead of going to the mills. When can I start?"

Ruby's family regarded her as if she were insane, but he just marveled. What a spirit she had. She would let nothing stop her. "Right away. We can work whenever I am free."

Lona nodded her agreement. "It's the answer I been praying to Jesus for. You a gift from the Lord, Dr. Morson."

"He surely is." Delie nodded in agreement.

"Let's stop talking. I want to get started."

"It's a good thing I kept my textbooks, then. I'll unload them and we can start after I return from the Winslows."

"What you have to go back up there for?" Lona's voice lowered to a whisper. "They don't need to know about none of this, do they?"

"It's none of their business what I do," Ruby insisted.

"No. That's not why. I'm not staying in the house with them. I have to speak with Paul Winslow about how much he's going to pay me."

The Bledsoes were relieved. "Good. Only I don't know about the pay part. He's mighty cheap," Ruby warned.

"You've said that before, Miss Ruby. I'm well prepared," Adam put in.

Though he realized his mistake later that day as he sat with Paul Winslow. "It was mighty expensive to send you to school," Paul said, sitting in his parlor surrounded by fine furnishings. "Although I'll give you some start up money for a place to treat them."

Adam cleared his throat. "I'll also need some funds for nurse training."

"Of course." Paul waved his hands. "I expected you would need some assistance."

By the time Adam figured in the cost for nurse training and an office space, which he was not going to have since he would use the Bledsoe's back room, his salary was more in line with what he had thought it should be. He prepared to send off a telegram postponing his appointment in the steel mills for an indefinite period of time.

Now with money, he could help Ruby get ready for her exams and see to the health of the community Ruby loved so much. Could Ruby feel a spark between them?

Maybe not. He would stay and help her. He wanted her to have everything his mother did not. Ruby deserved to be happy.

Thank God for all reading and writing she had done while she had kept herself at home. It had served her well. If high school should ever come to her, she wanted to be ready. In some subjects, she found she could take the exams now. She had a great skill set in writing, reasoning, science and math. However, she was less than adequate in foreign languages. She did not like them. "I don't see why I have to know all of this," Ruby grumbled as she reviewed her Latin primer.

"Do you see how many words have to do with these ancient languages?" Adam pointed out something on a page.

"Yes, but still."

"There are even more medical words that have to do with ancient languages."

Ruby nodded her head and continued studying. She had Solomon on her lap as she read Latin verbs aloud to him. No giving up. Just knowing what her own education had been, and knowing the poor education which awaited Solomon in a few years, made her want to study these horrid, difficult Latin verbs. It would be harder to watch her beautiful little boy be educated for only eight years and then work in the cotton fields all day. Or even worse, work in the mill where his own family would make sure Solomon led a limited life. She couldn't imagine her Solomon working in the mill, breathing in the fetid mill air full of lint. No. That was no life for her child. He would do better. And so would she.

Exhausted from a long night of visiting patients, Adam helped John Bledsoe work on the small back room to convert it for visitation. Adam knew a few things, but he was not the most proficient carpenter, so he was glad to have an additional set of hands to help him. The past week he had been in Winslow looking for one father. John Bledsoe was a pleasant surprise. He enjoyed being with this man, so at peace with his life and his choices. How did he manage it?

"They is all jewels," John kept repeating as they worked together. "Every one of them. And they going to be someone. Even Ruby. Folks round here think she's done. But she got something special. She always have."

He couldn't agree more.

Later, having displaced Mags out of the small back room and into the big bedroom with her sisters, he fell into a heavy dreamless sleep sensing something special which stirred him awake now. There were small grunting sounds that sounded vaguely human.

Ruby.

Adam sat up in the bed and looked out of the small window into the backyard. She was digging in the soil and she kept putting things into an old tobacco box that she must have gotten from her father since John had a few like it. Ruby's feet were bare and folded under her as she worked. Her jet black hair had been swept back into one thick plait which swung down her back. She wore men's work overalls and a white shirt underneath, and instead of covering her feminine shape, the masculine clothing enhanced it.

As he watched her, his lungs were on fire. There was something special about Ruby all right, and it almost threatened to capture him and pull him over into the abyss. He had to remember why he became a doctor, and to do his best to assist Ruby through her situation with Solomon, so she and the boy didn't have to struggle. He dressed quietly and stepped out onto the back porch.

"Are you trying to get out of lessons, Miss Bledsoe?" He tried to fold his arms and look sternly at her, but it didn't work. She was very captivating. She seemed to call a truce on her hatred of him since he had explained about a high school education and he was glad for it. He didn't want to think of a time where she didn't like him.

Ruby brushed the red dirt on her hands on the front of her overalls. Even dirty, her tapered fingers held a grace and elegance to them. "This is good fishing time. Before Solomon gets up, before anybody gets up. That's where I am going. Come along if you want, but be quiet."

She enjoyed telling him a thing or two. "You aren't afraid to go out by yourself now?"

Ruby shook her head and offered him a pole to carry as she gathered her own by the barn door. "None of the troublemakers are up now. They stay up late, they don't get up early like me. You got to get up early to catch Ruby Bledsoe."

"They sure do," Adam echoed and they walked along in the darkness, finally comfortable with one another. The comfort surprised him. He usually saw women as patients, an ailment to be treated, a puzzle to be figured out. Thinking of talking with a woman as a friend, and being with one—that was something else. She startled him when she asked him a question.

"Do you ever take your tie off?"

Adam cleared his throat and looked over at her. Her brown eyes shone at him in the darkness and were wide with innocence. "Didn't your parents ever teach you it was improper to speak with a man about his apparel?"

"How am I going to find out things if I don't bother asking?" Ruby shook her head. "And you say you teach me."

"That's it, Ruby. I'm just guiding your learning process. You're very smart. You've taken in a lot on your own. Just like Lincoln and Douglass, great men who didn't have an official education."

"So you saying I'm a great woman then?"

Adam stopped mid-stride. How did she keep doing that? Putting him off of his mark? "Ruby, I…"

Ruby threw her head back and laughed. "It's okay, Doctor. I get what you were saying. Nothing inappropriate from you, that's why the tie stays on."

"It stays on so people can see that people of our race can be proper."

"That's nice, but it's not just what we wear," Ruby insisted. "It's who we are. That's why I'm starting a chapter of the NAACP here. I want everyone to know they can have dignity and not be at the mercy of the mill. We can do it ourselves."

"It'll be hard for some who have families."

"We can start small, like with those who don't have families. What about you?"

"Me?"

"Yeah. You can be the first one to sign up." Ruby bent over and pushed some branches to the side, going onward to a small creek bed, and got some of her worms out of the box. She fixed the pole for him, presuming he didn't know how, which was sweet of her. "Here, Doctor. Throw it in like this. I'll keep an eye on it for you."

"Thanks."

"Like I said, you can be one of the first ones. Then the membership is bound to explode."

"So let me get this straight." Adam stilled himself. "It'll be myself and you as members in the Winslow chapter of the NAACP."

"To start. I'm going to be the president."

"I see. Well, I'll have to give it some thought."

"For what?" Ruby fiddled with her own line.

"To make sure there is no danger. I don't want to launch into a dangerous enterprise."

"I see. Part of the tie wearing you do."

"If it bothers you, then I'll take it off."

Adam loosened the stays on his stiff collar and it dropped to the ground. The thud the collar made in the soft grass echoed through the fishing place and made him sorry he did it. *You are her instructor. This is wrong.* An apology came to his lips when there was a tug on his line and he forgot to let Ruby think he didn't know what he was doing. In one swift movement, he pulled in a beautiful spotted trout.

He enjoyed the shocked look on her face. Her bright eyes were wide with surprise and the sprinkling of freckles across her nose seemed sharper and more prominent in the dawn light. "What? How did you…"

Adam reached over to the box now on the ground, fixed the pole again with proficient fingers and threw it back into the pond. "I was raised in Tennessee by a little creek bed. I know how to do a few things too."

The doctor could fish. Oh Lord.

Why did she have to kick him in the leg? If she took a dunk in the cold creek, it would not cool her humiliation at her behavior at Bob's.

It did not seem possible for him to be more handsome, but he was and freer without his stiff collar on. She could see his Adam's apple move up and down in his throat as he spoke to her in his deep and resonant voice.

Focus on getting some fish.

How shameful she had not caught anything yet. She could not let herself get caught up into the spell of this man—a man unlike any other she had ever met. Uncle Arlo had left her a great and powerful work to do. He would not like for her to be distracted for a silly reason. Determined, she stepped over and placed her bare feet onto some of the smooth stones of the creek bed, and focused on catching something.

"Moving closer to them doesn't necessarily help," Adam cracked as he pulled in another one.

"I know. We're fishing too close. Let's get on to another place. I do fine when I'm on my own."

Adam threw his pole in again. "I know. I've been on my own for a long time. But I have to admit, it is nice having companionship."

"Nice idea. It doesn't always work." Ruby laughed and the old times slid through her mind. "For instance, growing up, I was supposed to be David's wife.

What a joke on me."

Adam said nothing. She liked that. He was ready to listen. Maybe that was his doctor training, but she was glad that he wanted to hear her side of things. "I mean, we're the same color. Always running around when we were young, comparing our skin, all over." Ruby remembered those carefree days before she got to be a Negro. She and David played right up until the summer she turned fourteen..

Then, her changing body betrayed her. Suddenly, they couldn't be friends anymore. No more playing. "But we weren't the same color. Not in the eyes of everyone. People said, I thought I was too good for anyone else in this town, 'cause I'm light."

Ruby peered at Adam's quiet and dignified countenance in the dawn as he pulled in yet another fish. He added the fish to his growing pile and faced her again. "Folks were wrong. I just thought we were the same and it was the natural order of things we would be husband and wife one day. But I found out the hard way. I'm a Negro. Different. And now, I'm soiled for any other man."

Adam snorted which wasn't like him at all. "You don't really believe that, do you?"

"It's what people say, day and night."

"It's not true." Adam faced her as he paused in baiting another hook. "What happened to you was not right and not natural. You cannot honestly believe you ruined your chances. You're a perfectly lovely, smart woman. Once you decide not to be any trouble to any man, you will find a husband who will care for you and provide for you."

Now it was Ruby's turn to snort. "I don't want to be taken care of like a china doll. I want to help a man in his work. I could do somebody some kind of good."

"You have a lot you can do." Adam pointed out her fishing rod to her. "Look, I think you got lucky."

Ruby reeled in her catch, a small trout not worth eating. She unhooked it and threw it back in. "You." And with a finger, she touched his hard, thick, muscled chest. A delighted little shiver went through her, "Are bad luck."

The wind shifted and she sensed the change in the day, thank God. "Solomon's up by now. He'll want breakfast."

Adam picked up his five fish. "I think there is enough to go around for breakfast, thanks to me. If you clean them, I'll fry and give your mother a break."

Ruby hooted, "Fry?"

"I told you there were a lot of things I could do. Don't underestimate me." Their eyes met in the first spark of sunlight for the day, a new day full of hope and promise.

"I won't." Ruby gathered up the poles. "I just want to see for myself."

"Good," Adam praised her, "You have used the kind of language a teacher wants to hear from his student. You'll make a fine nurse someday."

Her heart sank. He didn't say a fine nurse for himself. No need to get excited about his hard chest. Despite what he had said about her not being soiled, he spoke one thing and believed another. A true hypocrite. He was no kind of person to be in her life and certainly not one to be an example to Solomon. Ruby resolved right then and there to make his words come true—to be a fit nurse for someone else despite the ever-pulling and ever-tightening bond between the two of them.

Chapter Eight

As they walked back to the house in the early morning dawn, Adam kept sneaking glances at Ruby's side profile and thinking how pleasing it was to look at her. She was eighteen, almost nineteen years old, but she looked younger with her luxuriant black hair tied back into one thick black braid. She had a fine mind as well, as she talked to him about the rights of the Negro people and how they had to fight. Her animated way of expressing herself made him get lost in the intensity of what she was saying. Any man would want to be caught up in her intensity.

He couldn't help but admire her. Those brown freckles scattered across her nose like nutmeg on a pudding of some kind—something which only enhanced her sweetness. David, his pseudo brother, was a fool. If he ever really loved this worthy, wonderful young woman, how could he have done her such a profound evil and wrong? He shook his head to clear his mind of the thought. One saw many such things in the medical profession, and David, in his weak sensibility, was just one person who had it in him. He wasn't a man, he was just a thing controlled by Paul Winslow. Adam would not be controlled.

They came up to the porch and her mother was standing there with her hand on her hip. "Solomon was looking for you."

Ruby grinned. "I knew he was up. I can just tell when he's awake in the world. Look at what we caught." She held up the string of fish.

Lona nodded. "A fine breakfast. Good job."

"We?" Adam choked out. "You mean me." He turned to Lona. "I can fry, Mrs. Bledsoe."

Lona waved him away. "Men don't belong in my kitchen."

Ruby's mother's offhand comment did not strike him as much as when Ruby gestured with her thumb at him in a careless way. That got to him right at his heart. Couldn't she regard him any better than that? "He had some beginner's luck down at the pond."

Lona regarded the fine string of fish. "He don't look like no beginner."

"I am not, surely. We had similar creeks in Tennessee."

"A Southern boy. And a provider." Lona took the fish and admired them. Adam could hear her as she turned to address Ruby who passed her by, "That's another kind of catch over there." She spoke to him in a stern voice. "You coming to church with us tomorrow?"

Lona held the door open for him as he went into the house. All of the Bledsoes were in a flurry getting ready for the day. Ruby grabbed a squalling Solomon in her arms ready to get him fed, and yelled over her shoulder as she went into the bedroom. "I don't know about church yet."

"It's getting past time," Lona yelled out after her. "You have to get over it. Solomon is nearly six months now. He has to be christened for the sake of his soul."

Adam handed off the string of fish to Mags who bustled off to the kitchen with it. John came to him and guided him to the table. "Ruby hasn't had an easy time with the church folk since she started showing with Solomon. Folks at First Water are real particular about how young girls behave."

"As they should be." Lona elbowed Em.

John insisted, "I ain't said that. But as I recall, the Bible says something about throwing stones. And as you say, we got to bring Solomon into the church. Any thing his mama did don't have nothing to do with him."

"Or his father." Adam did not hesitate to come to Ruby's defense. When he said those three words, something he thought of as a mere utterance, as his way of telling the truth, every one of the Bledsoes stared at him. What was wrong with what he said? Was it wrong to say Solomon had a father?

He was about to ask for some explanation when Lona asked him in a clear tone, "Will you come with us, Adam? Come to the church and stand in God's light?"

"I'm not usually much for church," Adam's mind went back to those long, boring Sundays when he attended in Tennessee. And to God denying him his mother.

Ruby emerged at the doorway, holding a satisfied looking Solomon so he faced outward. His little legs wriggled back and forth and Adam could see the blue veins working in his little skinny legs. A trail of milk went down his cheek. Solomon gave him a toothless grin that took his heart away. Who wouldn't, or couldn't bring themselves to welcome this child anywhere, much less into the kingdom of God? "Well, why not?"

Ruby jiggled Solomon up and down a bit, almost using him as a shield against the world. "You can meet more of your patients there. I can check on Agnes while I am there as well."

Her use of the first person plural did not escape him.

"There'll be lunch afterward too—they always do on the last Sunday," Delie chimed in. "You'll get to meet lots of folk and eat some good cooking too."

Everyone chuckled. Adam smiled at the love-struck Delie. "How can I refuse? Ruby?"

A sigh of relief went all around. All except Ruby, who had a stormy look on her face as she sat down at the table with the baby. Mags came bustling out of the kitchen with a plate full of crisply fried potatoes. "Fish will be out soon. Have a biscuit," she urged Adam. He obliged her.

Ruby sat down next to him. "No one is saying anything about Dodge."

"What should be said about Reverend Dodge?" Lona split a cathead biscuit and put some peach jam on it.

"He's the one who cast me out."

"And now you're coming in to have your child brought to Jesus. He won't turn you away."

"He didn't even come to see Solomon when he was born. Or when he was sick. He might have at least prayed for him. What kind of minister is he?"

"You know his feelings were hurt," Mags mumbled as she came back in with the platter of hot crisp fish.

"That's enough," Lona interjected. "No disrespectful talk in this house about a man of God."

"Even if he disrespects me by turning away my child," Ruby said.

"That was months ago, Ruby," Lona insisted.

"Eleven months and twenty-one days."

Pain etched onto Ruby's beautiful features. Missing the worship had meant a great deal to her. He reached over and held his hands out for Solomon. The baby pushed out his arms to him excited, and as they exchanged the holding of him, he and Ruby touched flesh. A jolt went up and down his arms.

But he would never drop precious Solomon. He accepted the warm, milk-heavy weight of him. He was doing much better. "Everyone will be there. I'll be there. If it is a true house of God as you say, then anyone should be welcome. Including you."

Ruby's warm brown eyes gazed back at him. "It'll be all right then." Her voice went soft as if she were praying. "God'll see to it."

Since she had spoken it, he was sure she was right.

Ruby's stomach was in knots. She told Adam she'd go to church in front of her family, but hadn't been in nearly a year. But she was ready. She wanted the Winslow community to see that Solomon, despite his birth, was worthy of God's blessing. Solomon was one of them—a child of God. If she were brave enough, she would make Reverend Dodge bless her son.

She had been brave about other things, why not this? Ruby tightened her grip on Solomon as Adam's car slowly and carefully navigated the bumpy, Georgia back roads to the little church on the other side of the Bledsoe's woods. Ever since Dodge came to the community to lead and establish First Water four years ago, his eyes had always gazed on Ruby with a burning intensity. He had been waiting, probably, until she was eighteen years old and a young lady, to ask her father's permission to court her.

Maybe he had been about to, but then there was the awful Sunday when he realized she was going to have a baby and he cast her out from the church in a very public way. She could have kept going if he hadn't made every sermon about sinning or low behavior. She couldn't take it anymore. That was when she stayed at home, and then her family, one by one joined her. It wasn't fair to the other fifty people who attended the church to have to hear the same sermons all the time. God had more in mind, and better goodness than that.

Adam pulled the car to the side of the little grey clapboard church, which needed a coat of paint, and stood away from all the horses and mules. Adam's car was the only car there. As he came out and opened the door for her, she got a full view of him in his suit. And just as before, the sight of him made her heart skip a beat, which irritated her. Why did she react to him in this way? The lighter linen color held a clean crisp edge. The beige didn't wash out his light skin, but enhanced it.

My, he is handsome.

As he extended his hand to help her get out of the car, a tingle went up her arm. She was a lady, clean and snow white, not dirty. Not anymore.

She held onto Solomon as she came out of the car and walked to the front steps of the church. A good portion of the church members of First Water, about fifty in number, stood in stunned silence as they watched this strange, light-colored man help her out of the car. Reverend Dodge stood at the top of the steps, staring, seemingly ready to condemn her once more. They moved to the stairs and Mrs. Bomead, one of the leading church women, fixed Ruby with a stare and then shifted her gaze of judgment to Solomon.

The whole church held its breath, Ruby was sure. This woman, next to her mother, was the foundation of the small church. She, without Lona's input, had decided Ruby did not belong. Even though it was somewhat apparent he had feelings for Ruby, he folded, not wanting to lose his high position as a minister. Just another reason Ruby wasn't too fond of Dodge, as she called him.

"Ruby Jean!" Mrs. Bomead boomed from under a ridiculously decorated daisy hat. "Let me see that baby."

Ruby stepped closer to the woman and held Solomon out. She really didn't want to give her son over to her. On the top of Solomon's head, his little veins throbbed faster as if he were nervous.

When Doris Bomead turned the baby around in her arms, Solomon stared up at her with curiosity. He reached a small hand out to the big woman, and grabbed at her dark brown nose.

Ruby let out her breath when Mrs. Bomead smiled. That woman probably hadn't smiled in years. "Look at this here little fellow." Mrs. Bomead grabbed his hand. "He's so handsome and friendly. And as white as a boll of cotton, bless his heart."

Her countenance became stormy. "Where's his hat? Got to keep a baby's head covered."

Solomon played with Mrs. Bomead's face some more and then searched for his mother. Ruby stepped forward for him, but it was Adam he wanted. Adam took the baby. Ruby foraged in her bag for a hat and a clean cloth diaper. She didn't want Solomon to be sick on his beautiful suit. But Adam rejected the diaper as she tied the hat strings together under Solomon's sharp little chin. His light colored suit was so beautiful.

Well, if Solomon got sick, she would wash his suit for him. What would it be like to wash his clothes? Such a personal thing. She warmed a little at the thought of it until she lifted her eyes and saw Dodge at the top of the stairs, watching the family-like tableau. His small black eyes narrowed and he peered down his large nose at her. He made sure he used enough oils on his person until he shone to the color of teakwood. Dodge could have been handsome, but he was vain. Vanity was not a good quality in a preacher. He wore his collars too often and insisted on being called Reverend.

She'd heard he may have gone to school in Tennessee or maybe he was from there? Maybe Adam knew something of his people. She would ask him later.

As a number of the parishioners gathered around Solomon to admire him, Reverend approached the baby, the crowd parting for him. "*Reverend* Dodge," Ruby put emphasis on the title he loved so much. "Reverend, will you bless my baby?"

Everyone quieted once again. Everything was still. "Sister Ruby," he intoned. "We have not had a chance to discuss your request."

Ruby said, "You're always welcome at the Bledsoe home. Solomon has been there. He's almost six months old now.."

"True. But this child is not the child of a sanctioned Christian marriage. His heavenly position is in jeopardy."

In the hot summer sunshine, a chill froze her limbs. Coming here was wrong. Poor Solomon should not have to deal with this. If she could only move, she would take the baby back to the car, or better yet, walk with him on down the road. Why were people staring and judging them? Why had she listened to Lona?

Adam turned the baby outward again. "I believe, Mr. Dodge, God said, 'suffer the little children to come unto me.' Surely you know life is a blessing. Perhaps you didn't hear Solomon has been sick recently. He's much better now, but this illness alarmed his mother. She wants to have her child blessed."

Dodge had the nerve to look shaken. "Dr. Morson."

"Glad to see you. We didn't get to meet at the funeral last week."

Ruby took a measure of pleasured delight. Adam didn't call him Reverend. He extended his hand to Dodge while still keeping a firm arm on Solomon.

Dodge didn't approach his handshake. "So you're still here? I believe the Winslows know you."

Adam took back his rejected hand and placed it more firmly on the baby. She could see Adam was fully aware Dodge was judging him, the same way he condemned Solomon, and Adam's narrowed lips showed his displeasure. "Of course. I'm a child of God too."

Dodge shot a glance at Doris Bomead. With her approval, Dodge said, "And welcome. Bring the baby in and we'll begin church."

"Come on, Ruby." Adam extended the crook of his arm out to her, still holding Solomon with steady hands. She slipped her hand into it, and taking comfort in the firmness of his arm, climbed up the stairs into the church building, which had provided her so much comfort over the years. She was glad to be home.

Adam despised the man the moment he saw him. Dodge's gaze at Ruby was full of unseemly lust, as if Ruby were a pastry in a shop window. Dodge's behavior was not appropriate for a man in his position. He had judged and practically condemned Ruby.

How many of these people truly understood Ruby's trials? He doubted any had. In his position, he had been witness to ugly behavior in the world. Because Ruby and David had known one another, people probably blamed her— thinking she had seduced him in some way—just as those who'd condemned him for his mother's low standing. It wasn't true. And Ruby wasn't a woman of low character either.

Despite Dodge, the service was beautiful and filled with welcoming words. His soul stirred as he looked into Solomon's innocent face and down at Ruby's hopeful countenance. She deserved hope. She deserved better. Lona clearly thought he was worthy, but she didn't know him.

As he sat there in the church, listening to the beautiful words of welcome, he understood there was something larger at work here. His palms slid off each other, slick with sweat. He pulled out a handkerchief, leaving the cloth wet. Ruby's newfound role in his life made him better. He was no longer lonely and there was the thrill of joy in his heart for the first time in a long time.

After church was over, the women went outside and spread the beautiful quilts Lona had made on the ground. The artistry in the quilts stunned him. The spread of food amazed him as well. Clearly, this Sunday picnic the church had once a month was an opportunity for many of these women to show off, and they did. The table nearly sagged, overwhelmed with all kinds of chicken and sandwiches, beautiful pound cakes and pies, and rainbows of jars filled with pickled vegetables.

Adam ate his fill and then went around and met the congregation. There were the Bledsoes, of course, but other families came forward, and he met them as well. He resolved to come to their homes to gain knowledge about their healthcare, something that had never been done, apparently. The only care they had before was Ruby and her predecessor, an old midwife clearly with very unsafe practices.

He pushed a fork into a triangle of peach pie and savored the buttery goodness of its crunchy crust mixed with the tangy sweetness of the succulent peaches. Such joy came to him in knowing he could be of purpose to these people, even at the behest of Paul Winslow.

"Having a good time?" Dodge's oily tone made him cringe. "Had enough to eat?" Dodge smirked at Adam's plate that held remains of his uneaten peach pie. Adam faced Dodge. The animosity coming from this man added to the heat of the June day.

"Everything here was delicious. A wonderful repast. Still eating." Adam held up the peach pie in hopes he would go away.

No luck.

Dodge spread his arms, trying to look like a prophet, but came across as something more like a charlatan. "These are my people."

Antipathy radiated off of Dodge. Adam threatened him, so he stood down, but just a tad. "They're in need of quality care. It was good I was sent for."

Dodge fixed him with another judgmental look, "Yes, I heard about how you came to our town. Take care you don't use the dictates of the white man to keep these people sick and unwell."

"The first time someone takes an oath to be a doctor, the first words you learn are 'Do No Harm.' I like the words because they remind us, as doctors, we cannot intervene in God's will by making the situation worse. I think these people, the Negroes of Winslow, will be better with more care." Adam put more pie into his mouth so Dodge could see he was finished with their talk.

"A man of God I see," Dodge's words came on the back of a turtle. He must not be able to process very fast. "And where do you stand, Doctor? With the Negroes of Winslow or the whites? In your situation, I suppose it would be hard to decide."

This man might know his entire history, but he didn't care. He didn't like the insinuation in this man's voice. He swallowed. "I'm here at the invitation of Paul Winslow. I had other offers, but I came here. I knew I was needed."

"Really? Or was it to pay your school money back? I hear it is very expensive to educate a doctor."

Adam didn't let any flicker of surprise register on his features. "I wanted to know my family as well."

"As long as you aren't here to make one, you're welcome." Dodge eyed Ruby who sat on a blanket and played with Solomon. His inappropriate behavior made Adam lose his appetite. He would have put down his pie but had no place to put it.

"Reverend, I'm a grown man and I'll do as I please, without anyone's approval. Excuse me." He smoothed out his waistcoat and walked away from the Reverend as quickly as possible. No wonder Ruby hesitated to return to this flock. Adam didn't think himself worthy of Ruby's goodness, but he was a much better man than Dodge. He had to do whatever he could to protect Ruby from him.

Walking toward Ruby, he smiled as she waved him over, smiling. He waved back, marveling at the warmth her smile made him feel.

If only he could be certain of its continuity.

Could he ask God for it? He might, but the sun seemed too large and too big a thing to ask an unlistening and unknowing God for.

Chapter Nine

The picture of Adam in his crisp summer suit provided some nice flights of fancy for Ruby over the next several days. She remembered how he had waved at her as he approached her and Solomon on the picnic blanket at church.

Could he possibly like her?

More than as a teacher?

A mentor?

Solomon's doctor?

Can't afford to be distracted by folly. And it would be folly to believe someone like her would be a fit woman for a doctor.

Delie came running in, looking as if she had rolled around in dirt. Ruby looked up from her task, readying some hand-decorated signs to give to some of the patients.

"What're you doing?" Delie poked at the artwork with a red-mud crusted finger.

"Don't touch. I'm making signs for my recitation of Frederick Douglass's 'What to the Slave is the Fourth of July?'"

Delie sat down on the bench across for her and scratched her nose. Ruby reached in her skirt pocket and handed her a handkerchief. "When you going to do that?"

"At the town celebration."

"But what about Archibald Melvin?" Delie blew her nose into Ruby's clean handkerchief. Delie was the sister most like her, a grubby little tomboy. Even though Ruby was not happy at having to launder what was inside the dirtied handkerchief, she loved Delie with a fierce protectiveness. "You start talking, we'll miss the music and the fireworks and the ice cream. No more trouble making, Ruby."

"No one wants to hear the Declaration of Independence. Not the way Archibald Melvin reads it."

"What does Douglass say?"

Ruby put her brush down. "He says the Fourth of July is not for Negroes. We can't be happy on that day, because we have been in shackles."

"But slavery is over." Delie put down the handkerchief and started to fiddle around Ruby's beautiful creations.

"To a point, yes. But in other ways, no. Stop touching."

"I ain't no slave," Delie insisted. "And I got to have ice cream."

"You're too young to understand." Usually, Paul Winslow had big celebrations for the Fourth of July for his namesake town. He hired a band to play music for the recently built bandshell in the town square. There would be ice cream, a rare treat, followed by the annual reading of the Declaration of Independence. And he did all of that so little people like Delie would believe everything was just grand. And would want to work for him in the next few years.

Ruby grimaced. The music was fine, and the ice cream delicious, but she hated they were forced to endure the reading of the document. She loved the soaring poetry of the Declaration, but Paul Winslow asked Dr. Archibald Melvin, minister of the First Presbyterian church, to read it. The man was older than Methuselah and the way he read the words made Ruby want to fall asleep. She usually did. The reading was only worth enduring to get to the fireworks Winslow would have in the cool of the evening.

Douglass's oration made much more sense. Ruby shivered at remembering some of Douglass's words. She had been in love with a dead man. Douglass had died a few years before she was born. Still, he was such a great man for her people.

What if Adam were as proud to be Negro as Frederick Douglass?

She shivered. Good thing he was not. She would not be able to resist him then. Better Adam continue on with his two-faced ways and his embrace of falsity. A man who looked like Adam, with those grey eyes and spoke like Douglass, would be too much distraction from her task to make Winslow better.

As she added some more color to a border with paint, a sharp knocking at the door startled them. Delie ran to the door to open it and was surprised to see Mary Winslow standing there. Despite the impossible Georgia heat of early July, Mary Winslow was dressed in a very ornate gown of pearl grey and had a matching hat perched on top of her head. As Ruby went to the door, Mary fixed her with a gaze of contempt. Dirty little Delie was far beneath her notice and Delie ran out the back door in response.

"Is your mother at home?" No polite preamble for her.

Mary Winslow clutched one of her beautifully designed reminders about her oration in her gray glove. Ruby opened her mouth to say something about it, without getting Lona dragged into whatever Mary Winslow wanted. She decided not to. "Why, yes, ma'am." Ruby went submissive on her. "Let me get her for you. You can make yourself comfortable on the porch if you like. The heat is something fierce isn't it? Lemonade?"

"This isn't a social call, girl. I want to speak to Lona, now."

Ruby turned on her heel and a little hand popped up in the air out of the cradle. Miss Mary's sharp tone made Solomon stir in his nap. Tempted to go and pat him back down to sleep, she stopped. An idea came to her mind. She went to the kitchen and told Lona that Mary Winslow was on the porch.

Instantly, Lona's face became a mass of worry lines. "What could she want from me?"

Ruby assumed all innocence. "I have no idea." Ruby followed her mother to the porch where Mary Winslow waited.

"Mrs. Winslow," Lona's voice floated back to her. She went submissive too. "Fine day, ain't it? Can I help you with something?"

Mary Winslow sat on the courting porch right under the window to the front room where Solomon napped. Her sharp upset tones were going to further wake the baby. Good. That was just what Ruby wanted. Mrs. Winslow popped up, confronting Lona, "What's your girl up to now? She's trying to ruin my husband's Fourth of July celebration."

"No, ma'am."

Mary Winslow waved the flyer under Lona's nose. "What's this all about? She's to give an oration? No one wants to hear her speak!"

Ruby skipped down the three front stairs to the car parked out in the front yard. The Winslow chauffeur, Bob, tapped his hands on the wheel of the car, waiting for Mary Winslow to be done with her visit. Ruby waved as she approached him. "How's Willie? I come to check on him soon. You want a lemonade?"

The sharp taps stopped. "Baby's fine. Right healthy. No lemonade, thank you, Ruby Jean. I'm right fine here in this car."

Ruby stood next to the car, and whispered. "Who gave her my flyer?"

Bob's long chin froze. "I needs this job, Ruby. You can't get that out of me today, no way."

"But you'll let me know when you can?"

Bob just nodded. Good, he understood why she needed to know the information. Ruby went back up the red clay path to the house, waving and shouting as she went. "Ok then, Bob!"

Her mother gripped at her apron corners and Mary Winslow stood over her, shouting at Lona, saying she would have her laundering done elsewhere and Lona would not have her business or her friends' business anymore. "It'll be all over for you, Lona, unless you get that girl in line, you hear me?"

Ruby and her mother clashed often, but it still twisted her up inside to see her mother, a pious if not mistaken woman, as Lona twisted the corner of her apron in worry at the loss of this income. She had to find a way to help her mother, to do better for them all. Ruby went past the little scene on the front porch, back inside the house and picked up Solomon.

He squirmed in her hold, wet and smelly in a bad way, but she picked him up and held him on her shoulder. Nowadays, Solomon didn't like this position as much, because he couldn't see anything, but Ruby rubbed his back to get him to be quiet. Patting him, she wandered toward the front courting porch to hear Mary Winslow. "You have been good and faithful and your laundering skills are wonderful, but I mean…"

Ruby stood in the open doorway and turned Solomon around so his little face was toward Mary Winslow.

The woman gave a sharp intake of breath.

So, that was it. Mary Winslow came down here to get a glimpse of her first grandchild. She didn't really care what Ruby did. Ruby stared down at her hands and arms filled with her child.

God's teachings had taught her to feel compassion for a fellow human being and she let the compassion for Mary Winslow sweep over her. The poor woman was in a cage of her own, in her house, in her hot, heavy and ornate clothing, and in her skin. She couldn't even come down to say hello and marvel at the beauty of her first grandchild without harassing Lona, who was innocent. Christian pity for Mary Winslow was only appropriate for her as a poor person who could not know the beauty and wonder of Solomon.

"Ma'am, I know Ruby will not offend. I think she just thought the young people would like to hear something a little different after Reverend. Marvin. I think all of the young people, even the white ones, wonder if something a little different couldn't happen on the Fourth, sometimes. That's all she was trying to do, not offend."

With the placating note of her mother's voice, Ruby knew Lona had also noticed how Mary Winslow's stern countenance had softened on sight of Solomon, who squirmed in his mother's firm hold. "Well, see she doesn't."

"I won't, ma'am." Ruby took a step onto the courting porch and turned Solomon back over her shoulder, gripping him more firmly as he squirmed. Mary Winslow couldn't see Solomon's face anymore, but his soggy bottom faced her instead. "I gots this boy to take care of and I can't let nothing happen to me like it happened before. Ma'am."

Then, Mary Winslow remembered herself, and her backbone straightened again. "See you don't." As she turned away, Adam Morson came up the walkway toward the front of the house. "Adam. Dr. Morson. What are you doing here?"

"The Bledsoes are patients who are part of my community, Mrs. Winslow. And I live here in this house now."

"Oh. Well. I can only caution you on the company you keep. I can speak highly of Lona, but the oldest girl of hers is trouble. Stay away from her."

"I'll treat anyone who is in need of my services, ma'am. I'm a doctor." Adam's voice was firm.

Mary Winslow paused at the bottom of the stairs and turned to look at her again. Ruby should have cast her gaze downward, but she couldn't do it. Not anymore. She stared right into Miss Mary's blue eyes.

"Yes. Of course you are a steward of their health, certainly, just as my husband intended. I mean in another way. She is temptation personified. She seduced my son. Don't think you are invulnerable to her charms."

Adam stiffened at Mary Winslow's accusations. "Ma'am. I'm sure you're suffering in this heat. Let me escort you to the car."

Adam led Mary Winslow to her car and opened the door for her, all without touching her. Ruby sniffed and a sharp odor entered her nostrils and she knew now her son was more than wet. She hurried him back into the front sleeping room and changed his diaper.

No one was going to malign her or tell her not to give an oration. As much as she loved the words of Frederick Douglass, she got another idea instead.

Yes.

Instantly, her spirits perked up at the way Adam had just defended her in front of a powerful woman and all but threw her off of their property. The good doctor was not meek about anything. Why did that surprise her? Would he help her with her plan?

If she told him about it in advance, he might.

She pulled her dry son up to a sitting position and reveled in his toothless smile of comfort. No. He had to appear as if he had no idea about it. It would be wrong to put him in harm's way.

Adam waited until the cool of the day to see other patients. He would miss dinner at the Bledsoes but the early July heat made this necessary. He also was aware some people were out at work and he could not see them as he might want. However, later in day, he and Ruby went out in the car to visit Bob's house again, deeper in the woods. They would also visit another house. The homes were closer to one another, but unfortunately, the car could not make the journey all the way into them.

"Here's the walking part," Ruby announced, carrying a bag with some of her belongings in them.

Small claws dug into his flesh and in reaction, Adam slapped at a mosquito or a chigger, it was hard to know which. All he knew was the insects of the deeper South had ferociously large jaws, far worse than Tennessee. "Don't kick me, Ruby. Who else is back here besides Bob and Agnes Turnman?"

"Bob's on this side," Ruby pointed, "and his brother Turnbull is over here."

"Turnman and Turnbull?"

"Turnbull's real name is John Turnman, but he stubborn, so everyone call him Turnbull."

Adam nodded. He enjoyed hearing these stories about how Negroes gave each other names more suitable to them once their personalities, or life stories, were better known. Very creative.

As they walked to the houses, his stomach clenched. Turnbull's house was more like his brother's than the Bledsoes. These homes were more like the ones he had been exposed to when he was growing up.

A doctor had to see many things. He cleared his throat to steel himself.

"Let's go see Turnbull first," Ruby urged, and Adam agreed. The visit went smoothly, thanks to Ruby's attitude to the family. She was such an asset for a doctor in this situation. Truly a jewel.

Once they were done visiting with Turnbull, wife and three children, they went further down the path to the other house. Bob was not home, but Agnes greeted them with Willie in her arms.

This time, Agnes Turnman welcomed them heartily, glad to see a Negro doctor examine her and all her children. Adam took note of everything she could remember about them. He gave the children and Agnes, some vitamins. They prepared to leave and Bob appeared in the doorway. His long and familiar-looking face reflected shock to see them both in his humble home. Ruby lit up at his appearance in the doorway and Adam knew clever Ruby had engineered this visit on purpose. "Told you we be by, Bob, good to see you," Ruby chirped.

Bob didn't seem so delighted to see Ruby. "Looky here. I got nothing to say to you. You see Agnes and my children here. Willie just come. I needs my job, and I ain't telling you nothing that I can get in trouble for."

Ruby's brown eyes seemed downcast at first, but then she looked up at him. "That's not what you said before, Bob, but I understand. We'll get along now."

"What's going on?" Agnes interjected with a very direct gaze at her husband.

"Mary Winslow had one of my flyers and Bob knows where she got it from. He don't have to say, though. Come on." Ruby, Adam could tell, spoke out loud on purpose.

"What?" Agnes's face was puzzled and Adam could not help but admire Ruby. There were other ways of getting this information, without getting Bob into trouble. "What she talking about?"

"Oh come on, Agnes. This here's men's business,"

Bob had not said the right thing, because Agnes puffed up. The woman who he had thought of as having a shy and cowardly countenance changed all of a sudden.

"I think we better be going." Adam stood from the hewn pine table to leave.

"This my business too, if it involve letting Mary Winslow know she don't run our business. She sending folk up in here all the time, all hours, thinking she owns you like it's slavery times again. Well, it ain't." Agnes folded her arms and faced the still-seated Ruby. "What you want to know?"

Ruby faced Bob and gazed straight into his eyes, unafraid. "Did you give her the flyer?"

"No."

"Who did then?" Adam asked, curious to know himself.

"Reverend Dodge." Bob spit out the two short words. "No more now. Go on home, Ruby Jean. It was nice seeing you, though, Dr. Morson. Thank you for coming and checking on the family." Bob stood and shook his hand with a firm, sure grip.

Ruby slapped a hand on the rough-hewn wooden table. "I should have known. Sell-out."

"Reverend Dodge is a minister of God, and you ain't got no right talking bad about a Christian man." Bob shook his head. "You got to go on home before my young girls see how you doing."

Agnes unfolded her arms. "They is a Christian man, and then there is Christian ways. Telling on Ruby ain't no Christian way. The Reverend, he get on my nerves sometimes."

Bob's eyes widened as he looked as his wife. "Girl, what you saying?"

Agnes stood next to Ruby's chair. "He try to act like he judge and jury over Ruby here when she had the baby. I didn't like it, not one bit."

Ruby stood and grasped her hand. "I appreciate it, Agnes. More than you know."

"Ain't no sin in having a baby. Especially if you love somebody. But it really ain't if someone forced it on you."

Bob was silent. "I don't know nothing about it."

"Yeah, I know we in trouble water now, since we talking about Queen Mary again."

"We had better go." Adam made a move to the door and Ruby followed him.

"Thank you, Agnes." Ruby hugged her.

"Bob." Ruby nodded to him. "We see you at church and for the celebrations on Sunday."

"Yeah, we see you," Agnes echoed and waved a little.

"Don't start nothing you can't finish, girl. This here community see you,"

Bob warned.

Ruby stood before Bob. "I know. And the reason I say what I do is 'cause I see them too."

Bob patted her shoulder. She and Adam made their way through the thick tall weeds down the road to the car. Adam ducked whenever a chigger came close to him. Ruby's mood shifted to the quiet as they climbed back into the car, and he started the machine.

"What are you thinking about?" Adam climbed in next to her and began the slow drive out of the thicket.

"What reason could Dodge have of telling on me to Mary Winslow?" Ruby's naiveté startled him.

"Revenge. He wants you for himself and can't have you. So he's doing his best to ruin your life. You need to stay as far away from him as possible." Ruby nodded her head and seemed thoughtful on the ride back.

The bad feeling in the pit of his stomach was not a bellyache. How much of what he said had she taken in? She needed protection from the forces at work against her, and from Dodge.

What was stopping him from providing the protection this admirable young woman clearly needed from him?

Rejection.

He knew that embracing him would be embracing the enemy—he was Paul Winslow's son, after all. And David's half-brother. Taking up with him would practically wed her to her attacker.

She might not like that.

But he was bonded to her, as if they were drawn together by an invisible force. Even the positive way they had begun to regard each other was still so new, he was afraid to take a chance on its permanence.

His training in science guided him in his work, as well as in his emotions. He was a scientist and he would proceed with caution. However, when he pulled up to the front porch of the Bledsoe house, a strange horse nickered at the car, rebelling at the tether holding her to the post. Ruby's creamy skin went a shade paler beneath her adorable cinnamon-colored freckles. "What is it?"

"Dodge…he's here to see Mama, I guess, to make my life more miserable."

Before Adam could stop her, Ruby climbed the front steps and he came behind her, standing in the doorway to overhear Dodge in his pretentious voice. "A woman like her needs a man of God for protection. She need protecting from the community and from herself. She need to atone for what she has done. And the boy need a right firm hand from a man of God to be brought up in the light. I'm here to be of help and service to you."

"What's going on here?" Ruby stood in the doorway, not in a reticent posture, but in full attack mode. Adam breathed a sigh of relief, glad at her show of spirit.

Lona wiped her hands on her apron as she sat as the family all were sitting at the front room table, eating peach cobbler and drinking coffee. Dodge had the biggest helping of all and scraped the plate clean with his fork picking up every drop. At least Mags wouldn't have to wash the plate.

Lona spoke up. "Reverend Dodge is here, Ruby. He has an offer to make things right for you."

"Right for me?"

For some reason Adam couldn't fathom, his heart started to beat faster, both at the Reverend's words and how Lona and John cowed in fear. Adam didn't like they had to be afraid in the comfort of their own home, but he guessed these matters depended little. Most Negro people had little control over their own lives.

"Reverend Dodge has come to offer for you, Ruby. He wants to marry you." Lona's usually harsh register softened as she spoke to her oldest daughter.

His heart shattered in a thousand little pieces.

Chapter Ten

So her sisters' teasing was true. Dodge did have feelings for her—why would he want to marry her otherwise? What could she possibly say? *Think, Ruby.* Then something occurred to her. "Oh, Reverend," she said with more enthusiasm than she thought she could ever gather at such a prospect. "I'm a sinner. How could someone like you be married to someone like me? I could never be a preacher's wife. I wouldn't want to get in the way of what you do."

Dodge ran a thoughtful hand over his mouth. "Well now, Ruby Jean. I've given it some thought. I suspect the people here in Winslow know your past. But we've forgiven you. And, as I travel, other churches will want my services. They'll have no reason to know about your disgraceful actions."

Adam Morson fairly bristled next to her, but she couldn't react just now. She had to think—think—think of a way to hold this man off. Dodge held out his plate toward the pan of cobbler. Lona obliged him with another big flaky piece. Ruby tried to keep her face straight as he picked up his fork and went to work on the cobbler as if his life depended on it.

He said, "People will see us, you, me, your child and they will take us as a Christian family. In time, we'll have our own. So it'll be all right."

"Umm." Ruby paused. She heard Solomon cry. *Thank you, God.* "I have to go and get him."

Her mother gave her a distressed look out of the corner of her eye. She didn't know what Lona was thinking of now—should she marry Dodge or not? Ruby could sense her mother didn't like him either, but Lona would never speak against a man of God. Lona went along with his dictate when he made it purposefully uncomfortable for her to attend church at First Water. And she thought it was because she had sinned.

Now, she understood it was because he was angry she had been with someone else in what he considered a sinful way, and Solomon was evidence of her sin. She went in and picked up Solomon, who smiled at her. She peeked into the back of his diaper and smelled him. Nothing wrong there. "Thank you for coming to my rescue, you old spoiled thing you." She kissed his little forehead.

Solomon gurgled and cooed while the rest of her family was out in the big front room, talking low, making plans for her life. Adam stood in the front door, blocking the daylight out with his tall and manly frame. He appeared upset, with both hands on his hips looking off into space. What was he thinking of at this latest turn of events? Could he help her in some way?

Ruby shook her head at the thought. How nice it would be if some great knight had swept down into her life out of Michigan and Tennessee to help her out. All she got was Dodge. Life didn't work out that way. She had to help herself out of this mess.

She smoothed Solomon's little dress down and placed him back in the cradle. She stood from the bed and smoothed down her skirt.

"Ah, here is Sister Ruby again." Ruby almost bristled as the Reverend used the Sister appellation, seemingly accepting her back into the body of Christ. "Baby okay?"

As if you really cared. You didn't even come back to pray for him when he was really sick. "He just wanted to say hello."

John smiled, but Dodge frowned at the prospect. "He can't always get his way now. He got to learn he can't get you to do whatever for him. Spare the rod, spoil the child. He got to know."

"Amen," Lona intoned.

"Actually, he is a very good baby," Adam Morson said. "One of the finest specimens I've ever seen."

Dodge shifted in his seat. "He's a looker alright. He look like his mama."

Ruby cringed inside. "Thank you, Reverend."

"You're right welcome." He stood and towered over her, smelling of bergamot oil and hair grease, gripping his hat. "I give him a good home. I make him a fine Christian daddy."

"Solomon need that. A daddy," Lona voice was low, so low only Ruby heard her, and the words went straight to her heart in slender shards.

Ruby forced herself to look at the Reverend and his round face peered at her in hope. "I never expected to be on the receiving end of such a proposal. I don't know what to say to it, sir. I wonder if I might have some time to consider what you say."

He clapped a hand on her shoulder as if he were a good buddy of hers. "I see what you are saying, Sister Ruby. And it is wise. I'll give you some time—maybe at the Forth of July picnic?"

Three days away. Ruby had to stop herself from breathing out a sigh of relief. She could think of *something* by then. "Yes, I could give you an answer then."

He edged to the door. "I'll leave you all, then." He put his hat on his head and gave a special tip to Adam as he left. What was that all about? She didn't have time to dwell on it or think about it. A proposal was too much to consider. She hurried back into the room where Solomon was and wished there was a door to close.

In the corner of the room, she just slid down and sat there frozen, feeling helpless, as if a big hand had closed over her and cut off her circulation. How would she ever consider marrying the very man who had made her feel as if she had done something bad?

She was not bad, nor was Solomon, and she would never feel any different. The problem was, if she said no to Dodge, then he would see to it her life in Winslow or anywhere else with him, was intolerable. Because of Dodge, she wouldn't be able to stay in Winslow. It wasn't a question of if she would leave her hometown, but when, how and with whom.

All of the ideas from her Uncle Arlo about making Winslow better were just a beautiful pipe dream.

Adam stood in the doorway. His chiseled features were slightly flushed and reddened. His eyes held a tightness that continued to his lips, as if he wanted to say something, but he stopped himself. She wished he hadn't, because his lips, as she could see them from sitting in the room, were full, lush and beautiful. Clearly, people saw what they wanted to. Adam might be as pale as pine, but he had the lips of a Negro man. What would it be like to kiss them? A rush of crimson warmth came to her face. By his downcast look, she could tell he was embarrassed to be there too.

"Your mother held dinner. She has plates for us."

"I'm not hungry."

Adam cleared his throat and she could see his Adam's apple bob up and down and wondered what it would be like if she reached up to trace her fingers over it. "I'm not either, but we could study afterward. If you like."

Would Dodge let her continue to study for school if she married him? She could never imagine such a thing. Studying was an opportunity to spend some time with Adam, a prospect which would certainly stop if she had to go off with—she swallowed—another man.

"Yes. Thank you." Ruby stood and went out to the large front room, where her sisters clustered in the kitchen, trying to act as if they were not listening in on everything. In her desire to spend time with Adam, she had not thought of Lona wanting to say something to her. Her mother emerged in the doorway.

"Dr. Morson," Lona said, "I would like a word with Ruby."

"I'll go get the study guides." Adam gave her an encouraging look as he left the room.

"Yes?"

"What you going to tell the Reverend?"

"I don't know."

"What you mean, you don't know?"

"She said she don't know," John echoed as he emerged in the doorway next to Lona. He folded his arms. "I believe her."

Lona turned on him fiercely. "I'm talking to Ruby Jean. She think she have a decision to make, but it's made for her."

Lona whipped around to her and came to where Ruby stood. "You ain't going to wait until no picnic. You're going to tell him tomorrow you say yes. It can be announced in church on Sunday before that picnic. Me and Mags will make a special cake in celebration."

Was the ground ready to swallow her if she fainted? She hoped so, and she was not the fainting kind. "I can't give up my life to that man."

"You can and you will. Being married to a man of God will cloak your shame."

"He'll torture me all the time for it. Even Solomon. You want your grandson to be tortured?"

John stood and shook his head. "No indeed. Ruby, you take your time deciding. Do what feel right."

"What if I say she don't have no place to live if she say no?"

John shook his head. "This here is my house when we come to to Winslow to live. I say she stay."

"She ain't even yours, John."

Stars burst in front of Ruby's eyes and pain as her mother's words entered her ears.

Every cell in her body was still.

Was her head going to explode?

Lona covered her mouth as if the action would take her words back. John sat down on their bed, all of the wind taken from his sails.

"What are you talking about? What're you saying?"

Lona sat down on the bed next to John too, covering her face with her apron, wailing. John slipped an arm about Lona's shaking shoulders and he drew closer to her.

Somehow, she had always known.

Not because of her too-light skin which was nowhere near an amalgamation of her medium-brown mother and John, who was a deep rich mahogany color.

No, it was always the way Lona was at arms length with her. She had been even more sure of it when Solomon had come.

Her mother always treated her as an embarrassment. Ruby thought it was because of how she had gone around causing trouble. But now, she understood, it came from something much deeper. The whispers behind her back in school, at church, they all made sense now.

There were tears at the corner of John's eyes, and seeing his pain made Ruby feel for him, far more than her mother's sobs. "It's true, Ruby. I'm not your birth daddy. But you know I love you like you my own."

"I know, Daddy. Thank you."

Lona took the apron away and her tear-stained face was a rebuke to Ruby. "You got to marry him, so it don't happen for Solomon. He got to have a daddy to take the shame away. Just like I did for you."

Ruby stood in the corner and pushed aside the curtain to let in a little daylight. She cleared her throat. "So who is my daddy?"

Lona dabbed at her eyes. "I wish I knew."

That was not the answer Ruby was expecting to hear.

Not at all.

Not the way Lona put herself forward as a pillar of the community.

"What you mean you don't know?"

"I was fifteen. I was coming home from a dance with John. We," Lona looked over at him, "We were in the courting buggy and it got taken over, by some men."

John waved and fanned his face. "They dragged me out of the buggy and I...I couldn't save her."

"I know they was men of the community. I couldn't recognize their voices. It was four or five of them. They all beat me down and had their way with me. I tried to fight them off, but I couldn't. I just couldn't."

The blood roared in Ruby's ears.

Before this moment, she had thought everything she had endured was terribly bad and awful.

Now she knew there was far, far worse in the world.

John took up the tale. "And they knock me out so I couldn't protect her. We was so ashamed of what happened. I had been saving my money, but I took what I had and we moved to the next state as soon as we could get married, way before you were born. When I saw you, I knew you were a child of God. I loved you, and I was your daddy."

"And," Lona said, through her tears, "when you came in here with your clothes all torn up, I knew what happened to you. I couldn't protect you. It was like it happened all over again."

Ruby couldn't help it, tears started to slip unbidden down her cheeks. She didn't want to remember that night. She had wept in her mother's lap. She just remembered how quickly Lona heated water for a bath. "Wash it away," she kept saying over and over. "Wash it all away." And she had. Or she thought she had.

"So we come here," John folded and unfolded his hands slowly. "We come to get away from them terrible men."

"So the way they scared you off worked." Ruby kept her voice flat, a pure monotone.

"It sure did." Lona's voice was equally flat. "Do you think we were fools enough to stay? We got the message." She stood up quickly and smoothed her apron down. "Sometimes, I wish you would as well."

"What message?"

"Stop causing trouble, Ruby. Marry him."

"I don't want to," Ruby wailed.

"See there. She don't want to. That's enough." John stood. "I'm going to bed." He started to turn down the covers.

Lona came and stood next to Ruby. Ruby was almost as tall as her mother, but now the older woman's strength and power towered over her. "I done told you what to do. You got to do something for this here family for your sake, for your son, and your sisters. Now."

"Yes, Mama."

"Marry him," Lona said, one more time then she and John went to the front porch, arms around each other, not wanting to talk to her anymore.

Adam came into the large front room holding two hot plates with towels in his hand and settled them on the wooden table. He slid a plate toward her and Ruby looked down at the pork chops, sweet potatoes and greens. Her stomach turned over, just like her world did.

He pushed a glass of milk toward her. "You've got to keep your strength up, for whatever decision you make for yourself."

"There is no decision to make," Ruby's back faced the plate. "I could never marry a man I don't love."

"I see."

"My problem is how am I going to tell him without him feeling rejected? I can't afford to have him feel as if I've done him a great wrong somehow. I have to get him to see I'm not worthy of this 'honor.'" She sighed. "I just wish I could go on away."

"My previous offer still stands, Ruby." Adam put down his pork chop. His Winslow gray eyes were very earnest and sincere. She loved how handsome he was in his glasses. In her mind's eye, they were standing in front of some other minister, with him holding Solomon. The fantasy made her feel good all over.

For just one second.

But she could not ruin his life. It would not be fair.

"Thank you, but I got to figure this out for myself. I'm not sure leaving Winslow is the answer."

There was silence between them and she spoke again.

"I'll have to figure this out."

Adam pushed the half-empty plate away from him. Now he wasn't eating and her stomach clenched. That was her fault too. "He'll never let you continue your studies. Not in any way."

"Why do you say that? I can do it."

Adam gave a short laugh and wiped his mouth with a napkin. His pink lips had been all shiny from the pork chop and the shininess made them so appealing. "He's not an educated man, no matter how much he told the congregation. I did some looking into him. He has no diploma. He told you all some far away, fairy story, never imagining someone from the real Tennessee would come and check him out."

Ruby shook her head. "I can't say I am shocked."

"People like him don't want to see anyone else get an education either. Were you to become Mrs. Dodge, there would be an end to all of that. He doesn't strike me as kindly either."

"I think that's part of the deal. My shame is covered up, I get to be seen as a good person and he does whatever he likes when we are alone." A chill went up Ruby's spine as she thought of the implications. Her life, which seemed so full of promise and wonder before, like Uncle Arlo told, and the doctor made her feel with nursing school, stretched out before her like an eternity.

Remembrances of her encounter with David came back to her mind, and the thought of having to live out the attack every day made her quake with fear. God was a kind, and protective force.

Had He turned His back on her again?

As He did in the day in the cotton field?

God would not ignore her cries for help, but she couldn't deny he seemed displeased with her. She didn't know what the truth was anymore.

Chapter Eleven

Loud, thunking noises woke Adam early in the morning a few days later, and raised alarm. Fear shot up his arms in horror and he sat straight up in the bed. Had another lynching occurred in the night? His heart began to pound. He didn't want to have to see another bloody face like Travis's again.

The noise was more than usual for Sunday morning. He pulled on his shirt and a pair of pants and made himself presentable enough to open the door. The noise came from Lona and Mags in the kitchen, rushing to prepare a meal. Mags smiled at him, but Lona did not. "Good morning, ladies."

"Good morning, Dr. Morson," Mags said. "I'm sorry if we woke you, but we got a lot to do today what with church in the morning and then the town picnic and fireworks and all at night. So we in here rushing around now. I hope we didn't wake you."

Adam held up a protesting hand. "I'll be fine. And I want to help you in any way I can."

"If you want to be of help, you need to marry my daughter." Lona stuck a long fork-like implement into a piece of frying chicken with extra special attack. Some juice ran out of the chicken and hit the pan with a resounding sizzle.

"Mama, stop," Mags begged. Mags's humiliation at her mother's remarks appeared as a russet undertone under her maple-colored skin.

Adam gave Mags a small smile and stepped over into the larger front room where the family was all in a bustle. The younger girls had dressed in navy blue middies and skirts. John had gathered himself to put on his best brown suit.

No Ruby. His heart sank just a little bit, wondering.

He sat down at the table next to Delie. "Miss Delie."

"Dr. Morson," Delie said, in the grown-up way she could talk. "Ruby is in our room feeding Solomon if you wanted to know."

"Can't I just sit here with you?" Adam smiled down at her.

"You could, Doctor, sir, but I know you wanted to know." Delie gave him her usual admiring glance. Adam reached for the jug of milk John had drawn from their cows that morning.

Was his admiration for Ruby so transparent? Even to a five-year-old? His regard showed too much. He should go to Ruby and just tell her they should get married, but Ruby would balk to any kind of heavy handedness. She had enough to deal with in thinking about her strategy to reject Dodge's proposal.

As Adam sipped slowly at a glass of milk, Ruby brought in Solomon to sit with them at the breakfast table. She dressed him in a little navy blue sailor suit. He looked so cute and welcoming, Adam couldn't compress a laugh at how eager he seemed. The baby held his arms out to him and Adam perched him on his knee. "He looks hungry."

"I know. I keep nursing him and nursing him."

"Remember, he needs food. As he grows, his stomach grows too. He needs something more substantial. Try breaking off some of the biscuit to give to him with some ham cut up fine."

Lona came out and slapped another pan of biscuits on the table. Adam's heart twisted a bit to see one or two of the fine, light biscuits leap out of the pan and land on the table. He had to admit, there were none lighter or finer. Adam picked up the ones that had landed on the clean table and put them on his plate.

"We ain't having ham this morning, we having bacon," Lona muttered.

As if on cue, Mags came right behind Lona with a plate of bacon. Typically, the family used the biscuits to make a sandwich for themselves. It would hold them until lunch.

"Bacon then, just avoid the fat."

Lona came around the table with a butter dish in her hand. "Ain't no fat on my bacon. I fry it out."

Adam cleared his throat. Lona was in rare form this morning. He thought of the pressures she was under and tried to be more understanding. "Of course."

Ruby went to reach for the baby but Solomon was quite comfortable on Adam's lap. Adam reached for one of the biscuits and crumbled it onto the plate before him. He gave some of the pieces to Solomon, who made some funny faces but ate greedily. Seeing Lona was right about the bacon, he gave some to the baby who smacked his little lips between each bite. Adam had such a good time feeding Solomon he didn't notice Ruby. When he adjusted Solomon on his lap, he looked up and a hangdog expression was etched across her freckles. "Are you okay, Ruby?"

He certainly hoped so. Was she still upset at the events of last night? Why couldn't he provide some reassurance that all would be well? Instead, he was making everything worse and more confusing for her. He longed to be the one to take the worry from her, and to let her know everything would be fine. Adam stopped feeding Solomon and gave Ruby his full attention.

This did not sit well with Solomon and he began to protest by kicking out his little legs with strength and vigor, much to the delight of his aunts and grandfather. Adam crumbled up a little more biscuit to give to him. "I just never seen him taking food from someone's hand, instead of me. He growing up," Ruby mused. "He won't even need me for food no more."

"I told you it was going to happen," Lona bit into her bacon sandwich with more gusto. "You would rather listen to some fancy doctor man than to your mother."

Ruby held out her arms for the baby and Solomon went into them. There were crumbs on Adam's pant leg and he absently began to brush them off. "Let me help you," Ruby said and gathered up a white napkin. She started brushing but stopped and blushed when she realized where she was brushing. Forbidden territory. "Sorry."

"Don't be," Adam whispered. He felt very stirred by Ruby's intimate gesture. He wanted her to help him, but knew where she was brushing was trouble.

"It wouldn't matter if he were your husband," Lona harrumphed.

"I would love a brother," Delie said out loud into the room, which had grown quiet at Lona's declaration.

Adam reached over and made a quick sandwich out of a split biscuit, peach preserves and bacon. "Excuse me, I'm going to make sure the car is ready to go this morning."

He sat down with his sandwich on the porch. Consuming the sandwich in equal quarters he thought of his mother, who, in many ways was Ruby's twin in fate and fortune. She too had been compromised by someone she knew. His mother, Matilda, had been a maid in the Winslow household in back in Tennessee. She was only fifteen when she started working there when the youngest son, Paul, began showing an interest in her.

What must she have gone through? Mattie was a smart girl, and an aunt of hers, Lizzie, had told him Matilda got the job to save money to go away to high school. None in the family wanted her to work in that house. However, Matilda, tempted by the ease of the money and the work, did her job well. She even knew how to do the maid work in an efficient and productive way. In her extra time, she accessed the library in the house, to keep up her studies.

Paul must have known this. Adam's gooseflesh came up when he thought of how Paul Winslow must have tempted her with those books, the very instruments of learning she so desired, and lost when she became pregnant.

People thought the pregnancy an absolute scandal and they cast Mattie out. The heartbreak of being treated so shabbily led her to let go of life just after having him. After his Aunt Lizzie told him the story, Adam became convinced he should make medicine his life's work, and sought to help others avoid such a sad and miserable end. Of course, the money Paul Winslow provided helped him as well as assuaging his own guilt over how he must have lured Mattie, however indirectly, to her demise.

Finishing his sandwich, he sat back and sighed, thinking it would be a very busy day. The Bledsoes began to trickle outside and he stood up to go back in the house to put on his church clothes. He hoped he would have time to explain to Ruby what he wanted to do with his life, so she could understand he had to help her and Solomon. He promised his mother's memory.

Knowing what the day held, Ruby dressed almost like her sisters in a navy blue skirt and a lightweight white middy so she looked like a feminine duplication of a sailor. She had a small boater of natural straw she wore, instead of one of her usual big hats. The naval look toned her down. She didn't need to call attention to herself with her plan.

When the Bledsoes arrived at First Water, everyone was very cordial to her. Too nice.

Did they know Dodge proposed to her? Or was it because of the way Adam had returned?

She glanced over at Lona, to see if her mother knew anything at all about this warm embrace of her, and her sin, but Lona's face was wreathed in sorrow. Her posture was as if she were at a funeral instead of a regular Sunday morning church service. Tears slid openly down her cheeks.

Ruby wanted to cry too, cry at the pain of being a constant reminder of the horror her mother had endured, but Ruby had to live her own life. She could do nothing to change her origins.

Dodge, of course, was giving her his best smile, and Ruby cringed. She had promised him an answer by the end of today, and she just didn't know how she was going to reject him. He had to see, somehow, being married to her would make his life worse, not better. Was he so infatuated with her?

She looked up at him once more.

He was.

He couldn't even keep the text straight on the prodigal son and did more of his improvising of the story. "Just because you have done something wrong doesn't mean God doesn't love you,"

"Yes, Lord," Lona echoed.

"God loves you."

"He does, yes He does." Lona would be his support today.

"I want to hear someone give a testimony today," Dodge went down in front of the church and spread his arms wide. "Somebody, talk about the love of God. Somebody, testify."

Ruby managed to refrain from doing so. What kind of daughter was she not to want to comfort her mother in her distress? What kept her from helping her mother, from being moved at seeing Lona's shoulders shaking from weeping, and John rubbing her back trying to comfort her?

Fear. At becoming Mrs. Dodge. She had wetness of her own collecting underneath her arms and in her bosom at the thought of it.

"I want someone to talk about the goodness of God. I want someone to say, Amen,"

Everyone in the church said it, but no one came forward. A whoosh of air went up in front of her. Now she couldn't see. Her view was partially blocked because Adam stood up. Why was Adam standing up in front of her? Why was he the only one standing? Oh no.

All of the clapping, whispering, praying out loud in the church ceased. Even Lona's sobs calmed down. Everyone focused on Adam, expectantly, and even Dodge had the good grace to look shocked.

"Yes, Brother Morson?"

Dodge didn't call him doctor.

"I want to talk about God's goodness in how he gives life. I'm a doctor. I've seen many things during my training where the situation seemed hopeless, and the person finds a way to pull through. It's a wonder and a blessing,"

"Amen," Doris Bomead said.

"There was a time when, a few weeks ago, I had the pleasure of taking care of little Solomon here. He was mighty sick. God led me to know how to take care of him. And I just want to say I'm thankful."

"Amen, amen," Doris Bomead said, supporting Adam and the emotion in the church shifted. To Adam.

"When he was sick," Adam warmed to his words, "he needed prayer. Some here, they didn't want to pray. Didn't want to visit such a child."

Not a sound echoed in the church.

Had First Water ever been really quiet with folks in it? Ruby could never recall someone who had the audacity to confront everyone in First Water. Or when the normally noisy church had been so quiet.

"Maybe they knew who his father was. But one thing," Adam intoned, gripping a pew in front of him, warming further to his task, "even if we don't know who his biological father is, we know who his Heavenly Father is."

"Amen," Mags nodded her head and giving Solomon a squeeze on his little leg.

"And it's his Heavenly Father who matters. That's who matters now, and everlastingly. This child."

"Yes!" Delie said aloud, urging Adam on. Some laughed.

Ruby didn't.

"This child is a blessing. We must never, ever forget it. He's here because of God's goodness to us."

The church quieted once more as he laid a hand on Solomon's little nearly hairless head.

"Amen," Adam sat down. To Ruby, he looked spent.

"Praise him!" Doris Bomead yelled, and the whole church joined her as they clapped. Clapping? Ruby squeezed her eyes shut. Things got loud at First Water all the time, but people very rarely clapped.

Adam, located a whole pew away from her, stared off into nothing and would not meet her eyes. He had sat next to Mags and not to her. He chose to sit so far from her today, which made her sad, but he must have had his reasons.

Yet, the distance gave her the space to contemplate him, to see him sitting there, looking pristine and crisp in his tan linen suit. Even as he sat back down, he took out a kerchief and wiped his forehead. On the edge of the row, people behind him clapped him on the shoulder as he folded the kerchief and put it back into his suit pocket.

"Yes, well, we sure thank our guest, Brother Morson, for his words, yes we do," Dodge said haltingly. Ruby could tell he was not pleased at just having been upstaged and laid out all at the same time. She wanted to put a hand up to her mouth and giggle, but today of all days, she must have the correct reaction and approach. She couldn't react like Delie, as her imp of a sister down the row, giggled just for her.

Ruby reached over, lifted Solomon and kissed the little wisp of light-colored hair on his head. As she situated Solomon on her lap, she wished Adam would look at her and see her as someone who was worthy of him. She wasn't proper nor was she an elegantly dressed doctor's wife, leading high society.

A doctor's wife would need to be educated and have pretty clothes. And to be that, it would take years to get her high school diploma, and nursing school. By the time she had her education, he would probably be long gone elsewhere.

Her best and only option was Dodge. He wanted her the way that she was now. She wouldn't have to change anything.

Ruby shivered. She didn't want Dodge or to be a minister's wife. And she wasn't going to change no matter how people wanted it, including Lona.

Then it came to her. How she could help Adam.

She could help him to see his purpose in life as a Negro, and be proud of who he is. He could provide so much help. He was a Moses, a great leader. *I could show him the way to be a proud Negro and he could show me...What?*

He could be more than a mentor, teacher or a friend. A life's partner? She warmed at the possibility.

Winslow was a small town, similar to where Adam had grown up with his Aunt Lizzie. But despite its size, it was big enough to draw big crowds from surrounding counties during celebrations.

"It's something for folks to do, to get out and see folk they haven't seen for a while." Ruby explained to Adam as he pulled his car up. "I thought you said you weren't very religious."

"I'm not."

"In church, you made a powerful testimony. From God."

"I don't have to be on some deacon board to know when I am trying to heal someone. I say a prayer to help guide my hands in the right way, to do the right thing."

"Did you pray over Solomon?"

"I wouldn't call it prayer. I asked for help. It's hard for doctors to see a little one suffer."

"Thank you."

When he faced her, a jolt traveled up his arm at the sight of tears gathering in the corners of her eyes. She seemed so resolute, and such a pillar of strength and fortitude. How amazing that she was touched by a simple prayer. "Of course, I still pray to let him draw sweet, even breaths."

"Me too."

Adam looked puzzled. "No one prayed for him?"

Ruby shook her head and a hurt look crossed her face, one he would have given anything to remove. "I did. So did my sisters and my father. But my mother," her voice sounded thick with emotion, but true to her way, she took it and kept on with the words that caused her pain. "She tried to act as if it were all for the best if he died. I guess I can understand now. So I came to the Winslows and found you there. It was God's hand," Ruby said, in wonder.

"Or Paul Winslow. Which amounts to the same thing in this town." Adam slowed down the car as Ruby laid a hand on his arm.

"Thank you," she said.

Trying to ignore the feeling rising in his arms, he pulled the car to a stop then made sure to come around and open the door for her, handing Solomon to her gently. "You are welcome." Gathering up all of the picnic things in the small trunk, he made his way to the picnic grounds with her and Solomon in his wake.

The center part of town, away from the mill, train station and general store made up the town square, crowned with an ornate, sand-colored county building, just built about five years ago on one side and the gazebo and the bandshell on the other. The largesse of Paul Winslow had set this large building and Winslow became the county seat of Becker County because of him. Other people of a much lighter hue gathered close to the bandshell and the gazebo.

The Bledsoes laid their quilts on the grass, far away from the bandshell. There had been some wooden picnic tables set up on the grassy area, and they put the food there, but everyone around them was from First Water. The separation was clear. "Why don't you all go closer to the bandshell? Don't you want to hear the music?"

The gathered crowd silenced and gazed up at him as if he suggested they should all take off their clothes and frolic the middle of the town square.

"This here is the Colored Corner," Delie piped up in a happy little tone— unhappy, ugly alliterative words she made sound jovial in her little five-year-old treble.

"Will we be able to hear the music?" Adam worried.

"Not really, but who wants to anyway?" Ruby tried to laugh. "The band isn't that good." She laid a calming hand on his sleeve. "We have a fine time here, among our own. We don't want to cause trouble."

Ruby wanted to explain more to him, but she didn't have time. She handed him the baby, even though Adam was still puzzled. He put Solomon down on a clean blanket for him to play. Ruby busied herself laying out the lunch of chicken, fruit and cold salads so everyone could help themselves after the long church service. She would have to take time to explain to Adam the white church services were shorter so they got the prime spots first. He seemed to take it personally.

Ruby gathered up a plate of food for Adam, who kept Solomon occupied. As she took it to him, two sources of trouble loomed on the horizon. Reverend Dodge had come in off to her left, and went around to various baskets, filling his belly like a grizzly bear, working his way to the Bledsoes' area. To her right, the Winslows drove past in their open-air car. Bob, their chauffeur, stopped the car in the shade of a tree and Paul Winslow stared hard over at Adam playing on the blanket with Solomon.

Was he looking at Adam? Or Solomon?

Both of them were his flesh and blood.

And when she thought it couldn't get worse, Dodge stepped over to the car on Paul Winslow's side and began talking to him in animated tones. His posture was so subservient she bit her lips at the sight, and tried to steady the queasiness in her stomach. He kept pointing over towards Adam and Solomon and ice water ran in her veins. David then maneuvered himself from behind his father and looked at Solomon for himself. For the first time.

Ruby's heart leaped in her throat as Bob came around to Paul Winslow's side and opened the car door, letting him out. The most powerful man in town headed straight for Adam's blanket—where, as she carried a plate full of food, her whole world froze in place, a thick fear clotting her throat at the thought of losing her child.

Chapter Twelve

Adam could see Solomon was a bright, cheerful child. He tried to trick Solomon with his little stuffed bear, but he wouldn't be fooled. In his residency, he had seen so much poverty and sadness amongst the children in Michigan, even in homes with married parents. The children wouldn't play games or show as much intelligence as Solomon did. So far, Ruby and her family had done an excellent job in raising this child.

What would it be like to have a child like this? With Ruby? As he played a hand clapping game with Solomon, he shifted. A certain physical act would have to take place for a child to occur. Ruby was certainly a beautiful woman, but he would not do anything to compromise her ability to get an education. As Solomon laughed at his clapping hands, Adam wished her mother would get rid of the idea Ruby had to marry him or anyone else, least of all, Charles Dodge, who was not worthy of her. Not at all.

Suddenly, Ruby came toward him with a worried look on her beautiful face. Dropping the plate of food in her hands next to him, she sank to her knees and picked up Solomon. In a swift motion, she put him over her shoulder and carried him away. His feelings were hurt. Did she hate him again? "Ruby, what's the matter? Did I do something?"

The curve of Ruby's retreating backside stirred him and with some pleasure he noted the womanly beauty of her shape, which was much more evident today in her plain top and skirt. He stood up to follow her, but then realized there were two shadows behind him. Dodge and Paul Winslow.

Dodge chewed on a large, smelly stogie, smoking it with fierce pleasure, as if someone would take it away from him. Adam coughed. Smoking was a detestable habit and he discouraged as many of his patients as he could from the practice. Many Negroes, though, enjoyed the diversion of tobacco in some form, whether as cigars, snuff or chew. A public health menace. "There he go." Dodge made a big show of gesturing after Ruby and chewing on the end of the cigar. "A right fine looking boy."

Paul Winslow had his own cigar, which looked just like the one Dodge was chewing. Clearly, he'd given Dodge one of his. Which had to be why Dodge made such a show of smoking it. It made him feel equal to Winslow.

Adam had a brief moment of sympathy for the deluded minister. "Adam," Paul Winslow acknowledged him.

"Good day, Mr. Winslow." Adam wished he could call him by his first name.

"Adam, is that Ruby's baby over there?"

"It was."

"My God." Paul Winslow didn't mind taking the Lord's name in vain on a Sunday or at any other time. "He looks just like David did as a baby. I wouldn't have thought it possible, less I saw it myself."

Dodge just stood there, smoking on the stogie looking satisfied.

"Is she taking good care of him?" Paul Winslow asked Adam, all of a sudden.

"I'm not sure what you mean, sir."

Paul gestured wildly with the stogie. "You know. You're a doctor. Come on, you have all of your education. Use it. Is the boy healthy and strong? Is he recovered from the time you had to go see about him?"

Adam regarded him. "I'm not in the practice of discussing the health of my patients with people other than their immediate families."

Paul threw down his stogie and stomped on it. "Listen here. I'm paying a lot for you to be down here to take care of these people. I paid a lot for your education. You tell me right now about her boy. You owe me some information."

Dodge was doing all he could to keep from smirking at this heated exchange. "Well, sir. While I cannot say what happened with the child, I can say he has fully recovered from his episode."

"Well, praise God."

"Yes, indeed," Dodge agreed grinning broadly.

"Charles, you got a point. The boy needs protection. He shouldn't be living down there on that farm, Lona and John got borders coming in and out all the time. Heaven knows what's going on down there at any hour of the day."

Dodge opened his fat mouth, but Adam stayed him with a hand. Clearly, Dodge was not used to this type of treatment. He would have felt satisfied by his gesture, if he had time, but he had to correct Paul Winslow. "As his doctor, I can tell you he is in excellent care at the Bledsoes. He has plenty to eat, and he's progressing on pace with his age, even ahead of his age a bit mentally."

Paul Winslow was the picture of a satisfied cat at this news and Adam could have kicked himself as hard as Ruby had done in the woods. What had happened to his control of his emotions? Had he lost his mind when talking about Ruby and her child? He divulged far more about Solomon than he intended. "Ahead, eh? Blood will tell, won't it?"

Adam gulped a bit. "Yes, sir."

"Well, I'm not surprised. Not one bit. He ain't no typical colored baby. He got good genes. Plain for anyone to see."

"Yes, sir." Dodge agreed, smoking like a smokestack, and looking like a fool.

Paul Winslow continued on, "I hear tell it was him being in the house what caused his sickness. Right, Doctor?"

Dodge had the nerve to look very satisfied with himself. He would have asked Paul Winslow where he got his information, but he already knew with his stooge right next to him. "The situation has been resolved. As his doctor, I find his current placement is more than satisfactory and allows for Solomon to grow and thrive. If it were not, I would have sought a different situation for him myself."

"Solomon, eh?" Paul Winslow reflected.

Once again, Adam could have kicked himself. He didn't know if Paul Winslow knew the child's name, but these pieces of information were making Solomon more and more real to Paul Winslow, something he certainly did not want to contribute to. "Yes."

Paul edged closer to Adam. "Remember who's paying you. If I need more information about that baby, you need to provide it. Otherwise, you can go on back to Tennessee."

Adam gave Paul Winslow a steely look. "I don't have to stay."

Paul Winslow clapped Adam on the shoulder, ever the benefactor. "There's no need to get all upset on the Fourth of July. It's a lovely day. We're going to have a nice concert, a reading of the Declaration of Independence, lots of game playing, ice cream later on. There's even fireworks after dark. We're here to have a good time." Paul projected, as if to reassure all in Negro corner who watched them, all was well.

"Good," Adam kept his voice low. "Because I didn't want to misunderstand why you sent for me. I graduated at the top of my class at Michigan and may I remind you of my more generous offers, sir. I don't have to stay."

Paul stepped back, surprised, either at this information he had divulged or that Adam had the guts to stand up to him.

"There's lots of towns what needs colored doctors, I guess," Dodge said smiling.

Paul Winslow was not smiling. "Shut up, Charles," he sneered. He turned back to Adam. "I heard all that from you before. You stay and take care of the baby, understand? I'll do what I have to do to make sure he's protected."

He stood back and was all smiles again. "Just like I did with you."

"Yes." Adam fixed him with another steely look, "I was well protected. But never loved. There's a difference. Sir."

Paul Winslow chuckled. "Love don't buy warm clothes, food, shoes, and a fine Michigan education, now does it? Money does."

He refrained from saying that a lot of that money had gone into liquor for his caretaker rather than food and clothes for him. The memory chilled him for just a second.

"The answer to everything as you see it," Adam spread his hands in a gesture.

Paul Winslow lowered his voice again. "The boy needs a daddy."

Dodge threw his stogie down on the ground and stomped on it in clear imitation of his puppeteer. "He sure do."

Adam nodded his head. "From what I understand, he has as much of a daddy as I did. I turned out just fine."

Paul Winslow locked his gaze on him.

Adam was more than ready for the challenge. As his father stared at him, he did not flinch.

Then Paul Winslow smiled again and clapped his hand on Adam's shoulder. "Keep up the good work, Doc," he said loud enough for all to hear. "You're doing a fine job taking care of the colored here. I hope you'll keep doing your job."

Adam said nothing. He stepped back and watched as the two men went back to the Winslow car where Mrs. Winslow and David waited along with their chauffeur.

Every person in Colored Corner watched their entire exchange. No one even pretended to do something else. Dazed, he walked back to where the Bledsoes laid out lunch, and sat down.

Had he been shaken out of a dream? The entire Bledsoe clan stared after the departing Winslow and Dodge.

"What's the matter?" He asked John Bledsoe, as he shook his head to clear him mind of the unpleasant encounter.

"He never came to Colored Corner before. Not for any picnic or any time."

"Well, he's gone now," Adam said grimly. "Does anyone know where Ruby went?"

"She took Solomon and ran off somewhere, I don't know."

When Adam made a move to follow Ruby into the woods, a hand stopped him. The touch was light but firm. He could shake off whomever it was who had stopped him, but he wanted to be polite.

David.

The need to be polite went clean away. "What?"

"Leave her alone. She likes to go there to think."

Adam looked at this brother of his who had been so pampered and protected all of his life, but still looked sad. A small pang touched him. He knew sad times well.

But David had cashed in any sympathy when he followed through on his father's mandate to hurt Ruby. He shook David's touch off of him.

In doing so, David nearly was flung back into the car. Those summers of hard labor he had to endure as he grew up made them both, fundamentally different. "That may have been the way she was before. Maybe she needs support and help."

"And you intend to provide it?"

"Do you have a problem with that?"

David's gray eyes darted over to his father and Reverend Dodge, talking and pointing after the piney woods where Ruby had disappeared. Mary Winslow sat in the open air car with a proper lace parasol poised over her head to block the July sun from her delicate skin and, as Adam supposed, to protect her whiteness.

"Mother and Father have talked about whether or not the baby is well cared for. When she saw him the other day, she said some things about how small he was, even though she pointed out that I tended to being small when I was little."

Adam's heart thudded in his chest.

For Ruby.

Clearly she had been able to see something that he had not been able to see. That was why she had run away. "Why in the world would your parents be concerned about one of the Negro children of Winslow?"

David waved him a bit away from Colored Corner and over to a stand of trees. There was a faint sheen of sweat on his forehead, and David, dressed completely in a suit as he was, pulled out a folded linen handkerchief and delicately mopped at his brow. "Mother had a hard time having me. There were a number of babies. A lot of them didn't live. So she's always been close to me. And now, she's concerned for Ruby's child given his origins."

"You mean because he's her grandson?"

The linen square made its way back around David's shiny, pointed features. "Well, yes. And how Ruby's been. You've got to tell her to back off of any incendiary activity. They don't like it."

Adam gave a short laugh, thinking of the fiery midwife who had won a place in his heart. "Are you fool enough to think anyone can control her?"

David gave a slight smile that turned Adam's stomach. What was he remembering? Was it a fond childhood memory of Ruby's persistence? Or did he harbor a memory of a struggling Ruby who had been firmly in his power as he compromised her virtue?

"No. But I'm just telling you that if Mother keeps harping on Father about the baby not being taken care of, he will find a way to solve the problem. He always will. And he has never resisted what Mother wants." David put his handkerchief away in a suit pocket.

A muscle twitched in Adam's chin.

And this was the man who had purported to love Mattie Morson. Clearly, Ruby had to be protected. "I don't know what you mean, the problem."

"Ruby making trouble for him. The mill. Anything. She's got to stop."

"She can't stand the sight of me." Even as he said it, things had gotten better between them, but they still weren't good enough.

"Why not?"

"She thinks horribly of me for passing for white at Michigan."

David shrugged her shoulders. "You would have been a fool if you hadn't. How else would you have gotten your education? At one of those colored schools? Please." David paused. "I often wondered why you would bother to come back here since doing so means you admit to that other side of you."

Adam gazed at his spoiled, pompous brother. "I had to know what he wanted."

David stared off in the distance at the trees as if he could see Ruby. And maybe he could. He had to go to her. What was he doing standing here, talking to this reprobate of a younger brother? "You'll regret coming here. You should have gotten away from him while you could. You could have gone somewhere, married a fine white lady and disappeared. You were a fool to give all that up."

"I wanted a family."

David jerked his chin off to the woods. "There's the one you want. Believe me, you want none of the Winslows. And you don't want Ruby's baby to have any of it either."

"He has a loving family who cares about him. He's healthy. I'm right there if anything were to happen to him—let your Mother know that."

"I will. But you tell her, this is enough. Father got her message. He's trying in his own way to make things better. Says he's going to build some housing for the workers closer in to town."

"A start." Okay, some improvement. But what would that mean at half the salary and no say in the community in which they lived?

"You don't know Daddy. That's huge."

And he didn't want to know him. Not anymore, after what he had just heard. "I'll tell her, but she doesn't listen."

"The thing to do is get her away from here."

"She loves this place for some reason." Adam's jaw was tight.

"You've thought about it?"

"I've offered it to her. Trust me, after a brief time in your little town, I would like nothing more than to leave myself."

"You would marry her?"

"She wouldn't have me. I offered to send her to nursing school and to be a nurse. She has a steady way with patients." Adam turned and stared down at the top of David's thinning brown hair. "Why am I telling you all of this?"

"Because you know I care about her. I always will."

"You can't possibly care about her after what you did."

"I can and I do. She was my only friend for a very long time and I'll always cherish that. It was a free time, a time when I could do as I liked."

"As if you can't now."

"I can't. I can't protect her. You can."

"Excuse me." Adam felt slightly sick as he thought of what David's protection might mean.

"Mother's in love with that baby. You've got to get them both away from here for their sake."

"You don't exist to tell her what to do. Or me either." Adam took purposeful strides to the piney woods where Ruby had disappeared, sick of seeing or talking to Winslows.

Adam took off through the woods, where he last saw Ruby go. He had to find her and talk to her. He couldn't explain it, but the whole exchange with Winslow and Dodge and David too, left him feeling very uneasy. Ruby had to make a decision about her life. And he would be the one to help her. They would do it…together.

Ruby didn't like the way Paul Winslow pointed and stared at her son. She took the baby to the woods on the edge of town.

"Let's put our feet in the creek, Solly, okay?" On the hot July day, she was relieved to take off her high button Sunday shoes and stockings and plunge her feet into the cool water.

She thrilled to hear his little laugh as the stream bubbled over his dear little toes. All of the tall Georgia pines swayed about her in a gentle breeze and she marveled at God's creations. He had spoken to her so often in such a place. She finally felt some peace.

"You want to stay here? Let's stay here in the woods. No one will be after us to get married. We'll stay here and God will take care of us."

Solomon fixed her with those Winslow eyes, laughing and happy. Were his eyes daring her to make it happen?

Whenever she left the woods, someone would be after her to make a decision about Dodge. Or Paul Winslow would fix his beady eyes on her son. Or Adam would be there.

When he came to mind, however, she wasn't upset, but rather comforted at Adam being there for her. If he only had the sense to accept who he was, she might be willing to go with him. However, it wasn't meant to be.

She pulled Solomon back onto the bank and they sat drying their feet in the sun. "Come on, Solly, I know you're hungry." Unbuttoning her blouse to feed him, she reached for Solomon but his little hand pushed her away. What happened? He wasn't excited or happy to nurse. She put him next her and pushed her blouse back together, then started at the sound of a familiar voice.

"He wants some food. Let me help you take him back. Are you decent?"

Ruby fiddled with the buttons on her blouse, putting them together. "Yes, thank you for asking." Adam approached with quick steps and picked Solomon up off of the ground. Ruby delighted to hear the baby giggle as Adam picked him up high in the air and brought him back down.

"I have to say, I agree with him. I want some lunch too." Ruby stroked Solomon's little arm.

Adam smiled at her. "Let's go get some together. You deserve to have a happy Fourth."

"Really?"

"Did you come last year?"

Ruby reflected on what had happened last year. People found out about her baby coming and she had begun showing. She stayed at home, the start of her long, long confinement.

All alone with her shame.

Thinking about last year, she was glad to be outside. "No. I would like to get back to the celebrations. Did they go away? I didn't like the way they were looking at Solomon."

A cloud came over Adam's handsome face. "I had some words with Paul Winslow. He was asking a lot of questions about the baby, his health, and such. I guess he wants to know if he's okay."

"It's none of his business," Ruby said angrily. "He don't care about him."

"He seemed to care enough to ask, Ruby."

"What are you saying?"

"I'm saying the man is a cold-hearted monster. And I say that knowing his blood courses through my veins. But when he first laid eyes on Solomon, he cared."

"He only cares for what he can get. He can't get my baby."

"I don't think he wants Solomon."

"Don't be too sure." Ruby's heart began to thud loudly in her ears.

"He wanted to make sure he was protected and in a circumstance where he can't get sick anymore."

"So why was Dodge with him?"

"I don't know. But I can't shake the feeling Dodge is with him somehow. If so, he may have said something to Winslow about you two getting married."

Ruby shivered and willed her heart to be still. "No. It won't happen."

Adam turned to her with Solomon in his arms. "Then what are you going to do?"

"I'm going to keep on with my schooling and get to be a nurse."

"Your ambitions are wonderful, and I would be proud to help you with them. But some of those plans may not be in your hands anymore because of Solomon."

"I put my trust in God," Ruby said as they approached the clearing at the edge of the forest where town began. "But I can't help but feel as if I'm in the woods, lost somehow, and I can't get out."

Solomon seemed too easy and secure in his arms. Her fingers itched to take him from Adam, but she didn't because she liked the way they looked together. Then he spoke the words. "Doctors work long hard hours. I chose the profession as a single man, because I knew it would be hard to have a wife and a family of my own. I didn't ever want my family to feel as if I were neglecting them because of the work I do."

"How thoughtful." Ruby stopped her steps to where a layer of trees came between them and the picnic grounds.

"I had a lonely life growing up. It would kill me to neglect someone else, knowing what I had endured. I couldn't do that to him," Adam stared down at the wisps of hair on Solomon's head. "And," his gray eyes stared at her, "I could never do that to you, Ruby."

"I see." Now, his Winslow eyes shifted to linger and gaze on her lips, as if he wanted to partake, as if he were hungry, but he just couldn't eat. The longing in his eyes wasn't helping her decide what to do.

She had to get away.

"I'll take him now, Dr. Morson. Thank you." Ruby reached for Solomon. "I would appreciate it if you just waited here for a few minutes. I know I'm ruined, but I still don't want to give folks something to talk about."

Adam's hand stayed upon her sleeve. "Are you angry?"

Ruby stopped for a few seconds, and her muscles quivered as she held the baby. Was she angry? Other men, if she had knowledge of them, would have taken advantage of the time they were in the forest alone together. They would have at least kissed her.

David had done it, luring her with the possibility there would be more, and then taking her virtue from her. She regarded Adam's soulful eyes and believed his admiration for her was true and genuine as was his concern for her. How could she be angry at someone who thought about her and about what was right before she ever did? "No, I'm fine. Thank you for letting me know."

Adam relinquished the baby. Ruby shushed Solomon at his initial protests. "Let's go and get some food, son. We'll be fine."

Walking out of the woods toward the picnic blankets, Ruby noticed Negro corner was much more populated than it usually was. She nodded to various folks as she made her way to the place where the Bledsoes sat.

Her family was busily eating lunch and she sat down and selected a small chicken leg, picking off shreds of meat to give to Solomon, who smacked his little lips at its tastiness. Adam came to join them a few minutes later and he sat away from them, next to John on the other side of the bench.

Good. Sit far away.

Even so, she didn't like the queer, hurt feeling in her heart at Adam's thoughtfulness. No one had ever put her first before. How could she put his kind of regard aside for anything else? Suddenly, she didn't feel hungry anymore.

Chapter Thirteen

Although he had objected to the whole idea of a "Colored Corner," the way the Negroes enjoyed one another's company was revealing. To be sure, he had his share of examining lumps, bumps, bruises and a headache, but he was glad to perform the service for so many who had never even seen a doctor before, let alone a Negro one.

It made him think hard about the things Ruby had said about the pride he could take in being himself, without having to resort to being something he wasn't. She spoke a powerful truth. However, for the rest of the day, Ruby avoided him. She kept Solomon from him too, always ensuring there was some other family member around.

Despite Dodge's best attempts, he was never left alone with Ruby either. Adam wanted to chuckle at his various frustrated attempts. Ruby paid no attention to Dodge, but instead, played games with the baby and her sisters, and made sure Solomon got his first taste of peach ice cream. At the taste, Solomon kicked his little legs back and forth, as if he wanted to run, but he could not—he was almost six months old.

Adam had to refrain from laughing at how the baby smacked his lips at the taste. *What a delightful little fellow. Such a blessing.* If he took that opportunity in Pittsburgh, what would life be like without Solomon? Or his mother? The vision of either one of them out of his life was a bleak one.

Soon, it was time for the reading of the Declaration of Independence. Paul Winslow stood up in the bandshell and, all of the town citizens quieted. Thus, the noise and laughter emitting from Negro corner became more obvious, but they quieted down as well. "Thank you," Paul Winslow's voice carried on the evening wind. "We're glad to have you at the town celebration on this, our beloved country's one hundred and twenty-ninth birthday." Everyone clapped. "And as always, we're delighted to have the Reverend Archibald Melvin come forward and read the Declaration of Independence. Everyone quiet now."

From his vantage point, all Adam could see was the top of a shining pink pate with wispy white hair creeping forward. Everyone had to be still, to hear the decrepit Reverend speak in winded, low tones.

Solomon, in the ensuing cool of the evening, was not poised to be quiet. Ruby kept shushing him, but he wouldn't hush. Lona and John, who were sitting next to her, couldn't get him to be quiet either.

Ruby picked up the baby and came over to where Adam sat with her sisters on a blanket instead of the bench. "Keep him quiet and still," Ruby whispered to him as she stood. "I'ma be right back." She strode with intent over to the red clay strip of land that separated Colored Corner from the area where the rest of the town citizens were seated, listening to the Reverend read the speech in his ancient and wavering voice.

Beautiful and dignified, dressed in her white and blue, with a red tie the lone accent on her middy, Ruby faced her people, with her hands behind her back and her legs slightly akimbo. She was going to open her mouth.

What was Ruby doing?

Gently, he handed the baby off to a sister, he didn't know which one, but someone had to hold Solomon so he could stop her.

And she spoke. She said the Declaration of Independence right along with the Reverend, word for word, and she, unlike him, did not need any paper in front of her. It was coming right from her out into the world with a strong, proud and resolute voice. Now the Negroes, shunned off into the corner, could hear the words.

Even as he tiptoed between quilts, preparing to stop her, the recitation she gave of the familiar words stirred him. She believed, wholeheartedly, in what she said and she recited it to all with everything in her.

Taller than everyone else, he noted the attention of the white side was not on the Reverend, rather, they were watching Ruby and her loud, proud, recitation of the well-known document. There were scowls on nearly every white face, including Mary Winslow, and he kept a smile to himself inside of his heart.

At the part of reciting the list of grievances against the king, Ruby would say the "He," with special emphasis. It came across, to Adam at least, as a heartfelt condemnation of Paul Winslow and his rule in the small town.

Adam turned his head quickly to look at Lona, who was terrified. Lona stood too, as if she wanted to go and stop Ruby, but John stopped her with his hand. John's pride in his daughter was unmistakable as they all watched Ruby speak.

Out of the corner of his eye, though, the sheriff was edging closer to Ruby. Adam tried to speed up his footsteps, but there were too many people between them.

With a beet red face, Paul Winslow had stepped off of the bandshell and directed the sheriff to where Ruby stood. Now it was time to pray.

Please protect her, God. Help me to get to her.

His heart started to beat faster—Ruby had really gotten herself into trouble this time. Nothing should happen to her. Solomon needed her. He needed her. How could he have been so casual about what had told her earlier? Had he spent so much time by himself, studying, so he didn't know how to talk to another person, another woman?

No wonder she hated him.

"In every stage of these Oppressions We have Petitioned for Redress in the most humble terms: Our repeated Petitions have been answered only by repeated injury." The sheriff had beaten him and stood right in front of her. Ruby did not flinch. She made her voice louder, clearer and stronger.

Please, God, let her be safe. Let her be safe.

His prayers creaked through his brain, probably because it had been a long time since he had prayed, but he needed to believe in her safety.

"A Prince whose character is thus marked by every act which may define a Tyrant, is unfit to be the ruler of a free people. In every stage of these Oppressions We have Petitioned for Redress in the most humble terms: Our repeated Petitions have been answered only by repeated injury. A Prince whose character is thus marked by every act which may define a Tyrant, is unfit to be the ruler of a free people."

She must have sensed him coming closer, because she held up a hand. Stay away, she seemed to say. Let me finish. Despite his typical good sense, Adam gave her her wish, and fell back at the edge of the crowd but his heart thudded in fear and worry for her.

As Ruby got closer to the end, the sheriff came closer but Ruby did not move, and did not appear afraid. As she ended the recitation, her voice grew stronger and more forceful.

At the end her voice almost boomed, "And for the support of this Declaration, with a firm reliance on the protection of divine Providence, we mutually pledge to each other our Lives, our Fortunes and our sacred Honor." She finished and Adam leapt to her. But there were strong men on either side of him, holding him down. She finished and a crowd of officials surrounded her, and pulled her off, deep into the town square.

Colored Corner did not realize at first what was happening to Ruby, because they were applauding, but when they realized she had been taken away, they protested in loud, angry voices. Adam tried to follow the white officials, but soon, they were swallowed up by the crowd who, he could see, were clearly condemning Ruby.

Bits of her straw boater were strewn on the ground, and with horror he understood the angry crowd must have ripped the hat from her head. What else had been ripped from her? The thought scared him, and he ran back to the Bledsoes, trying to think about what to do. "Where's Ruby?" Mags cried out as he came back.

"They've taken her away," Adam said, "probably to be arrested."

"She ain't do nothing," Nettie cried.

"Hush," Lona told her daughter. "They going to take her to jail. We got to get her out of there."

John gathered his daughters into his arms as they began to cry. The fireworks started and the loud sound made Solomon join in the crying as well. "We should get back home. I'll take as many as I can in the car, then I'll come out to see what is going on. Let's go."

Packing up baskets, he resolved to carry as many Bledsoes into the car as he could. Could he do something for Ruby to get her out of custody?

He would do anything, even trade on his associations with Paul Winslow, to keep her safe. As he balanced Solomon and picnic baskets in his arms, something struck him.

He had never been a part of anything before. And now, he was a part of something for the first time in his life. The answer, to him, shone clear and the possibilities of resolving everything for Ruby became immediately obvious. He knew what he had to do.

Her straw boater had been her only other hat besides her pink one and now it was gone. Warm hot blood rushed to her face. How could they be so mean to her?

Thank God the boater had not been secured with her usual hatpin, or they would have ripped her hair out by the roots too. She had grown up in Winslow and known these people for most of her life and they had ripped and clawed at her like animals, as if they wanted her torn apart.

In all of the times she had gotten into trouble, she had never been arrested before. Uncle Arlo had and she tried to be as brave as he must have been when they had taken him from the jail cell into the woods and...

Ruby shook her head to clear the vision of her dear uncle from her mind and ignored her racing pulse. When the sheriff had finally gotten her into the clear to a car and pushed her inside, she could see the hands of the crowd had dirtied her crisp white middy blouse. "Where are you taking me?" she asked Sheriff Baines.

"Hush up, girl." Sheriff Baines started the car and jumped inside.

"I should know where I'm going to."

"I said, hush. You done caused more than enough trouble today."

"Okay," Ruby sat back and breathed, "At least tell me what I did wrong, Sheriff Baines."

"You up here disturbing the peace during the Declaration speech. You heard Mr. Winslow. You should have been quiet. Up here making me miss the fireworks to deal with you."

Ruby sat in the seat of the car and was struck with a pure terror. Was Solomon okay? Would he be able to eat? Thanks to Adam, he knew how to feed him without her now. The thought made her sad, along with the alarm running in her blood at being taken to some unknown place.

Sheriff Baines pulled up to the courthouse building where Winslow's two-celled jail pen was located. "You can't put me in jail," she said with more bravery than she felt. Sheriff Baines came around the side of the car and grabbed her arm. His sweaty palm print would leave more marks on her blouse.

"I can do whatever I want, gal, now you're in my company. Come on here."

No. No more of whatever they wanted to do to her. There was worse and her mother had endured it. Uncle Arlo had lost his life over it. Was she in for the same treatment? Tears began to run down her face.

She didn't understand how brave her mother had been before, how strong in God's presence she had to stand, but now, facing the unknown, she knew. She would never question or disrespect Lona again. And she would always, always fight Uncle Arlo's good fight.

"Honor thy father and thy mother, that thy days may be long upon the land which the Lord thy God giveth thee." The words gave her comfort and the understanding of this particular commandment came to her for the first time in her life.

"Shut up." Sherriff Baines jerked her hard by her arm into the empty courthouse building. As he guided her down dark corridors where the jail cells were housed in the basement, she could see, luckily for her, there was no one in the jails.

Be brave.

"I still should know why I'm here."

Baines pushed her into the jail cell door he opened. "Creating a public disturbance."

"I was saying the Declaration so everyone could hear it. Have you even been in Colored Corner trying to hear?"

"I ain't colored," Baines snarled as he shut the door. "Praise God."

Now that she was in the bare cell, and out of his clutches, she could say what she really wanted. "We can't hear when you all push us away from the band shell. I was just making it so everyone could hear."

Her words gave Baines pause, as if he might let her go, but he shook his head. "You get into too much trouble 'round here. You tell it to Mr. Winslow. He'll be here to talk to you." He walked away.

"Paul Winslow is not God, no matter what he thinks. He's just a man, same as you," Ruby shouted after him. There was only one place to sit, on a saggy cot in the jail cell and she sank down on it, weary. "He's a person, just like me."

She laid down on the thin cot and said the Lord's Prayer to herself, over and over again to give her comfort. Solomon, her family, Adam—those thoughts would only make her cry.

Instead, wetness seeped through the front of her blouse in the form of two equal circles. Her breasts wept and she had no way of changing clothes. The thought of the wasted milk and what it meant for Solomon made the silent tears fall faster as she lay on the dirty cot. The boom, boom, boom of the fireworks sounded overhead, and matched the thudding fear resonating in her heart.

Ruby sat up at a slight scuffling in the hallway. She looked all around her. She was a country girl and could handle seeing most anything, but she really didn't want the scuffling to be people.

Or rats.

She clasped her hands. *Lord, please, please protect me. Please be there for me.*

I am sorry I was so foolish, I was just trying to help my people to hear, really hear the words of the Declaration so they could know, just as I know, it means me too, even though so many people here don't seem to know.

Her dry throat was full of emotion.

Then, Paul Winslow appeared in front of her. He held a tin cup in his hand. "How you?"

Pushing back at her hair, she knew she must look a sight with mussed hair, ripped clothes and large milk spots on her blouse. "I'm fine, thank you."

She folded her arms over the milk spots, which had dried by now and tried to look brave. Paul Winslow laughed at her efforts and she stuck her chin out, determined he would not see her broken. "Thirsty?"

"No." The shine of the tin cup sparkled in the near dark and she licked her dry crusted lips. Better not to drink. She didn't know what was in there.

"Are you sure, girl? It ain't nothing but water."

"No, thank you."

Paul Winslow stood there in front of her and drank most of it, then threw the rest on the floor into the jail cell with her. He wiped his mouth with the back of his hand. "What do you call yourself trying to do now, by ruining by celebrations? More of your organizing?"

"Sir, I was trying to speak the words so everyone, including those in the back corner, could hear. If the Declaration is for everyone, then it should be loud enough for all to hear it."

"And so you took it upon yourself to make it happen. Without asking, saying anything?"

She met those Winslow eyes of his, the ones like Solomon's, Adam's and David's. Those eyes figured too much into her life and she would not look away like she was supposed to. "You don't speak to me direct most of the time, sir. How would I know what you say?"

He flustered at this response. "It's the job of the Reverend to read the Declaration."

"He's getting mighty old, sir. That's why I did what I did."

"Not to cause no ruckus or scene like you do?"

"Sir, every problem I have with you and the mill, I take up with the workers direct. I don't mean to cause a scene; I wanted to help people out. Just like I helped out today."

Paul Winslow fixed her with a steely stare. "I don't know, Ruby. You've gotten yourself into a lot of trouble in the past."

"Some of the trouble, sir, was not of my making," Ruby stared back at him, thinking Adam's warm grey eyes looked very different in his father's cold, harsh face.

He cleared his throat. "Yes, well, you got you a baby now. You can't go around causing trouble. Got to settle down. I hear you've had an offer of marriage."

Ruby shouldn't have been surprised he would know, given how Dodge had informed them of her plans to do the oration and cozying up to him at the picnic earlier. Still, she was surprised at Paul Winslow's interference in the life events of his laundress's daughter. Someone who was supposed to be the lowest of the low.

The casual way Paul Winslow bothered to be down here in the jailhouse, telling her she needed to get married proved she was important, as she had always known. Ruby sat up on the cot a little straighter, and prouder. "Yes?" The one word was a question. Just what did he propose she should do?

"You need to go on and take it. Go on, get married and have some more babies. What women are supposed to do." He pointed at her. "You, you say now what you're going to do, and I'll call your intended in and free you from this jail right now. You can go on home."

So, that's what this was all about. He wanted reassurance she wasn't going to cause him any more worry or trouble. But marriage to the wrong man would be exchanging one jail cell for another. All she wanted to do was to go back to her son, almost worse than anything, but to give in now would set the whole course of her son's life back, almost back to slavery.

This moment, this confrontation with this terrible, powerful man meant allowing Solomon to go forward in this world. She wanted that more than leaving the jail. "I can't tell you I'm going to marry someone before I tell the man."

"You want me to call him down here? I get Dodge in here now, and you can tell him yourself and put an end to all of this. I can get a marriage license and even Reverend. Melvin too, make it all official." Paul Winslow looked all around him, as if he were going to summon Dodge now.

"No, don't call him. I don't want to talk to him now."

He hung on the bars in such a way Ruby knew he had to be intoxicated. Had that been water in the cup? Ruby's eyes followed the wet shape on the floor that the tossed away drink had made. As temperance herself, the disgust and alarm rolled in her threatening to empty her stomach. Had he been trying to get her drunk? "And why not?"

"I'm still thinking it over."

He stood and smoothed his thinning brown hair down. "You better do more than think, girl. You better tell him yes and get yourself married and have a bunch of babies with Dodge."

"And if I don't?"

"If you don't?"

"Yes, what if I don't, sir? What do you have to say to me, a local little Negro girl who is not married?"

"There's a whole lot more I could say. I could say, I could call David down here and let him handle you again Yes. I think my son's got some more celebrating to do on the birthday of the United States. I think he could have some more celebration with you." She gulped down the near vomit that rose up in her throat.

He believed he could rattle her.

And she was rattled. She wouldn't show him, though.

"David's got a few buddies up at school who would like to have a good time with a pretty Negro gal too."

Stay brave. Ruby swallowed hard again.

Paul Winslow held out a warning finger. "Then, I could say your fine boy should not be permitted to be with a whore mother. Yes, I could say, a white child like him deserves a chance in this world to live away from a whore mother. I could say plenty."

"Don't touch my son!" Ruby cried in spite of herself. "Don't you touch him!" The tears in her face threatened to break loose in a flood. He had gotten to her.

"You see? We agree. Your baby shouldn't have a whore for a mother. He deserves a solid, respectable home to grow up in with a father and a respectable mother. What about what he needs? Make up your mind." He slapped the tin cup against the bars of the door, making loud clanking sounds. "You think about what you want. See you in the morning." He turned on his heel and left.

Ruby stood and grasped the bars of the jail cell door. "Don't touch my baby! Don't touch my baby!" She screamed the words over and over as the tears slipped down her cheeks, her voice hoarse.

I don't care about myself, God, just protect my baby. Protect Solomon. The picture in her mind of Adam holding Solomon in his arms was all she had to hold onto. And it calmed her for some reason.

Chapter Fourteen

Adam and John decided to leave during the fireworks display, figuring the crowd would be too distracted to notice. As Adam drove, Lona's stiff and ramrod straight countenance cast a shadow in the darkness, as did Mags's worried face. Sad little Delie just sniffled. Delie, reprimanded with a slap at conveying her disappointment at missing the fireworks, wiped away tears with a grubby middy sleeve.

As punishment, Delie had been charged to keep Solomon. For a five-year-old, Delie was doing a great job. Solomon made light fluttering noises of sleep in the backseat as his young aunt clung to him. John had the other girls in the wagon and Adam hoped he would make a brisk pace home.

Even picking his way through the dark, the car got there first. He helped the ladies take everything inside and repacked his medical bag to make sure he had whatever he needed, if anything, to help Ruby. He worked swiftly, with fear-stiffened fingers, to make sure he was prepared.

Mags came to the doorway. "Mama wants you to go down to see about what they doing to Ruby."

"I'm just making sure I have what I need to help her, Mags. I have to wait until your father gets here to make sure you all are safe."

Adam turned around, ready to take his bag to the front room when Lona appeared in the doorway, her face still etched with worry. "You go on ahead and see to Ruby. We be fine here until John come home."

"You need a man to make sure you are protected. Leaving you here by yourselves puts you in danger. Ruby would never forgive me if something happened to you."

Lona showed him her husband's gun by the door. "I've lived through some danger a time or two in my life." The clear strength and resoluteness on Lona's face shone through and Adam understood where Ruby's stubbornness came from. "I can protect these girls and the baby. I knows how to shoot a gun. I'm more afraid for Ruby being down there by herself. Go on ahead."

As Adam moved to the door, Lona put a hand on his arm. "You care about her don't you?"

Adam matched the intense gaze shining from the careworn face. "I do. I want to make sure she's safe and protected."

"Please, help her."

"I'll do my best, ma'am. Excuse me."

"God be with you," Lona said. Adam passed Mags who sat in a chair in the front room, trying to soothe a fussy Solomon back to sleep.

"Take care, Doctor," Mags whispered as he went past her.

Adam calmed a bit as he heard the creaky sound of the wheels on John's wagon approaching the farm. He got the car going and drove off.

The shining tan stone of the courthouse, full of life and vigor just hours before, stood dim in darkness. This was where they would have taken her if she were brought here. The empty-looking nature of the building alarmed him. Then, in the still of the night, there were female shouts and screams.

Ruby.

Taking up his bag, he ran to a side door where the sound seemed to come from. What were they doing to her?

His heart beat fast in his chest. How could he get in? The door was made of heavy wooden beams that would not budge. He prepared to run around to the front to see if there were other ways of getting in, when the door swung open and Paul Winslow stood in the doorway.

"Why, Dr. Morson, whatever are you doing here?"

"I came to see if Ruby needed some medical attention." Adam tried to smooth down his tie and straighten his viewing spectacles. He figured Paul Winslow would have more respect for the posture his education afforded him.

"Really now? Come on in, since you're here."

Adam entered the dark courthouse and followed Paul Winslow down a long, straight corridor. Ruby's shouts sounded much more clearly now, and he could hear she shouted about Solomon. He could let her know her child was safe. Paul Winslow turned into a small office space and Adam stood in the doorway, impatient. "I want her out of here."

Paul Winslow went behind a desk into a cabinet and got out some glasses and a decanter and filled them with alcohol. "Join me?"

The strong stench of the liquor filled his nose and brought to mind Lucas's incessant drinking. All of Paul Winslow's caretaking money went right into those bottles, instead of food to fill his belly. He shook his head to clear the headiness of the memory from his mind. He had to stay focused. "I'm temperance," Adam said. "Where's Ruby?"

His father shrugged his shoulders as if he didn't care. He filled both glasses and looked prepared to drink from them. "I don't know how you ended up as temperance. Winslows have a long proud history of being able to hold our liquor. Must be Mattie's side." He held up the other glass to Adam in salute and drank it down quickly. "What's it to you for her to get out of jail? One night ain't going to hurt her."

"She didn't do anything wrong. You're infringing on her rights as a United States Citizen, rights she is guaranteed under the fourteenth amendment of the Constitution."

Paul held out the second glass before he drank from the other one. "I see. You using all the education I paid for to tell me I should let her go. You got a thing for her."

"I don't understand why you are keeping her," Adam insisted.

"You a latecomer to the town here. So you don't know or understand who's running things here. This is my town. What I say around here goes."

"So then you can see why she should be let go."

"You don't know what kind of trouble she causes."

Adam shrugged . "She's just a colored girl. What could she do to you?"

"She's a fine little piece, isn't she? Man, if I were younger…"

In that moment, he knew God must have stopped him from reaching over the desk and punching Paul Winslow in his drunk face. And he was glad for it because hitting the man would damage the hands he needed to heal others. So he clenched them in pure frustration instead. "She needs to go home to her son."

"She needs a husband who'll keep her in line." His father sat down again. "I told Dodge he could have her. He's willing to take the task on."

"You have no right to say what she does. Let her go."

"What will you do if I don't? You're clearly not doing your job, Doctor, in taking care of these Negroes if you're so interested in just one." He laughed. "I might could have turned her over to you, if I thought you would keep her in line the way a woman should be kept. But you wouldn't. No. Dodge is the one for her."

"I'll make sure she doesn't bother you anymore."

"How?"

"Just leave it to me. If she gives you trouble, then you can deal with me."

Paul Winslow took a deep swallow of his pungent drink. Adam kept from making a face at the nose-clearing stench of alcohol. His father took the jail keys out of his pocket and dangled them at the ends of his fingertips. "Here. Go get her and get her out of here. I'll be back to see you, down at that farm, if you don't keep her in line."

Adam snatched the keys and followed the sound of Ruby's sobs down the corridor. Paul Winslow was in league with the devil. How was he going to get Ruby and her son out of his father's clutches?

And himself as well.

Someone ran toward her down the hall. The fear should have impacted her stomach, as it always did, but it didn't.

Paul Winslow was too drunk and big to have an alert step. The person coming to her had to let her go—the clink and clank of metal sounded down the hallway along with the footsteps. She wished she had a handkerchief to wipe her eyes and face with. Straightening up on the saggy cot, she tried to look brave. Ida Wells-Barnett had been in jail many times. Ruby would not shame her heroine with sniffling.

Praise God. Adam Morson's tall body came into view and she had never been so relieved to see someone. With his shirtsleeves rolled up and his collar off, the welcome sight of his lean, muscular body appeared. She almost wanted to laugh with delight at the fact he looked less than his usual correct dress standard, but she couldn't. She bounced on her toes to reach as high as he was tall.

"Adam!" She grasped the bar doors with joy. "Where's your tie?" When she threw herself against the bars, she had practically launched into his chest, and the hardness of his body slammed against hers through the prison bars. His big body was reassuring to her, and she wanted to hold him, to bring those muscles closer. But her clothes were ruined.

She calmed down. What a sight she must be.

He leaned forward and tried one key after another. "He couldn't keep you in here. There were no charges."

"That's what they do down here," Ruby crowed. "Sometimes, they keep people on a trumped up charge, but I didn't think someone would be in here to get me tonight."

"It's after midnight, Ruby," he informed her as the door swung open. He grabbed her hand and pulled her forward. "Let's get out of here."

His voice was forceful and direct. His hand on hers felt like home, warm and caressing. She had held hands with David sometimes, before the attack, but his hands were always cold and clammy. Adam's hands were a man's hands, a doctor's hands, capable and strong. Lona was right. These were hands to take care of a woman.

"Is Solomon okay?" she asked him, forcing her attention away from his body. She shouldn't think about the doctor in this way.

"He's fine," Adam said. "He was fast asleep in the car."

Ruby breathed out as they hurried down the dark corridor. "I certainly hope so."

Adam stopped in front of a door and let her hand go as he stepped into an office. Through the slightly darkened door, Paul Winslow's head was down on the desk. Adam put the keys in Winslow's hand, and came back out to her. He grabbed her hand as soon as he returned.

Something inside Ruby became warm and wriggly, as if she were holding a new puppy, but much better. He escorted her outside in the dark, humid July morning, and opened the car door for her. She did her best Miss Mary imitation as she got into the front seat next to him. She watched him as he quickly started the car. "We have got to get out of here," Adam said. "I'm sorry if I am rushing you."

The stark and sad bare town square sagged. So empty of celebrating citizens. No more Independence Day. "No, I understand. I have seen enough happen with some of these men in the town. We should get back to the farm as soon as possible."

He jumped into the car and grasped the wheel with those capable hands of his and quickly, with a surety she had not seen in many Negro men of her acquaintance, drove them back to the Bledsoe house. What about her family? Were they all safe despite her escapades?

She didn't need to worry. When they got back, all was quiet. The farm still stood. No one had come to raid, or burn or pilfer. She breathed out a breath she didn't know she was holding in. "I was so concerned for them."

"Fortunately, they are all fine." Adam pulled the car over. John Bledsoe had opened the front door with a finger to his lips. Ruby alighted from the car and went to embrace her father.

"I'm glad you are okay, girl. You give us a scare."

"I'm sorry, Daddy. I didn't mean to."

John opened the door wider. "Come on in, daughter. You home now." They embraced.

When Adam came back in the house behind her, her father banked over the coals in the fireplace and made a gesture. "I'm going on to bed, since the cows will wake up in just a little bit."

"Good night, sir," Adam said.

John stepped over to him.

"Thank you for saving my girl."

"It was my pleasure, sir."

John shook his hand and went to his bedroom off on the other side of the house.

Ruby sat down on the davenport. She wasn't hungry or tired—she just wanted to revel in the fact she was home.

"What're you thinking about?" Adam sat in the chair across from her.

"I'm thinking I'm so glad to be here. I want to study a little Latin."

Adam smiled at her. He had a very nice smile. His handsome features were so serious most of the time, that his smile was a welcome surprise. "*Gaudeo te ipsum.*"

Now she understood what he was about. Something stirred inside of her as he spoke the dead language. The part of her stirring was a part she believed dead, killed by David.

Wrong.

His gray eyes twinkled at her. "What did you say?"

He shook his head.

He wasn't he going to tell her what he said? Tipping her head to one side as she spoke, she determined to figure it out. "I'm glad, you are here."

"Home, not here," Adam corrected, speaking low. "*Spero autem quad te curare.*"

Frustrated, Ruby leaned closer. "I can't hear what you are saying, come here."

What had she done? A flush of warmth went straight to her cheeks. She had invited him to sit on the davenport with her. Around Winslow, this kind of invitation was considered a courting move, but she didn't mean it that way. Not really. She did want to hear what he was saying, so she could translate it. Adam got up and sat opposite her. He repeated the words he had spoken.

Ruby concentrated. However, it was hard now since he was sitting closer to her and she could smell the pomade he used on his black hair to keep it silky. What would it be like to run her fingers through it?

Concentrate. I have to let this man know I can do this. "I hope you take care of yourself," she said with delight, a little too loudly. Everyone was sleeping.

Adam nodded. "*Quod tot curae tibi.*"

"Because so many care for you."

His gray eyes sparkled in the dying light of the main room. They seemed to turn a shade darker, serious. "*I fac ut.*"

"As I do." Ruby finished. What did he mean by that? Brushing aside any hope, especially since she looked so wretched, she said, "Thank you for coming to get me out. If it was up to Paul Winslow, I'm sure he wouldn't have minded letting me stay in there all night long."

"I'm glad I could help. I didn't want anything to happen to you."

"Thank you," Ruby's voice lowered, as they faced each other on the davenport in the dark room. She leaned in to give him a peck on the cheek to show her gratitude. It seemed appropriate, seeing he was her teacher, and mentor, and now, a guardian of sorts.

He backed away fast, too soon, making her feel embarrassed at her attempts to be kind. "Yes, um. I'm glad you are home."

She smiled a bit to see the calm doctor so ruffled. She couldn't resist teasing him despite her humiliation. "You just said it. In Latin, no less."

Adam stood up and smoothed down his pants legs. "I'm going to get some rest. You should too."

"Yes," Ruby said. "Before Solomon wakes up. Good night."

Once again, she was aware of how tall he was as she slid past him to get to the large room where all of the girls slept. She entered and closed the door quietly, intending to be alone with her thoughts, but in the darkness, she could make out the shapes of four very curious and nosy young women. She slipped to her bed and could see Solomon sleeping peacefully in his cradle, a beautiful sight which made her heart happy. "I'm glad you are safe, Ruby." Delie's voice piped up in the darkness.

"Thank you, honey. Go on to sleep now."

"We trying to sleep, but it's mighty hard with a Latin class going on in the middle of the night," Mags said, and they all started giggling.

"Hush up." As Ruby slipped off her dirty torn clothes and into the nightgown at the foot of the bed, she felt brand-new. "The baby's asleep."

They kept giggling. Clearly, her sisters cared more for their giggles than Solomon's sleep. "Y'all get on my nerves."

"You know you love us," Em said.

"We know who she loves," Mags said, which sent them into more giggles.

Ruby didn't respond since she didn't want to encourage them any more— and she really didn't want to wake Solomon. However, as she lay in bed, she remembered again and again, not the horrid jail cell, but that she had dared to kiss Adam.

How would she make up for her forwardness? She had a hard time going to sleep.

Chapter Fifteen

Ruby had been doing very well in her studies over the week, garnering A's in nearly everything she studied, even in subjects she professed to dislike. Her mind was particularly quick in algebra. When she obtained a 100 per cent on an exam he had given her, Adam was astonished. She must surely be ready for the bigger challenge of completing this portion of her high school diploma. She only lagged behind in languages. *A true jewel, just like her name.*

She worked hard and she deserved some reward. When he had marked her algebra paper, he sat back in the chair and asked her if she had ever been to a nickelodeon show.

"I have heard of them, of course. But no, I've never been. I would love to see one. They have a movie house over in Calhoun, but we've never gone before."

Admittedly the show was an expense, but why would a couple with such an expansive view of education and the world as John and Lona, deprive their growing brood of a show? "You put on your best dress and we'll go to Calhoun tomorrow, maybe even have a sundae at the ice cream parlor afterward."

"Really?"

"Why not?"

"Unless I've heard differently, Negroes can't go to the show or to the ice cream parlor in Calhoun."

"They'll let us."

She understood the implication of his words. "If we are discovered, we can be arrested. Or worse."

"I'm willing if you are," Adam shrugged . "These practices are silly and stupid at best. I refuse to pay any real attention to these rules and regulations."

"What if we see someone we know?" Ruby said.

"We can say hello."

"I want to go, but I don't know if I can go under those circumstances, Adam. I'm not ashamed of who I am."

"I didn't ask you to be. It's just a line to cross, just a way to get you to think you are less than what they say. And we're not."

"Okay," Ruby agreed but there was reluctance in her voice.

"Are you sure?"

"I want to go with you. I just don't want to go to church tomorrow."

Adam immediately understood. "It'll be easier if you just let him know."

A light came into Ruby's eyes. "Maybe when we go to church we can show him I don't want to marry him."

Adam sat back. Who knew what went on in the mind of an eighteen-year-old young woman? "You want to put me on display?"

"You want me to go into a movie house and pretend I'm something I'm not to avoid the crow's nest. I don't see much difference."

Adam did. Going to church as a couple would be a public declaration of their feelings for one another. A qualm of guilt went up his back. He was glad she didn't seem to hate him so much, but just to get to Dodge? "We'll see."

"Yes," Ruby said. "We will."

The next day, Ruby dressed in the rose-trimmed white dress. She left off the pink hat. Her sisters were very pleased to see her looking nice, and she told them Adam was going to take her to the nickelodeon for doing so well on her schoolwork. "I'm almost a high school graduate."

"I wonder what he will do when you *are* a high school graduate." Mags's usually graceful countenance turned sly.

Ruby made a face at her.

"I want to go to the nickelodeon with a handsome man," Delie opined. Her sisters started to laugh, but Ruby grew serious. She understood why her parents had kept them from the show all of these years.

There was nothing but humiliation by sitting up in the crow's nest, where the theater wasn't as clean or kept up and the seats weren't as nice as those on the main floor, where the whites sat. If Lona and John went, their darker brown faces would mean instant relegation to the crow's nest. Ruby and Adam might go in and sit on the ground floor, if no one knew who they were. Georgia towns were small, and there were so few of their acquaintance who had cars who might see them, it might be all right.

"What are you going to see?" Mags asked.

"*The Birth of a Nation.*" Ruby smoothed down Delie's braids with a hand. "I've heard a lot about it. Not all good."

"What do you mean?" Nettie's delicate features arranged themselves in concern.

"It shows our people in some bad ways. Other NAACP chapters up north have protested it. That's why I want to go."

"I heard it was a long movie. Maybe that's why Adam wants to go." Mags had her sly look again.

"Keep your opinions to yourself," Ruby told her younger sister sharply while taking Delie's face in her hands and kissing her little sister's smooth forehead in farewell. Ruby's heart, touched by the shiny brown eyes and the smooth pecan-colored skin of Delie, ached in her chest. All in all, it was best to go in anticipation for the day when she would protest such a show, and the crow's nest, as an appropriate place for any of her sisters. Or for her son.

Calhoun was about an hour away on the rough Georgia roads, and Adam made sure to take plenty of time to make sure they didn't get stuck in mud. There hadn't been any recent rain in the hot month of July, but with the country road being so rough; it was hard to tell what condition the road was in. However, the ride was uneventful, the most pleasurable being his closeness to Ruby for long stretches of time.

Ruby made such sense and understood so many things with wisdom beyond her young years. She was a pleasure to talk to. It would take a while to do her nurse training, but a man could do far worse than to have such a life's companion. Still, he hoped her desire to further her education was what she really wanted, and not because he wanted her to. It wouldn't be right.

Adam paid their way into the nickelodeon, and Ruby held her breath. If they were to go to the crow's nest, they would have to go back outside and enter the balcony from the side of the building. However, the ticket taker gestured over his shoulder for them to enter the front door, behind him.

With a knowing look at one another, they entered the front door and took in the beauty of the lavish decorations, the crimson deep plush carpeting and the ornate golden trim, touches that made the lobby area thrive with luxury and splendor. Ruby was awed. Could she be a doctor's wife, used to the finer things in life?

"I want to sit in the back."

"Good idea."

He got them an area in the very last row of a sold-out Saturday afternoon show where all of the downstairs seats were nearly filled. As they sat downstairs, afraid to speak, there was silence and stillness in the crow's nest. There were Negroes attending the show, dressed up as if for Sunday church, very proud and dignified. However, as he watched the movie, he could understand why they were so quiet. He was too.

Adam had been to the nickelodeon before, and some parts were wondrous with special effects which made the movie almost fit in the realm of pure fantasy.

But it wasn't.

He squirmed at the wrong-headed portrayal of Negroes as greedy and lascivious. Being with Ruby had given him new eyes and he didn't like what he was seeing. When the film turned to a Negro trying to rape a young white girl, Ruby began to tear up. He leaned over and whispered, "We can go whenever you want."

She gathered herself. *Such a brave woman. Nothing like his mother.* She didn't answer him right away. When the lights came up at intermission, Adam repeated his statement. "No, I want to see it all. I need to know the bad parts. I'm fine. I'm sure it will be better in the second half."

The movie did not improve, but there was a resolution of the white love story. The Negroes were not as much of an issue, but the image of Negroes as lazy continued.

Had Ruby ever thought about making a change for herself? About having the vote? He had never thought much about it, but Ruby could make a strong case for women's suffrage. All of her thoughts about an NAACP chapter could turn to something positive. She could run for office and change things without fear. Maybe some day.

When the lights came up on the second half, he shepherded Ruby toward the exit before her indignation could let loose. As he touched her arm, he was taken aback by the tightness of her muscles. Before they reached the exit, David Winslow strolled by with a young woman with blonde hair. Their eyes met across the plush space of the lobby and his brother's mouth hung open at seeing them there. Normally, in this type of situation, he might have panicked at being discovered. However, something about the scenario, and David's shock at seeing Ruby—and with Adam—made him smile.

It felt too good to be able to smile and nod at David Winslow, and witness his wonder at their treatment in the theatre as if they were all equal.

And they were. The little encounter proved it.

But was Ruby okay at seeing David? The look in her brown eyes was distant. "Are you okay?"

"Oh I am fine. The movie, I just…"

He escorted her out of the door before she could explode. So it was the movie. He was inclined to agree, and maybe she wanted to talk about it. They stood next to the car. "Ice cream?"

She opened the door and stepped inside. "No, thank you. Let's go back home and eat. I don't want to press our luck, not even for an ice cream. I'll be fine."

He drove them back to the Bledsoes having a little more confidence in the road than what he had before. "This was a great idea. I like spending time with you."

Ruby seemed shy all of sudden, unsure of what to say. "It was a nice time but I've had enough."

"Why?"

"It just left a bad taste in my mouth. I just can think of better ways to spend time. The revival is coming next week, for instance. I would rather go praise God. I hope you will come."

Ruby could see the reluctance on his face. She added, "They'll need a medical man there. It's always very hot and people fall out almost every night."

"I remember hearing your mother say something about it. Brother Carver and Sister Jane?"

"They've led the revival ever since I was a little girl. The revival is always in mixed company, white and black, where we are all equal in the sight of God. It's a beautiful thing to see."

"I would think Dodge wouldn't like another Negro minister in town."

"He hasn't nothing to say about it. Everyone loves Brother Carver," Ruby insisted. "Dodge wants to get married around this time because Brother Carver could do it without asking a white man to officiate." Ruby lowered her head. "He's going to have to be disappointed."

Adam reached over and placed his hand on hers, relishing in the feel of her skin against his. It was only when he touched her that he understood. He longed for her touch. "If you want, we can tell him together."

"We'll see."

He didn't like how quiet she was, so he tried to make conversation. "Did you know that young woman?" Adam hated how he had to shout over the motor if he wanted to talk to Ruby, but she seemed truly stunned by the movie, or was it the sight of David with a statuesque blonde?

"What?"

"David's young woman?"

Ruby waved a hand absently. "That may be someone Miss Mary got him set up with. She's been trying to pair him with girls from the counties for a long time now."

"Why?"

"She was afraid that he had what Mr. Paul had, a thing for young Negro girls I guess."

Adam gripped the wheel that much harder. And how was it when men who had a thing for young girls who were powerless were the ones who always ended up okay?

Things had to be different this time for Ruby, they just had to be. God's hand had directed so much of this journey to Winslow. Now, the God that his Aunt Lizzie had referred to so reverently as he was growing up set him on a path he never expected. A path that meant his life was changing in new and unexpected ways.

"I'm sorry. I'm sorry." Ruby kept shouting over the noise of the car. "Hey." She reached over and put her warm, small hand on top of his. Joy slipped through her fingers to his and took all of the sadness away.

"It's okay, Ruby. I mean, I'm alright."

"I didn't mean to speak ill of the dead. Your mama, I mean."

"I didn't think you did. It's when Paul Winslow spoke of her when I was first here, that it was hardest."

"And now?"

Adam pulled the car over to a grassy field. They had to get home, but he wanted to try something with her first.

"What are you doing?" she asked him.

"I want you to learn how to drive. This is the perfect opportunity. Dry road, clear ahead. Come over."

He didn't move fast enough out of the way to open the car and run around to the passenger side of the car. She slid her rounded female body over and she was, for a too brief moment, pressed firmly against his side. And in that moment when the full length of her was next to him, stars exploded in his mind. Aunt Lizzie had been right. God made women to stand strongly by the side of men.

And Ruby's shape, while substantially shorter than his, seemed to fit next to him like a puzzle piece.

He leaped from the car and slid in next to her, careful not to get too close. "Here. Pull on this. Slowly now. Easy."

"Like this?" she asked.

Such a good student. She took in everything so eagerly. "Pull out onto the road."

And Ruby did, with almost expert efficiency. She was so smart, so worthy, just as Mattie Morson had been, but she had never been given a chance. He loved to hear the sound of her laughter as she drove the Model T ever so slowly down the red, dusty country road, thrilled that she was moving the vehicle for herself.

He moved a hand on the wheel to pull the car over and stopped it. "That's enough now. I wanted you to try it."

"I like it. I always thought a big man like you should drive cars, but I could do it myself."

He slid back into the car next to her. Despite the effort it would take to get it started again, he turned the engine off. He wanted to hear every precious word she was saying. "Did you like the way that felt? To do things for yourself?"

"Hey, why you turning the car off?" Ruby's neck craned in all directions. "We got to get home before dark."

"We will. I just wanted to hear you answer my question. It's an important one."

"I liked it fine."

"You're capable of making your own life beyond this town." And when he said that, silence came down like a heavy curtain, emphasizing the crickets chirping as nightfall came.

"What about my family?" Ruby's voice was small.

"What about your son? You can do more for him by getting away."

"He needs his family. This is where he was born."

"Ruby, I didn't want to alarm you, but David and I, we spoke at the holiday celebration last week."

The freckles stood out on her blanched features. "You and David talked about me?"

"He knows he did you a great wrong."

Her beautiful eyes grew shiny and bright. "He does?"

"He does. I didn't like him talking to me about it, but, Ruby," he forced himself to touch her shoulder, dared himself to stay under control from wanting to touch her any further. "He says Mary Winslow has fallen for Solomon. She had a difficult childbearing history, and they were asking me questions to see if he was okay."

"I don't believe it." To his surprise, a slight flush came back into Ruby's pretty face. "She doesn't care anything about little Negro children, but to be seen as a generous lady like in slave times."

"Maybe," Adam said. "But some women can become unbalanced if they want a baby. I've seen it before on my rotations. I thought you should know."

"He—he might be in danger now." Ruby reached over for the wheel. "Let's go."

"My point is, he *is* in danger now. And you are too." He felt more alive every time he touched her and it struck him how normal that could be. Something in his heart grew and became alive. His loneliness seemed foolish to him now.

Why had he closed himself off to feeling this way? Oh, to become a doctor. Well he was one now. And he didn't have to be closed off anymore.

"I—I don't know what to do."

"You can go to nursing school. You can learn how to be a nurse and take care of yourself. But you have to leave this place. Can't you make a difference for the race by going and getting some education to better your life? Solomon's life?"

"I don't know about all of that."

"Because it would involve me? Helping you?"

Her eyes narrowed as she looked at him and she pulled his hand away from her arm. No. Did she just attack him in a small way and he didn't even know it? "I don't know if what you're saying is true. How would it make things better here? For my sisters?"

"Sometimes, things have to be about what *you* need."

"No, Dr. Morson. Everything is connected. If I leave, I have to take my sisters with me. Somehow. Someone like you wouldn't understand that, having been by yourself all of your life. I suppose that's not your fault, but that is what it is when you are linked with someone. You just can't leave them behind. Better start the car now. I want to see if Solomon is okay."

Well, she could be very decisive. There was a finality to her words and as he started up the car, and pulled back into the road, he mused. Was it still about David? Or did she really despise him that much? Him as a deliverer? Maybe God didn't know everything after all.

On Sunday, Adam planned to let Dodge see them sitting together, and see he how he handled Solomon. Now everyone would know where Ruby stood. Dodge would not be embarrassed—he would see how things were and back off. "I'm going to tell him." Ruby opened the door herself and handed Solomon to him.

"Ruby, I don't know if that is the best thing."

"I just want to get it over with." She left him and went right up the stairs to the minister by herself, who was there greeting people on their way into the church. And in speaking to him, her voice sounded a little high up at one point, but then she marched right into the church, leaving a dazed looking Dodge in her wake. The minister's flinty, cold, hard gaze met his as he held Solomon and handed Nettie, Delie, and Em out of the car's backseat.

Adam couldn't blame him. If anyone tried to hone in on Ruby, he would have been upset about it too. He didn't know what he would do about it, but he would have been angry. Dodge bore watching. Adam just tipped his hat at the minister and made his way into the church. When it was time to greet the remaining Bledsoes, Dodge made a big show about it being late, and sweeping everyone into the church without saying anything to him on an individual basis. Very clever.

He sat down next to Ruby. "What did you say to him?"

"I just told him no thank you."

"Why did you seem angry then?"

"He said something to the effect about how I'm going to hell," Ruby said rather brazenly not minding she was in God's house. His Aunt Lizzie would have dragged him out by the ear for such an offense.

"What did you say?" Adam said, speaking above the threadbare little choir beginning a hymn.

"I said he couldn't tell me about where I would go when I died. It's a matter for God and God alone." Ruby fixed him a look. "I didn't make it about us, if you were wondering."

Adam had wondered about it. "I'm glad you didn't. He might have gotten even angrier."

Ruby patted his knee, which was just under Solomon's little leg. She did it so artfully, anyone in the adjoining pew, like her father, might have thought she was patting Solomon. But she wasn't. She patted him. "I didn't want to presume too much."

Her wide brown eyes were so soulful, he couldn't question what she was doing. So, despite this depth of feeling, and Ruby's risqué behavior and willingness to cross a line of propriety, he adjusted the baby, just a little bit, to stop her from what she was doing. "You aren't." He cleared his throat.

But in the minx-like way she was staring at him, she had won the moment.

"I want to take my text this morning," Dodge boomed out in a loud voice making everyone jump, "from a different place. We been following along with the commandments, but I think I want to shake things up some, amen."

"Amen," the congregation agreed.

"I'm going on ahead to Proverbs, 31. When old King Lemuel learns from his mama. It's important to learn from your mama. I hope you got a mama who teaches you right from wrong. If you do, praise the Lord."

There were various people who agreed and opened their bibles. Adam glanced over at Ruby and her skin had gone a little paler, making her brown freckles stand out more than usual. "What's wrong?"

"It's my passage."

They should have expected such a reaction from Dodge, since he was so touchy and now, Adam could see, he was vindictive as well. She would have to sit there and take the humiliation Dodge doled out, claiming his right as a minister. Adam tightened his jaw and shifted his arms a little bit to comfort a sleepy-headed Solomon.

Dodge was going to use this opportunity to expound about why he couldn't find a virtuous woman. Like Ruby. Adam tried to tune him out, but the beauty of the passage beckoned to him and it made him think of Ruby even more. He wanted to feel sorry for Dodge, but this kind of confrontation in a place meant for comfort and solace was too much.

"Who can find a virtuous woman? For her price is far above rubies. The heart of her husband doth safely trust in her, so that he will have no need of spoil. She will do him good and not evil all the days of her life."

The description suited Ruby perfectly. Adam stared at the beautiful little freckles standing out on her face. "Favor is deceitful and beauty is vain," Dodge said with unnecessary force. "But a woman that feareth the Lord, she shall be praised." He shut his bible and started on his harangue. "Let us hear the word of God and know it's good and true. Let us hear and know to follow God is to obey. And for a woman to disobey God, to show she does not fear God by her bearing, and her attitude and ways is an abomination."

The congregation quieted. Strange. Usually, there would have been a great show of shouts praising God, but Adam could sense the tension in the people. Dodge went on, "A virtuous woman obeys the law. She does not get herself into trouble. She follows a righteous path. A woman who determines her own path, is not walking in the Lord's light, amen." He took out a handkerchief and wiped his face.

"A woman like this, who flies in the face of God's plan, and of God's desires is headed for sure and certain trouble, pain and heartache. A woman like this needs the hand God provides, of a 'husband who is known in the gates, when he sitteth among the elders of the land.' That's the kind of husband she needs. Anything else, anybody else, is asking for trouble, amen."

A rustling next to him.

Ruby. She was standing.

Parched, Adam tried to swallow for a second. Ruby was standing in the church, when everyone else was sitting and she stared at the Reverend, eye to eye. She then edged herself out of the row into the middle aisle. The murmurs in the congregation grew louder.

The only time anyone should be in the center aisle during the service would be if the person gave his or her life to God. No. Ruby dared to stand in the aisle and look at Dodge, eye to eye. She then, turned on her heel and walked out of the front doors of the little country church, in the most direct way. The sound of the doors shutting behind her sounded like a slap or a rebuke. The church congregation murmured then was quiet.

"There may be some who don't like what I say. But it's God's word, and cannot be denied. It's in the Bible. That's what it say." Dodge made a show of gesturing to the book. Adam took the sleeping Solomon and draped him over his shoulder. He edged his way out of the pew, down the side aisle and carried the baby out through the front doors and went outside. Ruby sat in his car, with her arms folded.

"I've had enough. I'm never stepping foot in First Water again."

Adam handed her the baby and began to start up the car. He would rather have walked through fire than to see Ruby disgraced again. Would people reject his treatment if she accompanied him? It didn't matter. Ruby did not resemble the elegant doctor's wife he imagined, but he did not care. She deserved to be happy. He slid in the car next to her. "I couldn't agree with you more. Let's go."

The reverberation of the engine of the car as it retreated from the little country church sounded like a parting shot in the still summer Sunday morning.

Chapter Sixteen

The family didn't talk or laugh at dinner after church, but she was determined to be joyful. "I don't know what is wrong with you all. The Carvers are coming. It's like Christmas time when they come." She had the baby on her knee, giving him a little ham in his mouth and a squeeze.

Her mother's face was morose at her disgraceful behavior, but Ruby did not care. She had never felt so free.

"Ruby's right." Mags took up some support for her sister and Ruby threw her a look of gratitude with pitched eyebrows. "We get off two hours early from the mill all week for the revivals. Mr. Winslow gets all generous because of it."

Ruby's heart sank a bit at having to hear Mags talk about being glad to be off for two hours. She insisted her work in the mill was going just fine, but it still bothered Ruby.

She folded up a corner of the tablecloth and said, "The tent goes up, and all the people go in, ready to praise God. When the sun goes down, people can go to the tent for five nights and worship God. As far as I'm concerned, this is our real church. I hope you will come, Dr. Morson."

"Sounds like something to see."

"Oh it is. We love the Carvers." Ruby shouted as she reminded her mother and father about what really mattered. Not being turned out of First Water.

Delie wriggled. "Brother Carver preaches and Sister Jane plays the music." She jumped on the bench and boomed. "We going to get right with God today, people!"

The family started giggling. Delie could do a fine impression of Brother

Carver. Lona was the only one not amused. "Sit down, Cordelia May." Delie obeyed immediately. Lona was not happy, Ruby knew, because she called out her younger sister by her full name.

"Should have waited for them to bless Solomon. That's the real blessing." Ruby looked up at Adam. "Each one of us. We was blessed at First Water, but every time they come, the Carvers bless us too."

"Solomon had to be blessed somewhere. Besides, they should be here by now. Revival starts tomorrow."

"Must be running late, Lona. Nothing to get worried about." Her father sipped at his coffee.

"Last year, when Brother was here, he wasn't looking so spry."

Her remark gained Adam's attention. "Do you think they would have gotten in touch with you if something were wrong?"

John shrugged his shoulders. "Might have sent a letter. Hard to say. I just know Paul Winslow wouldn't pay for no mill closings unless they coming. Did he say any different, Mags?"

Mags came back in from the kitchen wiping her hands on a towel. "No, we thought we were getting out for the revival like always. I hope we are." Her brown finely-etched features wrinkled with worry.

A few weeks ago, Ruby would not have dared to speak, but things had changed. "We aren't finding out anything by sitting here. I'm going to change and go into town."

Adam stood. "I'll take you."

"Thank you, Dr. Morson. She done caused enough trouble today." Lona echoed giving Ruby a fierce look.

Ruby handed Solomon off to John, and he took his grandson, willingly. "Let's have some Bible stories for this young man from his aunties. Em, you need to read. Come on now."

Adam wanted to laugh at Em's reluctant-looking face, but she complied immediately. "We'll be back soon." Delie looked after him longingly but he made her grin when he waved just at her.

After Ruby changed into her overalls, Adam and Ruby went down the steps to the car and Ruby brushed the red dirt from her feet, but she did not put on shoes. She probably should have. "I'll stay in the car," she promised. "Although poor Delie would not have minded if she'd been allowed to come."

"She had already been solicited by your father to help with Solomon." Adam slid in the driver's seat after he cranked the gear shaft to start the car.

"Poor Delie," Ruby chuckled. "I think she want to fight me sometimes, she loves you so."

Now Adam was embarrassed. "There's no need for resentments. I wouldn't want to cause any trouble between you."

Ruby waved him off as he turned the car down the street. "She knows she's too young for stuff." Her countenance turned serious. "I worry about her, though and Em too. Em'll be thirteen in three years and then they'll want her for the mill. They already trying to get Nettie in there with Mags. I don't want Em in the mill—her lungs have always been kind of weak."

"What do you think should happen for her?"

"She got to get into a high school somewhere. I got to work on my getting a nursing job. I can help out the younger ones. It's probably too late for Mags and Nettie." She stared out of the side of the car, lost in thought.

The thought of sweet Delie working in the mill turned his stomach and Adam thought again of proposing to Ruby, thought she might turn him down again. He still wasn't worthy of her. He couldn't face anymore rejection. They were quiet until they arrived into town and Ruby hopped out of the car and went into the store. "I'm sorry, Adam, I did forget. I got to go into the store to see what the word is."

Her pretty feet and trim ankles retreated into the store. If he bought her high topped boots with buttons on them, would she wear them? He had thoughts, rather impure ones of helping them onto her pretty feet, one little hook at a time and of Ruby's laughing brown eyes looking at him seriously as he had the pleasure of unhooking them and touching the rounded bump of her little ankle. Before he knew it, Ruby had come in the car and pointed northward. "They're coming in on the train this time. In about thirty minutes."

"Let's go. Hopefully, we will be able to see them there."

They drove to the depot and clearly, the word had gotten around because there was a good portion of the Negro population, about twenty people, at the depot as well. "Unless there is a convention, or Mrs. Ida Wells-Barnett coming in, they must be for Brother Carver and Sister Jane."

"You're the one who would get excited about Mrs. Wells-Barnett coming in."

"Did you just make a joke?" Ruby amazed, continued, "There is hope for you yet." Once he drove the short distance to the train station, she hopped out of the car to exchange conversation with those who waited on the platform, leaving him to contemplate her pretty feet, out in public, once again.

What could he do to help her, to keep her son and her sisters away from Winslow? If he only had the courage to do so. He gripped the wheel. What would give him the purpose? Could it be the God Ruby relied on so much? He didn't know, and as a doctor and a scientist, the space of the unknown made him feel very, very uncomfortable.

When Ruby climbed the steps to the platform, everyone who was standing there got very quiet. She was used to that kind of response from people when she approached them, but going back to the way things were last year was a bit of a shock. She cleared her throat. "Hey, good to see you up and about, Agnes. This where Brother Carver and Sister Jane coming in?"

"They is." Bob's Agnes spoke to Ruby, guarded and distant. What was wrong with her?

"I'm looking forward to seeing them. Hope they come and stay with us."

"I would say you all have enough company right through here," Bob moved Agnes over a bit, away from Ruby. "They probably need to find someplace else to stay."

Ruby started down at her bare toes. "We don't mind. Although we don't want to hog up any attention from anyone else. If you all can accommodate."

"If we can what?" Agnes asked her, looking as if she had two heads.

"You know, if you all got the space for them. Don't want you to be crowded."

"We do fine and plenty right by Brother and Sister, Ruby," Bob said.

"Fine then. I'll just wait down here until they get in." Ruby walked away from the small crowd quickly. Agnes had stuck up for her before. Now she was so cold and Bob was acting strange. What was going on? Who knew what Dodge was saying about her. Or maybe it was about her abrupt exit. She just wasn't going to pay any attention to it all. Adam came behind her as she walked to the other side of the platform.

"What's the matter?"

Ruby tucked her hands into her overalls and tried not to feel the sting of tears behind her eyes. She had been treated this way many, many times before. That was why she stayed in the house, to avoid the hurt. Now, after she had been treated so nicely by so many, it was startling to go back to the old way. But she didn't want to stay in the house, not anymore. "I'm just down here waiting for Brother and Sister."

"Did they say something to you?"

"They let me know they were not going to allow some soiled dove to tell them about where Brother and Sister were going to stay." Despite herself, the tears began to fall. "They have always stayed with us, and they said we already had company."

"Well, you do, after a fashion. Me."

Ruby wiped at her eyes. "I don't think of you as company."

"Well, that's how I'm seen in the community."

"No one else has a house bigger than ours. I don't know what can be done. Brother and Sister can't stay in the hotel."

"No. I guess not."

"It'll all work out, Ruby. I can go back to the Winslows, or the hotel." Adam informed her.

Ruby's eyes got big as saucers looking at him. "Oh, no. It'll all be okay. I'm sure of it. It's summer now, and not cold at all. I would sleep outside before you had to go back to the Winslows."

Adam put a warm and comforting hand on her shoulder. "Thank you, your hospitality means a lot, but I've slept in a barn or two in my time. We'll work it out. It's only over a week."

What did Adam mean? But then, the train whistle sounded in the distance and everyone turned toward it. The sound of the engine increased and grew bigger and more ominous until the train was upon them. It took some time to unload the train of its mail, luggage and passengers, but finally, a small couple got off, nearly at the end of the train on the Jim Crow car. Ruby was closer to them, so she was able to get to them first.

The Jim Crow car didn't have regular seats and would have been a hard trip. They usually came by use of their mule, Old Casey, because they didn't have to deal with the rules on the train. However, as she came closer to them, Brother Carver walked with a bit of a stoop and Sister Jane had new wrinkles at her neck. They were getting old, and as hard as the train trip was, it was an easier choice than having to travel with bumpy Old Casey all the time. Ruby spread out her arms and embraced the couple. "I'm so glad to see you both," she exclaimed.

"Lookee here, Sister," Brother Carver held Ruby out from him and marveled. "See how pretty Ruby is now."

"I see," Sister Jane smiled at her. "I always knew she would be, God bless her. She a woman now."

"Who this?" Brother Carver peered behind Ruby at Adam. "You courtin' Ruby Jean?"

"This is Dr. Morson, who has come to Winslow to doctor on us."

"Lord, don't You provide," Sister Jane shook Adam's hand. "What a blessing."

"Thank you, ma'am."

Sister Jane kept an arm around Ruby and pulled her to her side so she could see the rest of the people who were approaching them. "Are you sure you ain't courting him? He's pretty too."

"Here come everybody," Ruby waved at the other folks to come down. She wouldn't be as small to them as they had been to her. "People sure missed you all."

"We love coming to Winslow, for sure." Brother Carver kept up a steady inspection of Adam. "We never know what we going to find, but we always know there's a warm welcome and plenty of God's people, right here who crave the word."

"We made the trip special." Sister Jane hugged Agnes and Bob. Ruby was still at her side, despite Agnes fixing her with a cross look.

"Special?" Ruby said.

"Can't get so many places by train. Some folks don't want revivals no more, God bless them. So we just coming to places where we know we will be welcome."

"I see," Ruby said, as Sister Jane walked down the platform with her. Adam and Bob followed with the luggage. "You'll staying with us, ain't you? Like always?"

Bob overheard and stood before them, stopping their path. "Them Bledsoes got a whole lot of sinning going on there. You don't want to stay in a house of sin."

Ruby took in a sharp breath. What in the world had gotten into Bob? "What you talking about?" Sister Jane's tone and disposition showed she could match Bob for meanness if she had to.

Bob was ashamed for a minute, then stood tall. "Ruby got a baby. Everyone knows."

Ruby felt as if the blood had drained from her, but instead of Sister Jane dropping her hold on her, she pulled her closer, "Yes? What of it? I knew. Remember what the dear Lord say 'Judge not, that ye be not judged. For with what judgment you judge, ye shall be judged.'"

Ruby's head throbbed, nearly seeing stars at her astonishment. "You knew?"

"'Course I knew. I been knowing you since you was little. I saw last year, something in your eyes. Something wasn't right, but you look like you was full to bursting. I knew—didn't I, Brother?"

Brother nodded his head, "I recollect Sister saying to me, something was not right with Ruby. It was a reason we come special this year. Cut out a lot of other stops, but we had to see about this dear child. You all right?"

Ruby nodded, too much in shock to say anything.

"And the baby?" Sister Jane demanded of her.

"Fine, ma'am."

Sister Jane drew herself up. "Well, then, what's the problem? If we all stood up to the measure, most of us would fall way short, and why the dear Lord said what he say. We could do much counting on our fingers when some of these babies come, but they is all blessings from the Lord, no matter how they come." She squeezed Ruby once more. "And I wants to see this dear little blessing of Ruby's. Come on."

Ruby could see that Bob was cowed, but looked like he had a whole lot more to say. She ignored him and helped Sister Jane down the steps to the car and the men followed with the luggage. "Oh my, Carver, we riding high style today," Sister Jane said in delight.

"This is Dr. Morson's car." Ruby helped her inside in the front seat.

"He the baby's father?" Brother Carver said from the backseat where he sat next to Ruby.

"No, sir."

"Is he married?" Sister Jane fixed her a look over her spectacles.

"No, ma'am."

"It's done. He's all the daddy your little one need. I don't know how or where you got him, and why the real one don't want the baby, but this is why he's here. I done prayed it to God already and he done answered. Claim on it, Ruby Jean."

Ruby laid a finger to her lips as Adam came back around to get in the car next to Brother Carver in the front and Ruby sat in the back with Sister Jane. "You all had better behave," Ruby admonished her.

Sister Jane gave a high-pitched squeal. "We is about the Lord's work, child. There ain't no better work than seeing a family being made, Amen."

"Amen." Brother folded his hands together. "It all going to be all right."

The rumblings of the car shook underneath her body, warm and reassuring, and she believed what Brother and Sister had said for the first time in a year, could be true. "Mama got dinner hot for you all, she was mighty worried about you."

"And we was mighty worried we wouldn't get here in time for some of Lona's cooking." Brother patted her hand, and Ruby was comforted in the love of these two older people.

"She got fresh pork, mashed potatoes, green beans and peach pie."

"I'm sure glad we is traveling by car, so we get there faster," Brother said, and Ruby smiled.

"Don't get too excited, Carver. Remember what the doctor man said about your pressure and things."

"A man got to eat to live, Jane."

"I knows. But I'm saying, you better watch, now."

"I am, honey lamb. I wants to be around to bug you up some for a good long while."

A small smile tugged at Adam's lips, and Ruby could tell he liked the older couple too. "Is the baby at home?"

"Yes, ma'am," Ruby answered Sister Jane.

"What is the child?" Brother said to her.

"A boy, sir. Solomon David."

He slapped her hand some more. "A boy. Oh my. I can't wait to see this little one and bless him in the name of the Lord."

Ruby smiled. "Thank you, sir. I was so hoping you would do it. We had him christened a few weeks ago, but Dodge did it."

"Who we? Who stood up at the holy fount with you?" Sister Jane said.

"Dr. Morson did."

Sister Jane touched Adam on the arm. "You his God papa?"

"Yes, ma'am," Adam said.

Sister Jane clasped her hands together and her eyes heavenward. "It done already happened, praise him."

Sister Jane leaned forward, but the sharp old lady turned to face Ruby again, "I know Solomon is after the wise king, but David, the wicked one?"

"Ma'am." Ruby's response was more of a confirmation. Sister Jane covered her mouth.

"Is the daddy the Winslow boy?" Sister Jane spoke through her fingers.

Ruby could only nod. "Yes, ma'am. But not how you think."

Sister Jane fixed her with wise eyes. "I see, child. My word. It's more than a notion being a colored woman, isn't it?"

In the past, Ruby might have had tears prick the corners of her eyes at Sister's words. Now, Ruby nodded again, and a warm blanket of protection surrounded her. "In any case, I am glad, so glad you all are here."

Sister patted her other hand. "Me too, child. Me too. God never fails to put us where we are needed. You must have faith."

Ruby could believe her, even as Bob's strange reactions pierced her heart, washing away any hope that the town would feel better to her one day. It would never go away. Solomon would have to grow up in it and the feeling hurt even more. Could Adam be an answer to all of that?

Something began to sprout in her heart that had not been there for a long time. Hope.

Chapter Seventeen

Adam recoiled.

He couldn't help himself.

Paul Winslow seemed to appear to his mill workers as the great benefactor. Mags couldn't stop talking about how he allowed them time off to come to the revival tent, which was, handily enough, pitched high up on Winslow land and could be seen from the Bledsoe's front porch.

Mags's young brown face was full of excitement as she cleared away the dinner dishes from Brother Carver and Sister Jane after they ate. "We get to leave at five for the revivals all week long. So when Mama said she was worried about where you all were, I started to get worried too."

Sister Jane pulled her piece of pie closer to her. "We's here now, honey, and are doing real fine, looking at this piece of pie here."

Solomon gurgled and she squeezed his bony knee. "It's mighty good to see this young one here," Sister Jane continued. "Knowing the spirit of our dear Ruby will go on."

Lona snorted. "Please, God, I hope he isn't the kind of trouble maker his mama is. Do you know this girl was in the jailhouse just last week?"

Sister fixed Ruby with keen eyes. "I'm sure she had a good reason."

Lona waved a hand. "Sister Jane, you always had a soft place for Ruby. We all know you got to keep quiet as a Negro woman. You can't start no whole lot of trouble. If she hadn't started trouble—"

"Solomon would not be here." Sister Jane raised a hand. "And out of terrible trouble, came a blessing."

As if on cue, Solomon smiled, revealing a small white tooth in the front of his mouth. With his mouth open, he produced a long trail of drool, which ended up on his grandfather's pants leg. They all laughed.

All but Ruby.

Her light was dimmed, just a bit and Adam smiled at her, to give her heart. Her half-hearted smile in return showed the goodness radiating inside of her. He had not known it, but he had traveled in a long, broad, endless desert and he finally happened on a refreshing pool of water.

Ruby.

He could feel the blessing Ruby, and her son had brought into his life—and he had genuine sorrow in his heart for Lona who didn't agree with this view. "Amen," Adam's face warmed a bit as he adjusted his gold-rimmed spectacles.

Brother dug into his pie and gave Adam an amiable glance. "You never said how you was brought up in the Lord, Dr. Adam."

"I went to revivals with my aunt in the summertime starting when I was nine. I was first brought up by my cousin, Lucas, and he wasn't a church goer. But when he died and I went to my Aunt Lizzie I would go with her every night, faithfully." A flash of memory of the revivals came to his mind. They were an outlet for people who were looking for excitement in their lives. They came to see the spectacle.

"I'm sorry for your losses, son, but thank God Aunt Lizzie came on the scene," Brother Carver intoned.

"Yes, well, she was much better for me in a lot of ways. Lucas wasn't the kindest person, but I think people in the family thought it would be better if I was brought up with a male influence. Sometimes that can help an orphan, but Lucas had no business raising children. He had a fondness for the drink."

Ruby's spark came back a little bit and she regarded him with something resembling pity. "You never said. I'm sorry."

Adam was touched that she cared. "It made me who I am today. Seeing so much, at such a young age, kind of steeled me for life. I've been glad to be here at the Bledsoes. It has been the first time in a long time to see what a real family looks like."

Sister smacked her lips over the peach pie. "Amen. It's a blessing a lot don't have." She reached over and patted Ruby's knee. "And it's clear, at least to me, Lona, you has done a wonderful job bringing up these girls in God's light. They will make wonderful wives and mothers for some lucky men."

Lona lowered her head over some quilting piecework she worked on. "I appreciates you, Sister, but some of them still have a ways to go."

"And the Lord will bless them with every single step."

"Amen." Ruby's brown eyes had the light back in them again. Clearly, the words uplifted her. "We look forward to when you come, it helps us get through the trouble times."

Ruby brightened quite a bit, but he still longed to take her worry from her. She deserved better. Better than a vagabond existence going from place to place.

She deserved a home, stability and care. Things he didn't know he could provide to anyone, and he didn't want to promise them to Ruby, and by extension, Solomon and have everything end up in sadness. No, he could better prepare her to be able to stand on her own two feet as her own woman. He could do that much for her before he moved out of her life.

Adam agreed to vacate the little room in the back for a cot in the barn while the Carvers were in town. The Carvers insisted they take the barn, but he was used to sleeping outside. For he had slept in the barn with the animals before. Lucas kept him out in the barn while he drank away the generous money Paul Winslow sent for Adam's support. And he had to, somehow, find food to feed both of them. It was all a difficult proposition for a young boy.. Now, with his scientist's sensibility, he could see he had been malnourished. Fortunately, within a short space of time of drink and women, Lucas drank himself to death and he was handed off to Aunt Lizzie who provided him with a home. The memories still lingered, though.

After he had set up the cot in the corner of the barn, he sat down on it. As he did, a figure hovered in the door. Brother Carver approached him. "I just want to thank you, Dr. Adam, for giving up the bed. Sister Jane is getting kind of old, and she need a bed to sleep in at night."

Adam rose from the cot to talk to him. "I think, if she were to come out here, she would say something similar."

Brother chewed on the stem of a pipe. "We got to look out for one another. I come out here to you to ask you about it. I think, with my sugar sometimes, my fingers and feet feel kind of numb sometimes."

Adam nodded. "Sugar can cause a dead kind of feeling of necrosis in the limbs."

Brother Carver's eyebrows met together in the middle of his face. "Yeah, you got it. What's to be done?"

"I think what Sister is saying is right. You got to limit the sweets. Get more exercise. Maybe walk back and forth to the tents this week. It isn't far."

"Dr. Adam, what is wrong with you? You can't never tell no woman she right, even if she's as special as Sister Jane. She'll never let me live it down."

Adam couldn't help a chuckle. "She's looking out for you. One piece of peach pie—that's it. When it is time to leave, maybe you can have another piece."

Brother Carver groaned and rubbed his belly. "Whenever you come to a place like Winslow for the revival, the ladies make all kinds of special things for us."

Adam made his voice firm so Brother could understand the gravity of his situation. "You have to tell them about your sugar. They'll understand."

"You're sure making it hard for a man, Doctor. I'ma say goodnight." Brother Carver pocketed the cooled pipe. "Unless you got something to say to me. I see something good in you. I know that's why you are a doctor. But there's a pain there too, some hurt inside what don't have anything to do with the body. It's about the spirit. I just want to tell you, God sees. He's ready to heal you."

Adam nodded, not sure what to say to this quiet man who radiated contentment with his life, even though his life as a Negro could not have been easy.

Brother continued, "God gives us marriage to love one another. It's how Jesus was joined to the church. It's the center of our life, and it's the safe place for children to come. Ruby has suffered a great deal. I see you and your pain. Maybe when you comes together, you can heal one another. Think on it. Good night."

Adam secured the barn door as Brother Carver left. What if the pain was too big for one person to heal? He could never put all of his pain on Ruby, not after all she had been through. It wouldn't be fair to her. Not at all.

Ruby had to shade her eyes to see, because the glare of the white revival tent could blind her. So many happy memories had taken place in the white tent. She nearly danced with excitement because it had been almost two whole years since she had been last time. She didn't go last year everyone was just learning about her shame. *God, give me strength to go there and see for myself, I'm whole in myself. I have to do this. I have to do it for Solomon.*

She smoothed down her dark skirt and donned her high top shoes. "Every time I feel the spirit, moving in my heart, I will pray," she sang. Her father's deep bass voice joined hers and she smiled as he boomed out the words of the old spiritual over and over. She picked up Solomon and straightened out his little dress.

She would survive. John and Lona's people weren't from here, but the old slaves who worked this land, who had cleared Winslow out of the heavy pine forest had survived. With God's help, she would survive too.

The Bledsoes all gathered on the front porch, wearing their second best to attend the revival. Adam pulled the car forward, but John waved him off. "We walk to the revival. We be okay."

"I can park the car if you think it is a good idea,"

Ruby leaned in carrying Solomon, who was getting heavier and heavier by the day now that he was eating solid food. "No, I think maybe Sister Jane and Mama should ride with you. Take them on ahead and they can get some things straightened out."

"I'ma get in my exercise going up, praise God," Brother Carver proclaimed out loud. "I probably ride back later on."

"Give me Solomon," Lona directed Ruby reaching for the baby.

"I don't want him to be a trouble to you, Mama."

"He ain't no trouble child, he can be our escort." Sister helped to hand the baby to Lona and started to play with his toes. She loved little Solomon and Ruby was glad. She wanted the Carvers to bless her child so he would not have to carry the sin of his creation with him.

Adam's car pulled off with the women and Solomon inside and something did lighten in her heart. She could have felt terribly about going to the revival, especially where it was located, the scene of the attack, but it was revival time. Her heart was light and free and as the family walked up the red dust road, they sang and laughed all along the way. She wished her mother could have taken part in the good times, but even more, she hoped her mother could receive some peace from the revival tonight. They both deserved it.

As they arrived, several families sat in chairs and on blankets already under the airy tent, setting up chairs. Lona sat in one of the chairs with Solomon on her lap. Sister Jane played a tune on a mouth organ, and people began to sing. The start of the revival was always very informal, and as they entered the tent, Brother Carver moved into place, taking up Jane's song, "What a Friend we have in Jesus."

Ruby went into the aisle and slid next to Adam, enjoying the spectacle of Sister Jane playing on her mouth organ. Sister Jane, a very talented musician, could take up anything and play and sing. She was very enthusiastic in her playing and moved her elbows up and down as she blew into the holes, producing the melodious sound. Solomon, sitting placidly on her mother's lap, was also fascinated by the way Sister was playing the music. Music, at the start of the revival, drew the folks in, and Ruby could see there were about fifty people, mostly Negro, but some other white families who worked in the mill, came to sing, clap and to enjoy the music.

After five songs or so, Brother began his appeals. Ruby went to her mother and took Solomon in her arms. She stepped forward to Brother Carver and he laid his hand on the baby. "Where is the child's godfather?" Ruby gestured to Adam, who seemed a little shy, but came forward. They began to say a prayer over the child.

"I done already blessed this boy." Dodge. He stood at the edge of the tent leaning sideways. Would this never end? Why did he have to come and ruin things?

Suddenly, the revival got quiet. How strange, because the revival was never quiet. There was always clapping, shouting or singing. The noise was the point of revival time, a special time of release. "Well, now, Charlie. It is okay to bless him another time," Brother Carver reassured him.

Dodge nodded his head and Ruby was shocked. From the wobbling way he had come into the revival, he had been drinking. A minister who wasn't temperance? Who dared to drink?

If she had agreed to be his wife, he would have shown her his power over her all of the time. Maybe he would have beat on her. With a chill, she realized that was the point of why Paul Winslow wanted her to marry Dodge.

"Yeah, but she," Dodge pointed to her, "she thought it wasn't good enough. My blessing wouldn't take on her precious little white child. So she come to you to do it again, since it wasn't good enough."

Ruby's feet filled with heat and she sprang up to speak, even though Dodge believed women should be silent. "When you bless him, you say he was born of sin. So I bring him to Brother. Brother don't put no sin on Solomon. He's an innocent baby and how he got here ain't his fault. I want God and everyone to know it."

"Listen to her," his voice raged and his eyes were red. More church wasn't meant to make folk angry, but to compliment. God couldn't be praised enough, truly, but Dodge did not agree. "She thinks she can tell me, a man of God, about scripture. How to run my church. How to be. She thinks she got it all in control, even me."

He pointed at Ruby and Adam. "She ain't nothing but a whore. She was a whore for David Winslow, and now she whoring for this one. She only want to whore for white men. I be just a little too dark for her."

Adam stepped forward, and grasped Dodge by the arm. "*Enough.* This way."

Dodge shook free of Adam's hold, but Adam put his body firmly before Ruby to protect her. "Reverend. Just like you a fine, upstanding Doctor. Do not forget it."

"Just come this way," Adam escorted Dodge out the side of the tent, and the revival went stone silent. Sister Jane took up a tune on her mouth organ and played it low and sweet, "Amazing Grace." Everyone joined the singing in halting voices, but there was a lot of tension in the room.

Brother started speaking in low tones to relieve the tension. "Lord, we is all here with heavy hearts. Help us to relieve the troubles in all of our hearts. Brother, please be there for Reverend Dodge, especially. He has a terrible sadness in his soul, Lord, and he needs you to heal it. Please touch him tonight with your healing power."

"Amen," Sister Jane took her mouth off of the mouth organ and emphatically agreed with her husband.

"Amen," Lona Bledsoe said.

Ruby's sisters said it too, but Ruby could not bring herself to say it for Dodge. He wanted to make her pay for rejecting him. His daring to come to the revival, drunk, and confront her, only proved the point. How terrible would her life have been if she married him?

In her work for the men in the mills and as a midwife, she witnessed what alcohol did to men with families who had spent all of their pay on spirits and the woman and children were left to fend for themselves. She had to be temperance. She never wanted to be part of that kind of existence. Children went cold, hungry and miserable and the women became shrunken shells of themselves. A terrible way to live.

She peered at Lona to see what her reaction was to Dodge's drunken appearance, but she couldn't tell what her mother was thinking. She never could. Lona almost never betrayed any emotion—but at least now Ruby understood what made her so dead inside. She just didn't want the same life. She pulled Solomon's little body closer to her and was about to give him some comfort in the music time, when they heard loud shouting outside. The noise came in the same direction where Adam had taken Dodge.

She handed Solomon off to one of her sisters and, on bare feet, ran up the aisle to see what was going on. Several of the men followed her as well, and she covered her mouth at the sight in the diminishing twilight of the summer evening. Dodge, spread out on the hood of Adam's car, did not move. The doctor, the peaceful doctor stood over him, looking angry and ready to beat him down if he rose up again. "Adam!" Ruby screamed out to him, "Stop!"

Chapter Eighteen

Adam stopped where he was. Hearing Ruby's sharp cries snapped him out of his rage. She couldn't be in danger, it registered in his thoughts, since he was taking care of Dodge. He looked down at his hands, the hands he always thought of as healing hands. They were split and bleeding. His knuckles were beginning to sting from the feeling of bone and flesh interacting as he held down Dodge with one hand and connected with the minister's chin and soft body parts with another.

"Are you okay?" Adam lifted his hands from Dodge's portly body and began to examine him.

"Get your hands off of me," Dodge coughed. "You a doctor and all and you trying to kill me."

"I wasn't trying to kill you. I was stopping you from hurting Ruby."

Dodge wiped blood from the corner of his mouth. "And what right do you have to her, coming in here and trying to claim her? If you going to claim her, be man enough and do it."

At Dodge's words, Ruby raced to the car and grabbed Adam's hands, examining his knuckles. He couldn't help it, he warmed to her touch and the pain lessened. He started healing in spite of himself. Brother was right.

She began to rub his damaged hands, "Adam, what're you doing? You can't hurt your hands. Why did you do this?"

Her plaintive tone touched him and he had to respond to her truth with truth. "I didn't want him to hurt you anymore. I had to stop him."

Ruby's warm agate brown eyes stared into his. "They are just words. I have stood up to words before."

"That doesn't make it acceptable. You don't have to keep being a martyr."

"Oh, Adam. I'm so sorry."

Dodge gave a snort and began to act more hurt than he really was, Adam could tell. Other people from the revival approached Dodge and started trying to treat him.

Fine. Dodge shifted away from him, sitting on the ground. *See how he does without expert care.*

Adam let go of the worry since he knew Dodge's wounds would eventually heal. Since the pain in his hands hurt him, he might have felt warm again in embarrassment, but Ruby's attentions to him soothed the pain.

The air crackled with the sound of loud honking horn down the long red road from town to the tent. The sheriff? How had the sheriff known what was going on?

Adam groaned. He and the sheriff had not parted on the best terms, when Ruby had been taken away at the picnic.

The car pulled up and the sheriff stepped out. Adam stood, ready to greet him and trying to look as if nothing had happened.

Since nothing had.

Dodge writhed on the ground, making it look as if he were seriously harmed.

When Baines saw Adam standing up over Dodge, he smiled. Baines had made it crystal clear earlier how much he despised Adam coming into town and using his familial relations as power over someone like him. Pure rage radiated from Jim Baines's beefy countenance. How could someone who was a small-town sheriff afford enough food to get to such a size? "What do we have here, Doctor?"

"A tiny scuffle."

"It don't look so tiny to me. I see the good Reverend is here on the ground. You okay, Dodge?"

In answer, Dodge groaned. Something about the whole situation seemed fake, but Adam understood how this all must look, so he focused his efforts on getting this sheriff, who was not so bright, to see reason, if possible. Baines said, "This situation is quite serious. You cause harm to the Reverend here?"

"We had some words."

"Look like more than words," Sheriff Baines looked at Ruby standing next to him. "You set out to hurt this man, a man making an honorable proposal of marriage to a woman of questionable honor."

His words, spoken so casually, made Adam angry. He glared at Baines who only smiled at him. Ruby's gentle touch on his arm stopped him from advancing further. "What? Did I say something wrong?" Baines asked.

"You know who I am, Sheriff," Adam said in measured tones. He hated having to trade on his familial relations, especially given how he felt about Paul Winslow, but he had no other choice.

Baines's eyes grew small and beady. "I see an uppity colored doctor who just came to my town and causes trouble at a religious service. Pretty clear cut to me."

"Leave us alone, Sheriff Baines," Ruby spoke in measured tones. "We're just here to praise God. Let us be."

"Wonderful. And I would be willing to leave, except the good Reverend is lying on the ground and bleeding. I would be abandoning my duties to leave just now."

Someone in the gathered crowd shouted out, "You ain't never cared about arresting no Negro man for beating up on another one."

"Maybe I'm getting to see you alls side of things. Maybe I have been abandoning my duty before this. I intend to do it now. Get in the car," Baines snarled at Adam.

"No!" Ruby held Adam's arm with a more firm grip. "Don't get in the car with him."

"Ruby," Adam disengaged her arm from his. "I have to go and get this all straightened out."

Ruby's eyebrows heightened with alarm and she began to cry. "You don't understand. Please, don't get in the car with him. We might not ever see you no more if you do. Please."

He did not understand her worry. Adam patted her hand and squeezed it. "I'll be all right, Ruby."

Her strong fingers dug into his flesh. "Please, Adam." The service had come to a complete stop. Now everyone surrounded them with worried looks on their faces. Only Dodge was apart and sat up against the wheel of Adam's car.

"Remember as I showed you, Ruby. Drive the family back home in my car. Take care of Solomon. I'll be back very soon."

Ruby sobbed harder and more insistently than ever. "If you get in his car, he'll lynch you on the way to the jailhouse. Just like Uncle Arlo. Oh God."

The delighted look on the sheriff's face matched Ruby's words. This man was willing to hurt him now and risk Paul Winslow's potential displeasure later. Adam's mouth grew dry. Could his life be over? And for what? He hadn't really done anything.

All around him people stared with concerned looks stamped on the faces of all of the Bledsoes, their neighbors he had come to treat, and Brother Carver and Sister Jane. Even Solomon's little face was very serious even though he couldn't possibly know what was happening. Then there was Ruby's tear-stained face and her hands clinging to his arm.

Bless her, she was the one who had been saving him since he first came to this God-forsaken town, just to obtain the approval of his father. Now it came to him. His entire pursuit of his father's approval was a fool's errand.

Foolish, not for coming to Winslow, but for trying to get the approval of a man like his father. Being a doctor mattered, but he had wasted his life chasing after something invisible. He had given up his humanity in holding up ideals, having dignity at all times, putting on a brave face, and living with no emotion. Now, these things didn't matter. What mattered was right in front of him.

He grabbed Ruby's shoulders. "I'll be all right. Don't worry. Take everyone home and wait for me there." He looked around at all of them. And at her. Into those brown eyes—a safe place. This was the home he had been searching for, after looking for one for so long. "God'll take care of me."

She sniffled. "God'll take care of you," she repeated.

"That's right," He tipped up her chin. "I love you. Do you hear me, Ruby? I love you."

"I love you too."

He reached down and he touched her lips with his, something he had been longing to do. Her lips were so soft and she smelled so sweet, like a fresh summer day. If something were to happen to him it would be all right if this first kiss with Ruby were one of his last moments. He never wanted the kiss to end.

But end it did. The beauty of the moment was shattered by Dodge's sharp, hoarse laugh,

"Do we have to witness these scenes of sin? In front of good Christian folk? Take him on out of here."

Dodge's sarcastic tone conveyed something was going on, and this was all intentional. He had been set up. Despite all of his education and smarts, he played into the hands of these men who hated him. Now, he would pay with his life. Too bad. He nearly laughed with joy at knowing her lips. He had won. His life didn't matter. The love he felt for her was the reality.

A prayer came, unbidden, from the recesses of his heart. *Thank you, God. Thank you for letting me see love before I die. If it's your will for me to live to see it again, I will honor love with all that is in me. But if it is your will and I should not live, then at least I am glad I have seen it, and felt it, once before I die.*

Baines shoved at him. "Get in the car."

"I love you, Ruby," he said once more.

"No! Don't get in his car!" Ruby's cries sounded out full-blown now. "I love you. Please, don't leave us now."

As Adam walked toward the sheriff's car, Dodge had a small smile at the corner of his lips.

Adam ducked his head to get into the car, a peace settled in his heart he could not explain, even as it tore at Ruby's wails and Solomon's little shrieks. "I love you," he said again, not sure if she heard, because she sobbed so loud, fighting against the restraints her father and Sister Jane had placed on her by simultaneously embracing her.

Baines said to Dodge. "If you pressing charges, you got to come too."

Dodge, still inebriated like his cousin Lucas, wobbled and tried to get in the car in the front seat next to Sheriff Baines. "Get in the back with him." Baines snarled at Dodge. Adam wanted to laugh in the midst of trouble. Dodge was in such deep cahoots with the Sherriff, he believed he was as good as him, but Baines made it clear where his alliances really were.

Dodge gestured at Adam, "You need to cuff him. He might attack me again."

Sheriff Baines gave a sigh that reverberated in the summer air and got out of the car to reach over the back and put handcuffs on Adam. The click they made hit Ruby and she wailed even louder in reaction.

The pain in his hands was nothing compared to the pain in his heart at Ruby's cries. Little Solomon too. Then, his resolve grew louder and stronger. He would live to come back to her. He was smarter than both of these men put together, and he would find a way to defeat them to come back to her. And at the thought, the beating of his heart slowed and he calmed. What could he do to get out of this situation?

Sheriff Baines hopped in the car to drive it up the road. He drove past the Winslows, and Adam noticed he did not slow down or stop. "I want to stop here to talk to Paul Winslow," Adam demanded.

Baines gave a snicker and Dodge accompanied him. "You didn't know? Paul Winslow leaves town every time the revival comes. He left this morning. He won't be back until the end of the week."

Dodge leaned over. "There ain't no saving you now, fancy doctor. There ain't nothing worse hated around here than an uppity Negro and they hate you." Dodge leaned forward and yelled out companionably to the Sheriff. "Where we going to string him up? Closer to town."

"Don't tell me how to do my job, boy. I know what to do with this man."

Dodge sat back in his seat again, like a whipped puppy. "Just warning you, boss man. He's one of them smart ones. He'll get away if you let him."

"There ain't no way he's smarter than this white man. I know what to do. It's easy now with Winslow away, where he can't ruin things with his emotions and money. I'm the law in this town."

"Yeah," Dodge echoed.

He didn't like the sheriff's response. Whatever the sheriff had in mind, could be worse than a lynching. His shoulders drooped. Just as he had come to know real love, he was going to be in dangerous circumstances that might mean the end of his life. He didn't know what was coming.

Ruby tried to keep calm and remember all Adam had taught her about his car as her mother got in the car with the baby, Sister Jane and Brother Carver. She drove carefully down the road, keeping her walking sisters in sight behind her, going very slowly. When she pulled the car in front of the house, she didn't turn it off and stayed inside.

Her mother directed her. "Get in this house, Ruby Jean. Now."

Ruby looked straight ahead. "Sister, will you see to it my mother gets proper rest?"

"Yes, of course, child."

"If my mother doesn't want to take care of Solomon, then my sisters will be along shortly to help. You can keep an eye on him in the meantime, will you?"

"Of course, Ruby Jean."

"You can not go on off to see about him now. It's getting after dark, and you know it's too dangerous." Lona handed the baby off to Sister Jane. "Listen to me now. He's important and all, but what about Solomon? You know he wants you to take care of Solomon."

Ruby cleared her throat. "I've always know Solomon would be taken care of if something happened to me."

"That's my point, girl. Ain't nothing going to happen to you if you wait here until the sun come up again," Lona pleaded.

"You want me to pace the floor all night wondering if Adam is dead or not?

I can't just sit here, Mama, I got to go to help him. I love him."

The tears started coursing down Lona's cheeks. "I'm happy for you. Solomon gonna have a daddy, but the only way it can happen is if you stay here."

Ruby's sisters entered the yard, so they were home safe. "If I don't go tonight to see about him, I'll always wonder if I did right."

"You should be living your life to protect your boy."

Her father broke away from her sisters and went up to the driver's side of the car. "You still here, Ruby Jean?"

"I'm trying to explain to Mama, why I got to go." She turned to her father. "Can you help?"

John went to the other side of the car and put his arm around Lona's shoulders. "Let her go on, babe."

Lona started screaming and her sisters gathered around their mother. "Something terrible is going to happen to her if she go, I just know."

Ruby's eyes started to fill with tears, but she wiped them away to be able to see as she drove. Brother Carver came around to the driver's side of the car. "How about a prayer before you go?"

Everyone quieted as Ruby bowed her head to receive Brother Carver's blessing. "Lord, please look out for this child as she do your work. The good doctor ain't harmed no one—help him to come on back home so he and she can marry and live in your word. In your name, amen."

"Thank you, Brother."

Ruby pulled away in the car and tried not to look behind her to see Lona being dragged into the house and Solomon nearly inconsolable in the arms of Sister Jane. Solomon was surrounded by enough love—he would be fine. She hadn't known her mother, though, loved her.

As she drove, Ruby thought about all that had happened in the past hour and marveled at how quickly her life had changed.

An hour ago, she hadn't known if her mother loved her and had only thought about her as a reminder of a horrific crime committed against her. An hour ago, she hadn't known if Adam loved her, but thought of her as some young woman he was trying to help. Now, she knew both of them loved her.

With this knowledge, she could face whatever she had to. She had the strength to do what needed to be done to save Adam, even if it meant facing the horror of a crime like her mother had faced or being lynched herself.

This is what love can do. Love. It all seemed so simple, yet it was all so difficult to grasp. She set her chin and drove a little faster in the darkening twilight. Now she was ready. It was love, love from God, her mother and her man all formed into armor for this battle.

She could not, would not, let those who didn't love win. She rejoiced to be a child of a loving God in this, the most difficult hour of her young life.

Chapter Nineteen

Her life had changed. Her life was in her own hands. She did not have to listen or follow what Lona said, just to get Lona to love her. She did not care anymore—she was grown now. There was great empathy in her heart for why Lona had frozen her out most of her life. She understood it but didn't support it.

She would never, ever freeze Solomon out, and now, as an adult, driving her man's car away to help him, it came to her in a rush of emotion that her desire to stay in Winslow was the fulfillment of a childish wish. If she stayed, she would remain a child and follow what everyone wanted her to do or say.

Winslow was home, but not her home anymore. Her home was with Adam.

God, please look out for him, she prayed as she drove. Her eyes began to swim with tears as she thought about him and his potential danger. How in the world could she help him? As much as Ida Wells-Barnett wrote about the horrors of lynching and how they had to be stopped, she had never written a guide or manual about how to approach stopping one without jeopardizing one's own life.

She swiped at her wet face. Now she understood. David had chosen rape as his weapon of choice, purposefully. She confided in him, foolishly, as a child would, about Ida Wells-Barnett. He used her own words about morality and truth against her, and tried to make her immoral. But it wasn't her fault, and Adam did not hate her for her mistake, or for what happened to her, so she could deal with it. There was strength in that. She ran a hand over her silky black hair and gripped the wheel again. She had everything she needed, right with her.

The town's lone police car was not visible along the path she had taken into town, but when she approached the courthouse, it was parked in front. *Whew.* She parked Adam's car along side it and went into the side door of the ornate building Paul Winslow built in tribute to himself.

Sheriff Baines was in his office and he rolled his eyes. "Good gravy, girl, what do you want?"

Ruby stood as tall as she could at her height of five feet. "I want to post bail for Dr. Adam Morson."

A sick feeling emerged in her gut as the evil grin moved across his face. "What makes you think he is here, gal?"

Ruby mind raced. A trickle of cold sweat dripped down the back of her neck. "There's due process. Once you arrested him, he should be able to get a lawyer and a bail set."

The sheriff leaned forward and fixed Ruby with a look. "There ain't no due process for you people."

"What about the fourteenth amendment? It say in the United States Constitution all American citizens are entitled to due process."

"Ain't the case in my county, girl."

"Too bad, Sheriff. I always thought you was fair, but I see something different now."

"He came in here, riding on his white charger like a knight to save you. Used all his connections, everything, just for you. Well, now since Winslow is gone, I've something to say about where he is going to be."

"Where?" Ruby tried to draw herself up even more.

The sheriff fixed her with a look and made Ruby's blood run cold. "Winslow said his boy would fix you, but you're just as sassy as ever. Coming in here, making demands like you do. You don't need to know nothing about men's business. Go on home and take care of your little bastard, if you can."

Ruby tried not to shrink at the insult to her baby. People were going to call him names if she stayed here in Winslow. She had to gather up her son, and leave here as soon as she could—with Adam if he were still alive.

"You haven't lynched him, have you?" Ruby said with more confidence than she felt. "I'll bring the full force of the NAACP into Winslow if you've harmed a hair on his head."

The sheriff gave a harsh laugh. "I'm not interested in the ways you uppity coloreds think you can do something in my town, about my business. Go on home, before I arrest you again for interfering with the business of the sheriff."

"I want to post his bail." Ruby started to dig through a bag she bought. Her laundress money. "I have money." But it wasn't much, she knew. "And Dr. Morson's car." Which she knew was Paul Winslow's but she would think about that later.

"There isn't any amount of money or a car you got I want," the sheriff stood over her and fingered a loose curl tumbling down on her shoulder. Why did her hair misbehave? Now was not the time to have loose hair. She did not flinch or move one inch as he came closer and closer and she could smell his breath.

"What do you want?"

"Stop making trouble in my town. Stop stirring up trouble."

"If you help me find Dr. Morson, I will."

The sheriff still stood over her, in her personal space and folded his arms. "How?"

"He's going to take me away. I'll leave Winslow with him and I'll never come back, ever again. If I stay here and marry Dodge," she swallowed and turned her brown eyes sideways to him. "Do you think he can control me? Please."

The sheriff laughed and put the curl back on to her shoulder. "Dodge could be a real man once he got you into a house as your husband who have dominion over you, be master to you, and control you, sure enough. Break down your sassy ways. It might take some time, but it could be done. Winslow's idea about his boy was wrong. He wasn't the one to take care of you." He moved the half inch closer and whispered into her ear. "I could break down them sassy ways. I surely could."

Ruby did her best not to recoil at the sheriff's hot, wet breath in her ear. "Where is Dr. Morson?" Ruby repeated, drawing out the words, as if she hadn't heard him. As if she weren't afraid he was going to take up what David hadn't finished properly, according to him. "He'll take me from here and you'll never have to see me again."

"What a shame."

"It would end your troubles." Her stomach gripped her with fingers of fear as she waited forever for him to say what had happened to her love, the only man she ever cared for as a woman would a man.

They stood there, facing off, seeing who was stronger, judging who would make the first move. Ruby did not flinch even a little bit.

The sheriff backed down first.

"I turned him over in the next county."

"What do you mean?" Ruby's heart began to race, thinking "turned him over" was some type of words for dead.

"I owed the sheriff in Calhoun a little favor. So, I sold off the doctor there. He's over there working for him."

Something in her head throbbed as she informed him, "Slavery ended fifty years ago, Sheriff. President Lincoln freed us."

His sly, creepy smile came around again. He moved behind his desk like a snake. "Did he now? How come I am just finding out? And you the one who's telling me."

"You cannot sell a free man."

"I can sell any prisoner I want to the chain gang."

A cold wave of fear came over Ruby.

A chain gang.

It was almost preferable Adam be lynched. "He cannot do hard labor. He's a doctor. An educated man. The chain gang wouldn't work for him."

"Then he should not have gotten into folks' business. There is nothing worse than a stranger coming into town getting into other people's affairs."

"Since when do you care about who Negroes marry?"

"Since the Reverend promised he would keep you under control."

"And you believed him?"

His gaze was hard and cold on her. "I'm sheriff in this town. No colored tells me what to do."

Ruby leaned over and looked him in the eye for a second time. "That may be so. But I wonder what'll happen when Paul Winslow comes back to town. I hope I'm here long enough to see what'll happen to you then."

She walked out the door. Then, when she was sure the sheriff did not see her, she grabbed a fistful of her skirt and ran to the car, got it started and hopped in. The drive to Calhoun was a long one, over bumpy country roads. She had tried to avoid being alone for this extended period of time, but Adam's life was at stake. Life on a chain gang was too horrific to think about for a man like Adam. She had to find him.

Chapter Twenty

"Get over here," the Calhoun sheriff barked at Adam, who went over to him, adjusting his glasses. Adam could tell this sheriff was in no mood to bargain or to negotiate. "Why haven't you eaten your food?"

"It's not fresh."

This was the wrong answer.

The sheriff, who had eaten too much of any kind of food, put his face close to Adam's and Adam could tell, from the scent of his breath, that the man had many dental problems. "I don't like no uppity coloreds on my work crews. You eat, so you can work hard. I got to get my money's worth out of you—do you understand?"

"Fine." Adam picked up a shard of the smelly country ham and started to gnaw on it. The salty ham was a long, long way from Lona's food, but he had to keep up his strength. An opportunity to get away might come up. He couldn't stay here. Deep in a piney wood, where the gang was retrieving turpentine, he knew it was going to be difficult to find his way through.

The rough denim pants he wore scratched him and short white shirt they had given him was too tight. The clothes took him back to his childhood when he was exposed and open, often without enough clothing.

As soon as he could, he wore suits and ties because they underlined his status so he wore them relentlessly. These clothes were too ill fitting, and his chest looked strange to him. He had done hard labor before, while he was growing up and during the summers of college and medical school to earn extra money. And every time he did, he was reminded about why he wanted to be a doctor.

"Enough, captain." A kind-faced man who was the color of warm cocoa spoke to him. "He ain't looking now."

Adam put down the shard of ham and sighed. "People would work better if they had better food—why don't they realize?"

"They buys these pigs cheap, cook them fast, and give it to us."

"People could get trichinosis."

The man regarded him closely. "How did you get on this here gang, boss? What did you do? Kill your wife?"

Adam tried to see himself through the man's eyes. He probably had not had close kind of contact to someone like him before. The other men in the room were waiting to hear his answer. "I was looking to ask a young lady to marry. I beat up someone who wanted to marry her instead. The sheriff in the other county sold me over here. That's how I got here."

"The other man dead?"

"No."

"You musts made someone mad. They don't puts no white on the chain gang for hurtin' somebody."

Adam took a deep breath. He released it, thinking about Ruby's brown eyes and slightly parted pink lips, wondering if he would ever feel their warmth on his ever again. "I'm a Negro."

"What you say?" All the other men leaned forward and looked at him.

Adam repeated the revelation, seeing the men elbow each other in surprise and wonder. The kindly man spoke up, "You about the whitest Negro I ever seen. You sure?"

"My mother was the maid in the house where my father was the son."

"Whoa. Yeah. He one."

"That explain it then. They wouldn't put no white man in here for just any kind of reason," the cocoa brown man offered his hand. "James. Nice to meet you."

Adam shook it. "Nice to meet you."

"What you do?"

Adam frowned. Some other man leaned forward.

James clarified, "No, I mean, what you does. For work."

"I'm a doctor."

The men breathed out. "I ain't never heard tell of no colored doctor afore," James breathed out.

"I knew he was somebody," another man said under his breath, but the room was so quiet, everyone heard it.

Adam ran his hand over his short curls. "Well, I'm in here with everyone else. Trying to figure a way to get out."

They all stared at him. "There ain't no way off of the gang, captain. You got to work your time off."

"Until when?"

"Until the sheriff say you can go." Some of the other men shifted and laughed at James.

"What's so funny?" Adam looked around.

"We don't go. Some of us been here for years. Working from place to place. Doing whatever they say."

"Don't you know how much your debt is for?"

"We don't know. It's whatever they say."

"How do you know then?"

"We doesn't. They knows a lot of us can't read or write. They just brought us here. We go from place to place, working, doing what they say."

Adam had heard of chain gangs and peonage, but he never believed he would be part of it. Peonage sounded like a nightmare, being stuck on someone else's say so and having to work however much someone else wanted.

Slavery, all over again.

The thought of going around and around Calhoun County without seeing Ruby depressed him, so he tried to clear his mind so he could think of another time and another reality.

"Was your girl pretty?" James spoke in a low register. "Was she worth it?"

"Yes." Ruby was worth it. Without a doubt. The picture of Ruby in her big pink hat and white dress formed in his mind and comforted him. If he had the courage to ask sooner, maybe she might have worn the dress to marry him. He could see it, in his mind's eye. Next time, he would ask her to take off the hat, so he could see her beautiful brown eyes shining at him.

"Ruby?" Adam turned his head at the sound of his beloved's name on another man's lips. He hadn't even realized he had spoken her name.

"Yes, that's her name."

"Does she live over in the next county?"

"Yes, in Winslow."

"I used to work at the mill. She be the little bit, coming around trying to get the workers together." The other man's face softened. "Feisty little bit, even though the boss man keep trying to throw her out. You see her all the time, and then she stopped coming around."

"She had a baby."

"Your baby?" All the men leaned forward. A muscle twitched in Adam's jaw.

"No. They had someone take advantage of her to get her to stop going around organizing."

"What you say?" James breathed out. "Awful."

"It is. She had her baby and she loves him, but Winslow's attack didn't stop her." Adam still couldn't bring himself to believe Paul Winslow was his father. If Paul Winslow came to save him from this hellish existence as a Negro man, would he want him to do it?

No.

He could have a purpose in his life by being what Ruby wanted. Even though it meant she couldn't be with him, and he would never see Solomon again, he would take comfort in being a Negro man.

"It's mighty hard when you can't protect your woman," James said.

Many of the men around the table nodded, agreeing. "Don't nobody blame you."

"Thank you. While we are waiting here, does anyone need any medical help?"

The men presented, one at a time, almost shyly, one problem after another. There were a lot of upset stomachs and gastrointestinal issues—which didn't surprise him if they had to eat this swill every day. He was able to help more with the cuts he saw they suffered on their hands from slashing the pine to get to the turpentine.

His hands were sore, but the pain was small compared to what these men had to suffer. Not using his medical training meant all his time and education would have been wasted. But then, as he patched up another cut on another man's hand from the turpentine knife, it was all Paul Winslow's money wasn't it?

No. It was God.

There it was, the truth, right in front of him. All of the deception, lies and blood money it took to get his medical degree. To make it right, his education had to be turned over to serve God.

And even though, it hurt him to the core he couldn't see his beloved, she would be proud of him for treating these men who had been treated so despicably. He could do this, he could perform this service, before they succeeded in breaking him.

But they wouldn't break him.

The men turned at the rough door opening, letting in the hot steam of the Georgia day. "What is going on in here?" the sheriff asked and Adam's heart sank. This was it, the beginning of the downward spiral. When and if he laid eyes on Ruby again, she would love him and be worthy of him. Just as he was making himself worthy of her.

Going home would be fruitless. Lona would cry and beg her to behave. She had to do something, but ever since the sheriff made his revelation, she didn't know how. She hated the thought, but she had to go to the Winslows again. She didn't know if Paul Winslow was home yet, but she had to check and see. This time, she made sure she went to the back door and Bob opened it.

"Ruby, what's going on?" Bob and Agnes had been at the revival, too, Ruby remembered.

Ruby ignored his behavior from before at the train station and just said it. "The sheriff sold Adam to a chain gang."

"Jesus, keep us near the cross. The doctor wouldn't last on no chain gang."

"I know. Do you think Mrs. Winslow would see me?"

Bob shook his head back and forth. "I don't know. She mighty cross at you."

"If I can get Adam back, I promised the sheriff I would go away with him and never come back to Winslow."

Bob's face became a mass of wrinkles. "Afore God, Ruby. Where would you go?"

Ruby's eyes blazed. Now he acted concerned about her after his behavior at the railroad station.

The nerve. *Please God, help me to be patient. Bob is just a confused soul.* She calmed down. "I got places. The doctor said I could go up north with him and finish high school. Maybe even get to be a nurse and help him out."

"Maybe he marry you, and be a daddy to your boy?"

Ruby lowered her head and blushed a bit. "I hope so."

"I take you in."

Ruby followed Bob in through the kitchen to the parlor where Mary Winslow sat. All corseted up and sitting in her chair, with a bit of needlework in her hands, Mary Winslow was in her own prison. Ruby had pain in her heart for her. Her entire existence was sitting there in her prim, grey dress and purposeless needlework in her hands.

"What are you doing here, Ruby?"

"Ma'am." Ruby stepped forward and smoothed down her skirt in supplication. "I need your help. They've taken the doctor to a chain gang, and I don't know what to do to get him out. Please help him."

Something flashed in her eyes—she couldn't label it. Was it sorrow? Sympathy? She didn't know what to make of the look. When Ruby came close to identifying it, the empathetic look went away. Something aloof showed up in her eyes as Ruby knew she had reached her "I don't know what you mean, Ruby. I cannot help you."

"You can go to the sheriff and let him know he needs to get Adam back."

"Why? If the sheriff sold him off somewhere else, I have nothing to say about it."

Ruby narrowed her eyes. "I never said he sold him off. This must be a way of doing things, isn't it?"

Mrs. Winslow had the grace to look shamefaced, at least. "Well, yes."

"When is Mr. Winslow coming home?"

"The end of the week."

Ruby breathed a sigh of relief. Any time he was on a chain gang was long. Still, but they couldn't break him in three more days. They wouldn't be able to get their money's worth out of him. "Well, if you are convinced you couldn't do something to help Mr. Winslow's son—"

"David is Mr. Winslow's son, or have you forgotten?"

"I could never forget. He's the reason I have Solomon." Ruby stood still and stared Mary Winslow down in her own parlor.

Mrs. Winslow stood up. "I've had quite enough of your coming in here and making trouble for my family. I'm sorry, I cannot help with your request."

She was protecting her family, as Ruby would have. She couldn't blame her. "I –I don't have access to the kind of funds it would take to buy him out." Mrs. Winslow's blue eyes reflected her powerlessness with money.

Ruby believed her. She stood a little taller than her short height would let her. "Too bad. Whenever the doctor comes home, I'm going up north with him. I'm leaving Winslow for good."

"Go north with him? Leave Winslow?"

"Yes, ma'am. For good."

"You would take your baby? With a strange man? What about your child?"

And the same look of longing showed now in Mrs. Winslow's eyes as when she first saw Solomon on the Bledsoe front porch. The look appeared again at the picnic. Mary Winslow wanted to be a grandmother to Solomon, but she couldn't upset her little world.

Everything was in order, and for Mrs. Winslow, her world was a place of the nineteenth century. She still belonged in the old times, a time where women did needlework and waited for their husbands to come home to deal with financial matters, because they didn't have enough means to buy people off of chain gangs. Mrs. Winslow's blue eyes showed such sadness, trying to keep up the façade, trying hard not to show emotion when she shouldn't.

Ruby understood now. They were complete equals. They were women who were concerned about their families. "He'll be fine, ma'am. Even before the doctor came to Winslow, the world was changing. Took some time after slave times ended, but things are changing now, ma'am. Solomon," Ruby spoke her son's name softly before this woman so she could share in his name, just for the moment, "Solomon is part of a changing world. Dr. Morson has offered me a chance to finish my education. He says I have smarts, and I can get to be a nurse and help him in his work."

Mrs. Winslow gave a little laugh. "And be what to him? A paid companion of some kind, no doubt."

"No, ma'am. I would be his wedded wife. We would be married before God. He might not have had it in his mind when the sheriff come and take him away, but he has it now. We're bonded in a way only God would come to know and understand."

Mrs. Winslow's face crinkled up in disappointment and confusion. "I thought, if you married the Reverend Dodge, you would stay here. He told me so."

"It was very wrong of Reverend Dodge to tell you something about my life. I make decisions for myself."

"I see." Mary Winslow sat back down in her overstuffed chair. "You've certainly never done anything less. Well, this is a blow. That so-called Reverend took a donation for his church on his word."

Ruby smoothed down her skirt. "I don't know where Reverend Dodge is. If I see him, I'll tell him you looking for him, ma'am. I'm going to go now. The revival going to start soon, and I want to go and pray. Thank you for letting me know when Mr. Paul will be coming back."

"Certainly, Ruby. I'm sure when Mr. Winslow returns, he will do something to help the doctor. It would be a shame for him to lose his investment in all of his education." There was Mrs. Winslow. The aloofness was back. No need to stay to see that show, so Ruby turned on her heel to go. As she did, David stood there on the steps, having heard every word she said to his mother.

Ruby dipped her head at him. He was not the childhood friend, who, back in the distant past, she thought would be her husband. The divisions of race and class were too strong for them to overcome. She felt sorry for him, too, needing to adhere to those divisions. He didn't look well, standing on the steps staring after her with his mouth open.

Quickly, as she walked past him, out of the back door, she did something she had not done in a long time. She prayed for him.

Bathed in sweat and completely confused, Adam bumped his head on the pine bunk above his. Breathing deep, he inhaled the stench of a dozen unwashed men in the large roughened cabin. The smell was a slap in the face, reminding him he was on the chain gang, and might as well be far away from the Bledsoes as the moon.

Touching his head, he felt no bump. He could still think and reason as a doctor. He would be okay.

Thank you, God.

The prayer of gratitude came to him, even as he had to smell unwashed men instead of the clean earthly scent of Ruby's long silken jet black locks.

Carrying Ruby's smile inside of his mind, and thinking of her keen, curious eyes learning some new skill, he wondered at her beauty. An unfamiliar emotion inside of him hungered to see her again. He wanted to sob like a child at being on a chain gang instead of with her. His days as a trained doctor were at an end. It was workhorse days for the rest of his life. He might as well rest up.

Soon, the sound of scraping on a washboard made a loud clanging noise to wake them up. The camp did not have proper facilities for washing. Adam looked around him with disapproval. No wonder there was so much disease in the camp. How could he get more leverage to be able to tell them the filth of the camp impacted the workers by keeping them sick?

Of course, it didn't matter to them about what the workers needed. They would just get more workers if they died off. An endless supply of labor was the point of a chain gang. He had to laugh or he would have been sad he never got a chance to live the kind of life with Ruby he now realized he wanted.

"Are you okay, Doc?" A young man asked him.

"I'm fine. Do you know what they will have us doing today?"

"Hard to say. Might be turpentine, it could be clearing out a field. Who knows? They got breakfast for us." The young man looked at the grits and sorghum they were dishing out in a chow line and Adam joined in too. His stomach rumbled with hunger. Grits. Better than nothing.

He ate the grits from a tin plate with more rapidity than he would have liked. They gave each of them half a biscuit. Lona's peach jam would be perfect with this dry biscuit. The memory of the peach jam made him think of how Ruby let Solomon taste peach jam for the first time. The delight on Solomon's young face was like a sun.

He had never known what it was to care for someone else more than himself. He had never had the opportunity. So many people, relatives, his father, all had wanted something from him and couldn't love him the way he deserved. Something inside him warmed knowing he now belonged to someone. When he had come to Winslow, he wanted it more than anything, but he had been afraid to hope for it. All he could do was pray for Ruby and her son. Their well-being mattered more than his own health and safety.

They made him do a variety of things on the first day. They were watched over by deputy personnel of the county, armed with guns. How many citizens knew their tax money went to pay for these illegal endeavors? He chopped wood, helped to clear out a barn and dug holes. They gave them more biscuits and some sorghum molasses for lunch, not very nutritious fare, but cheap. They got to drink water from a water pump, which was fresh at least, and continued with their work.

Adam was struck by the looks of despair on their faces and he understood why. This would be their lives. This would be his life. For the rest of his life.

He began to sing. No one stopped him, but some of the men joined in, singing an old church hymn with feeling. He had to believe God would not leave him in this by himself.

They sang songs over and over as they worked until no one could remember another church song. The singing made him feel as if his existence were bearable somehow. As they worked, a car pulled up. He squinted in the hot Georgia sun to see who had come.

To his surprise, David Winslow stepped from the car. His doctor's eye noticed David stumbled a little as he got out of the car. Adam tried to see more but the deputies were watching. "Keep working, boy." One of the deputies gestured toward him with the gun.

He had learned enough to know not to tell the man David was his brother, so he kept chopping wood. David went into the small camp house where the sheriff was. Was the brother who he despised there to save him? Half of him wanted it to be so, but the other half did not want to be in David's debt. He kept working, toying with the possibilities in his mind. After about a half an hour, the sheriff headed to him and gestured with a thumb. "You, you been bought out. Come on."

"What about them?"

"Bring yourself on. It was enough for this man to buy you out. Be grateful and go with him and do what he say."

Adam put down the ax, happy at being liberated, but guilty at leaving the men behind. "Go on, boss man," James said. "Good to see someone getting liberty."

"Take care of yourself, James."

"You go on back and do right by Miss Ruby. She special."

"Yes, she is. Thank you."

Adam walked behind the sheriff to where David stood in the hot sun. David's skin was covered in a thin film of sweat, his pallor was off and he did not look normal.

"Hot day," David waved a lightweight boater in front of his face. "Thank you, Sheriff. I know my mother will be most grateful to you."

"Tell her I say hello," the sheriff waved off. "I hope he doesn't give you any trouble."

David got in the car and started it up. Adam slid in the front seat next to him, not sure what to say. "Thank you for getting me out of there." He could start there.

"You couldn't be there for long. You don't belong there."

It was a monumental effort for David to drive the car.

"Do you want me to drive?" Adam reached out to grab the wheel.

"Wait until we get down the road a way. I don't want them seeing you drive—it wouldn't be safe."

Once David drove down the road a bit, he stopped the car and he and Adam switched places. David slumped over into the passenger side, clearly unwell. "I'm so tired."

"Feel free to rest. You look as if you need it," Adam advised. Then despite himself, he asked. "How did you know I was here?"

David gazed at him with Winslow eyes. "Ruby came to the house and asked my mother to help. I overheard. She said no, so it gave me the opportunity to do something for her." He wrapped his arms inside of his jacket as if he were cold. "Some are luckier than others. I just wanted to do something to make it all up to her."

"Why would you bother?" Despite what David had done for him, the anger still rose inside of him at the way Ruby felt about herself. Because of what David had done.

"Because I love her. I always have." David slumped down even lower. "It's unfair. You're just as light as I am, but you're a Negro and can live with her and love her. I'm white and it would be against the law for me to love her."

"Is that why you raped her?"

David sighed. "I've lived under the thumb of Paul Winslow all of my life. You, at least, had the chance to make your own way in life and your own decisions."

"You've said that before."

"How else could I know how she was if I couldn't marry her?"

Adam's stomach turned. The complete picture of a spoiled child.

"You don't do certain things to people you love. That's not love."

"It's all I am ever allowed," David whispered, and put his head back on the rest behind him. "If I were allowed more, like you, I would do it."

"How much did it cost to buy me out?" The irritation in him came to the surface of his skin and made him hot and prickly. "I'll pay you back, every penny."

"You will not. I told you, I did it for Ruby, not for you. I could see the way she was when she begged Mother to help her. I always wanted her to look at me that way."

"She had feelings for you."

David turned over. "Crush feelings. The way she talks about you, thinks about you—she's got a woman's love for a man. I wish I could have her woman's love. All I could have was the one time in the cotton field."

"My. You just turned an attack on Ruby into being a victim."

"There are worse things in life than what you think. Like being Paul Winslow's only true son. Take your opportunity at liberty seriously. Take Ruby and the baby and get as far away from here as possible. Ruby told Mother she would."

"She did?" Adam looked confused.

"Yes. She told Mother she would leave Winslow with you and never come back. Mother wouldn't help. I think, in part because…" David stopped talking and out of the corner of his eyes, he swallowed hard. "She likes the baby. She won't admit it, of course, but it's like I told you. And she was angry when Ruby said she was taking the baby away. I think she didn't want to help Ruby so she could see the baby sometimes."

"He's a capital little fellow." Adam remembered how Solomon's little face lit up with joy and he drove a little faster.

"Mother was not happy to find out about you. It was galling to her to think—just a couple of tumbles with a maid and Dad had another son."

Adam tried, really tried to feel some sympathy for Mary Winslow, but it was too difficult. He marveled at her self-centeredness. David probably got it from her and Paul Winslow. A double-dose. He supposed he couldn't blame her for feeling hatred for Ruby, but at the same time, didn't countenance it. "What a shame," was all he could muster.

"So, are you really going to take her away?"

"If she wants me to. I had several offers at graduation. I'll send a telegram to find out if any of them stand. One offer I was most interested in was in Pittsburgh."

"Far up in the north in the cold." David began to cough and had a hard time stopping. "But I'm sure even as a colored doctor, you'll have enough to buy a coat to keep her warm."

"I'll take care of her, however she needs me."

David's coughing fit slowed down and he smiled. "If you think you are going to take care of Ruby, well." The smile left his face. "Take care of one another. Love one another." He laid his head back on the seat. "Brother Carver, always talked about that bible verse, in Corinthians II—the greatest of these is Love. Love her."

Adam didn't want to know how David knew about Brother Carver. He bristled at the thought of Ruby's rapist telling him what to do, too consumed with driving as fast as he legally could on terrible roads to get to his beloved.

"I will," he said. He could keep such a promise.

Chapter Twenty-One

When they came close to the Bledsoe farm at the Winslow home, Adam stopped the car. "I appreciate what you've done, David. Thank you."

David slumped on the front seat, napping. The motion of the car and Adam's voice stirred him awake.

"Are you well?" Should he check him for a fever? David's attack on Ruby staid his hand. Were his feelings reflecting a Christian attitude? Probably not, but Adam needed a bath. His need to be free of the grime of the chain gang seemed to be more of a priority now.

Still, his doctor's training kicked in. David wiped at his face with a handkerchief. "I'll be alright. If there is anything else I can do, please let me know. She deserves to be happy."

With the bereft look on David's face, something inside of him turned over. He couldn't imagine what it must be like to want to love Ruby, and not be able to. Well, yes he could. "Yes. I'll help her."

David gave a faint smile and sat up, getting ready to exit the car. "I don't see why not. You reflect everything possible for her in this life."

"Ruby has aspirations. If she marries, she could compromise her goals. She wants to finish high school and become a nurse and help me in my practice."

David nodded. "I could see her as a nurse. She's very smart."

The Bledsoe farm was down the road, and he wanted to run to it, and into Ruby's arms, but all of a sudden, he was afraid. "She has so much potential, I don't want to destroy it by asking her to give all of it up."

"Then don't ask her to," David offered. "A wife is a helpmeet, as much as anything. Why can't she still help you in your practice? Dr. Trywell, over in the next county has his wife help him. It's all possible, Adam. You have to put it just like that. She'll say yes."

Despite his misgivings, Adam reached a hand out to David, and slowly, ever so slowly, David shook it. "Will you be all right?"

"I will. Please, take care of them." David fixed him with a look. "Do what I can't."

Adam got out of David's car and started the walk down the pathway when he heard, rather than saw David's car pull off toward the Winslow house.

When he opened the gateway into the front yard of the Bledsoe farm, Delie's little face was the first one to greet him. She rushed out onto the porch in her bare feet. "He's back!" she cried and ran down the pathway to hug him. "I told them you would be back, no mean old chain gang could hold you back!"

Delie's shouts caused everyone else to come running, everyone except Ruby. Mags came out holding Solomon and he squeezed the baby to his chest, who seemed happy to see him. Lona stood in the doorway smiling, but shouted out she was glad to see him. "Got breakfast going," she said, "Come on in to eat."

"Where's Ruby?"

Everyone, all of Ruby's sisters, her father, the Carvers and even the baby quieted on his question. His heart started to thud. Was he too late to see her? But Solomon was still here. She wouldn't leave her son behind.

John spoke up, "She's at her spot near the creek. She been there for some time now, trying to figure out how to get you out. She been feeling mighty bad she didn't have no other way to get you off of the chain gang."

"How did you do it?" Delie asked in her childish voice. "I bet you fought your way out?"

Adam handed the baby to John. "I'm going to go find her. I need to talk to her."

John's eyes met with Adam's and tears stood in them. "Whatever you going to say to her, I agree and I approve."

Adam looked squarely at him. "How did you know?"

"Anytime a man been on the gang, it makes him think about life. You want to have the same thing in your life, day in and day out. You don't take as much risk. They won't mess with you as much then."

"I love her."

"I knows," John put Solomon's young cheek next to his older one and they both bent to their eggs.

"Yeah, we know," Delie said. "Go on and get her so there can be a wedding."

Adam looked down at her and smiled. "It's okay with you?"

Delie checked the red dirt on her feet. "Ruby's great. I can't wait around for you forever, so you might as well marry her. By the time I'm old enough, you might be too old anyway, so I'll go for someone else." Everyone laughed as he bent down and gave her a kiss on her forehead.

"And whomever he is, he'll need to come through your big brother."

Brother Carver raised his hand in benediction. "Go with God, good Doctor."

Sister Jane nodded. "Go on to her. Claim it. She loves you."

Adam nodded then went off through the woods in the direction of the pond, his heart pounding with fear, joy, excitement and trepidation all at once. How was it possible to feel so many things at once? Ruby made such a difference to him.

She had changed his life.

No luck without Adam. And no fish either. The fish were not biting this morning and since the sun was up, she should head home. However, something stopped her. She felt like a failure. She couldn't go home to Solomon and see his grey eyes searching hers anymore, wondering where the man who held him as if he were precious and mattered had gone. For the first time in her life, she regretted all she had done.

Why did she have to be such a troublemaker? Big, fat, hot tears slid down her cheeks and landed on her overalls-covered lap. If she had been more of a lady, if she had not caused so much trouble, Mary Winslow might have been willing to help her. Goodness, Adam wouldn't even be on the gang, and she wouldn't have been attacked to begin with. It was all her fault.

Ruby swiped at her tears, trying to clear her field of vision. She resolved to finish her studies and become a nurse. She would seek out the chain gangs to help the men on them stay healthy and strong.

Maybe one day, she would run into Adam and let him know how sorry she was.

She pulled in her line. It looked like biscuits and gravy for breakfast.

Guilt ate at the edges of her conscience and the tears began again. She stood up to go back through the trees to go home. She didn't even try to wipe them away.

Her sight was blurry, so when the visage of a tall man with light skin like hers, who was also dressed in tattered and rough denim overalls, appeared she couldn't believe it. She wiped her tears away and, praise God, it was Adam, with his arms folded over his barely covered chest in a too-small shirt. "I see you didn't catch anything. Did you ever catch anything before I came into town?"

Her mouth flew open and she gasped. She couldn't help it. She rushed into his arms. "Oh, Adam, I mean, Doctor. How did you ever get out? No one gets off the chain gang."

"I guess it's pretty rare." He leaned down to embrace her and whispered into her braids. "But I had to find a way to come back to you. You're such a rare jewel, everyone in the camp was cheering me on."

Despite what she wanted to do, she held him out from her, looking at his beautifully shaped pink lips and wanted to kiss them, but she had to ask the question through her tears, "Who was cheering you on in the camp?"

"Big Jim, he said his name was."

Ruby's eyes widened in recognition. "Big Jim Sawyer, from over Caton way? I know him."

"You've done so much good for so many around here, Ruby. I had no right to judge you and to condemn your crusades. I'm sorry."

She wrapped her arms around the long trunk of his body and a rush of warmth came over her when he reached down and embraced her in return. Tightly. "I'm the one who caused all of this trouble. If it hadn't been for...the attack," Ruby swallowed, "It wouldn't have happened. You wouldn't have felt like you had to protect me. So many things are my fault."

He pulled back and took her chin into his big hand. Even his hand seemed better. His hands were so important to so many. "You must never, ever feel as if you deserved to be attacked. The things you do, what you fight for, are good. You bring good in this very dark world. It's what makes you virtuous. You don't just take things in. You do something about it. And make you special." He ran a hand over her cheek. "It's one reason I love you."

"I love you, too, Adam."

He reached down and covered her lips with his, kissing her with his wonderful, delightful juicy pink lips. If she died right there on the spot, God would take her straight to heaven and she would be glad to tell him of this happiness she had found here on earth. Then, as he lifted his lips from hers, a little cloud edged in on her happiness. She had to speak her concern—even if this was the only chance she ever had in her life. "But, Adam. You said I was virtuous."

He smiled at her. "You are."

"Virtuous means, virginal. It means you kept yourself pure. I'm not pure."

He ran a thumb over her lips and Ruby wanted to pucker them, just a little, to kiss the pad of his thumb, but she stopped herself short. "You have the wrong understanding, my precious jewel. You didn't willingly give yourself to David. He did a great wrong doing what he did to you. He knows it."

Ruby pulled back from him a little more. "How do you know?"

He pulled her into the crook of his arm, and tightened his hold on her, just a little. "He told me. He's the one who freed me."

Ruby made a face and stood apart from him even more. "So I owe him?"

"You owe him nothing. He did a very terrible thing and he knows it. He said he came to help me because it would help you. I didn't want his help, but there was no other way off of the gang without him. And I wanted, no, I needed to come back to you, Ruby. I thought about you day and night while I was away. The thought of you kept me going, despite the hard, hard work."

"Really?" She looked up at him.

"Yes. I thought even if I died, or lost my capacity to be a doctor, I wanted to let you know I love you. And." Adam took her hand in his and kissed it. Please say you will be my wife. I want you to finish your education, and even keep going to school to be a nurse and help me in my practice. I would never take your education from you."

The prickle of tears at her eyes startled her. She would have never thought, mere months ago, someone like this man could come and ask her for her hand in marriage. Her breaths came shallow, as if she had been running in a race. "Your wife?"

She didn't quite know what to say. It was as if she had been presented with a great big sumptuous banquet and she didn't know what to eat first.

Adam's face was almost half sad, almost yearning. "That's all you have to say, Ruby?"

She looked up at him. He was the answer to so many things. And she said she would go away with him, but she didn't want to cause trouble in his life. He didn't deserve trouble. "Let me think about it."

"You mean thinking about it like with Dodge?" She couldn't tell if, in his response if he were being funny or if he were angry.

"No, no. No. I mean it, I don't want to bring you any more trouble."

"Ruby, I just said—"

And she put a finger to his lips.

"I heard what you said. It's wonderful. It's too wonderful for someone like me." Ruby stared ahead, almost dazed. "I have to get used to being treated in such a fine, fancy way."

Adam wrapped his arm around her shoulders. "There's nothing else I can say to convince you?"

"No. Not right now. Let's go back to the house and get breakfast."

"With no fish."

She smiled at him and put her arm around his waist to show him she loved him. "No fish. Just us."

"Everyone knows I came out here to ask you to marry me."

Ruby fixed her chin in a defiant way. "They know me. They know I would give such a wonderful proposition the serious consideration you deserve."

"Of course. Let's go back to the house for some biscuits and gravy. Too bad I couldn't get here sooner, or else we could have had some trout." She gave him a light punch on the arm.

"We can always come back tomorrow." Ruby guided him through the trees back to her family's farm, wishing for his sake, she was more comfortable eating at the banquet he had laid out for her.

"And many more tomorrows," Adam said, "just as long as we are together."

"I'll be just a second," Ruby stood up on tiptoe and kissed his lips then went back through the woods the other way looking for the answer to help her be free of her sins.

Chapter Twenty-Two

Ruby couldn't believe Adam's proposal. It would mean really leaving her home. Winslow was a childish pipe dream. It was time to put it away. But how, how would she do without the piney woods? The creek? The quiet and loneliness of this beautiful land? She took a deep breath of air and inhaled it. She would never, ever forget this, even as she returned to it.

When she came to the wider part of the brook, closer to the beginnings of town, she startled to see David sitting there, picking apart pine needles and staring into the creek.

Her heart leaped in her throat. Despite the preeminence of her heart, she turned back and tiptoed away, quietly as if she were a deer.

"Ruby!"

Then, she became a deer as she ran.

No.

No more.

She had been caught before. Flashes of that day swept through her mind, coming home after delivering Jacob's son, relishing in the joy of that family, David seeing her there on the road, offering her a ride on his horse. And she accepted, thinking she would get home faster, sooner before the dark.

Save me, please, save me.

"Ruby!"

Why didn't she move faster? Run harder? Had the ravages of childhood compromised her body? No, something else made her feet leaden and weighty, fear.

God will protect me. He will keep me.

But once before, one time sixteen months ago, David and she were on the back of his fine horse, with Ruby using one hand to grab him around his waist, so she didn't fall off and grabbing onto her birthing bag with the other.

Could David feel her heart thudding? Was her heart thudding as it did now? She had not felt alarmed when David said he was going a different way, because he wanted to show her something.

When they had been friends as children, they spent much of the day tearing through the woods in bare feet and patched-together clothing until her body betrayed her and became something strange and foreign to her.

And after a space of a few years of ignoring her, he noticed her again. Now he was a sophisticated college man coming home on break. She was his old childhood chum, from back when they would hang out together all day long and they didn't know who was white and who was black.

Or at least she didn't know.

She didn't know, until David took her to the vast fields behind the cotton mill and bothered to tell her.

"What you got to show me? You know Mama, she going to worry."

David helped her down off the horse, and his hands around her waist made her feel grown up. Like a young lady. "Just this way, over here."

Why was there such grimness in his voice? What was wrong?

"I be glad to help you. But not for long, you know how Mama is, so I got to get back."

But she wasn't scared. Not for one minute. This was David, not his father. They used to spend whole afternoons talking about the difference.

David, not his Daddy.

Ruby, not her mother.

They were never going to be like their parents of the same gender.

Except, Ruby was. And she didn't know it.

"Come here, Ruby."

"What for?"

Ruby went over to him in the field. "Hey, this is just where the old cisterns were. But your Daddy's crop is doing fine. That's good for you all."

And she lost her voice, because David had taken down his pants and stood there, exposed to her in the warm March day.

At first she wanted to laugh. What was her old chum up to? She had seen him before. They used to go skinny dipping all the time in the creek, didn't think anything about it. They had to look at each other, just to prove that Ruby was as white as he was. They were both white all over and that satisfied her to know that she was as she thought she was, white.

She lived in some type of sustained workplace, and would stay there until David graduated from school and would come and marry her and sweep her up and take her to live in the big white Winslow house.

That was to be her life. That was her dream.

Now, she was forced to wake up because David stood exposed in the warm March day. And it came to her, in a way she hadn't understood before, that she was a Negro.

Everyone kept telling her.

And she hadn't believed it until that moment.

And now, David asked her to do something, vile and terrible.

He might as well have slapped her. And she stood there. But then he did slap her and the sting of it resonated on her face. "Do it."

Ruby backed away. "Are you okay?" She asked him. What was wrong with him?

He grabbed her wrist and began to twist it in his hand, hard enough to bring Ruby to her knees in the hard red dirt. "Do as I say."

"I can't do what you say. I can't."

"If you don't, there'll be worse."

"Worse?" Ruby repeated as if she didn't know what the word meant. Except she didn't. What was worse than the filthy thing he wanted her to do to him? What had college done to him? This wasn't her old childhood chum. He was different, acting different.

And he joined her, on his knees, her wrist still in his hand and faced her, angry at her as if she had done something to make him mad. What could she have done to make him upset? "Lift up your dress to me."

"David, I ain't lifting up my dress to nobody until I'm married before God." Was that what he had brought her out here to the cotton fields for? To get her to marry him? All he had to do was ask, so why wasn't he asking proper-like on the courting porch with John Bledsoe saying yes?

Ruby tried to use her other hand to free herself, but David's strength was too great. She could smell liquor on his breath and all of a sudden he frightened her. She kicked him in the thigh and, startled, he let go of her wrist and she scrambled away in the dirt, not caring if the red dust ruined her shirtwaist and skirt. She had to get away from him.

Just as she was now. She had heard stories about how when white men had a Negro woman, they couldn't stay away, that they kept coming back. She had no intentions of being David's play toy. Childhood was over.

Now, with the Bledsoe home looming in the clearing, where Adam had gone back to the house, everyone laughing happily with the Carvers eating biscuits and sausage gravy and Adam was disappointed that she had said no to him. After all he had endured being on the chain gang and everything, how could she say no? It hurt her to her soul that she had hurt the doctor, because she truly loved him, but she wasn't worthy of him. She was dirty.

"Be still, Ruby. Come on, be nice."

David pressed himself on top of her, deep into the red dirt, ripping at her work skirt with one hand and holding her down with his terrible, powerful strength with the other. "Stop it, David. Stop. Don't do it. Please."

As he ripped her underdrawers, intent on his goal, Ruby screamed, but she knew it didn't matter. No one ever came out here to the edge of this field. She was alone and the spiky cotton bolls and dirt pressed deeper into her back.

He slapped her again. "Be quiet. And still. Do you hear me? Don't make me have to hurt you worse."

Worse? What was worse than him doing this to her in a dirty smelly field rather than in a bed in the big Winslow house with a wedding ring on her finger? There was worse than this?

When it was over, he stood over her, and adjusted his clothing.

"That's what they teach you up in college, I guess?" Her voice shook.

David was over by the horse. "Get on."

Get on the horse? As if she could. The pain was too much to bear, and she couldn't imagine wrapping her arms around him to stay on the horse. Ever again.

"I don't want to."

"I can't believe you are acting this way. All of your kind like it. Come on. Stop being mad."

"Give me my bag."

David tossed her the bag and her tools clanged in the dirt. She picked them up and silently put them back in.

David got on the horse's back and stood over her, taller and bigger and stronger than her. "You better not tell anyone, Ruby. And you need to stop doing what you are doing to hurt my Daddy. And the mill."

What? What did Paul Winslow have to do with this? "Your Daddy too big time for any little Negro gal to hurt him."

"That's right. So stop it. I mean you to understand."

He rode off, leaving her behind in the field to fend for herself in the darkness and to make the long, long walk home by herself in the dark. Which was easy. She herself was a part of the dark now. No matter how light her skin was, she was a part of the dark in a way she never understood before.

Now, he was here again, and loomed in front of her. "Ruby. I just got to tell you…"

Ruby screamed and she ran toward the house away from the memory in her mind's eye, straight into the protective arms of Adam. He cradled her to him tenderly and she never, ever wanted him to let her go.

There had been few times in his life when he had been so disappointed.

Just a few. Ruby's missing acceptance of his proposal felt like a failure and he didn't fail many times in his life. Only when he had been very young, and was not able to get his cousin Lucas to feed him more or treat him better. Ever since then, he had been on a roll and this failure, in particular stung.

He had fallen in love with her.

His brief exposure to life as a Negro man in the South was enough to convince him. He wanted away from here as soon as possible and he wanted the petite, soft roundness of Ruby next to him for all his life.

"Where is she?" Lona fixed upon him with intensity.

"She went off into the woods."

"She's just thinking," Mags said softly as she put the biscuits on the table. "She be back soon. No fish?"

He shook his head. "I didn't stay long enough to help her and she didn't have any."

"She upset?" Lona asked.

Adam nodded his head and sat down in the awkward chain gang clothes, eager to change back to his suits. "I told her I wanted to take her away from here and marry her. She ran off."

"She thinking she don't deserve better." Lona wiped her hands on her apron. "I find her and talk to her."

"We needs to pray for our Ruby," Sister Carver intervened. "I expect she got something in her mind got a hold of her and don't want to let her go."

Sister Carver may have been a simple preacher woman, but she was right. There was a lot of wisdom in country folk. They were teaching classes at Michigan. Psychology—treating medicine of the mind. He wished he had paid closer attention to them.

"Fine. Let's pray."

"You going to pray with us?" Delie sidled up next to him on the bench. "You believing in God's word?"

He looked down at the small, heart-shaped face and all of its innocence. "Yes, Delie. I understand now, these things that have happened, me coming here, finding Ruby, getting to know her despite the way my mother died, I'm a part of something much greater than myself. God's plan. I'm not ashamed to say it."

"Praise him," Sister said. "Let us join hands. Brother?"

"You was doing good, Sister." Brother put down his biscuit and wiped his lips. Some of the girls snickered a bit. They all joined hands and prayed.

When they were done, they let go of each other's hands and the fluffy cathead biscuits were split and coated with thick gravy. But he wasn't hungry. Twenty-four hours ago, he would have jumped on the food. Now? All he could think about was the turmoil of his beloved and how he could relieve it.

He got the plate that Mags served him and started in on it, reluctantly and accepted a cup of hot coffee.

A scream from the woods echoed through the still of the summer morning. "It's Ruby."

Adam stood and on fast feet made his way to the direction of the scream at the edge of the farm where the woods began. What had caused her to react so?

He started to part the trees, calling her name, over and over. Anyone or anything that dared to harm her would have to answer to him.

The thudding fear in his chest, that was what love was. It was in his soul to be attached to another human being. He understood now. And he was not going to let it go and he would not let one more thing happen to her. She had been through enough.

A heavy weight smacked into his chest. Ruby. He pulled her into the circle of his arms and held her. "It's okay. Whatever it is. It's all right, Ruby. I'm here."

"The dirt. I was in the dirt." She sobbed into his chest and he could barely hear her.

"No, love, you're here with me. You're with me now."

The pines parted and David, with that fine sheen of sweat on his face came through. "I didn't touch her."

Adam spoke in a loud voice, but his nerves pricked his fingertips, making him want to curl his hands into fists and pummel them into his brother.

"You did something to make her upset. And you'll answer for it if you did."

"Dr. Morson, Adam, I'm telling you."

He pulled Ruby under one arm and put his body in front of hers to shield her from the sight of her rapist. "You don't look well, David. Go on home."

"I just wanted to let her know—"

"She doesn't want anything from you. Leave her alone. Come on." Ruby's petite frame shook and tears fell fast down her face as they made their way back to the Bledsoe farm.

"You can't have a dirty wife, Adam. That's why I can't say yes. I-I'm dirty."

He stopped her and put his hands on her shoulders. "I want you for me, just as you are. I love you."

"I love you too, but I just can't." He put his hand under her chin and put his lips to hers again. But she trembled still and he pulled her close to him and held her tight.

Then the idea came to him about how to make it alright. Today.

"I want to be baptized. And you must sponsor me."

"What?" Ruby wiped her tears away and looked confused.

"In the creek. Won't Brother Carver baptize me?"

"I don't know. We never done anything like that before. Usually if it isn't babies, Rev—"

"And we know he won't want to do it. Let's ask."

His request seemed to perk her up. And it perked him up too. He wanted to get into the creek to wash away the grime of the chain gang, and everything else that had been holding him back. As they went into the house, Adam said, "I want to be baptized. Ruby is going to sponsor me."

"I never said I would."

"Who else would do it? You're perfect."

"I haven't done no baptism in years." Brother Carver's round face was a puzzle. "Ain't got no robe."

"You don't need no robe, old man," Sister Jane said. "I'ma be right there to hold up the Bible for you."

"It's a fine idea."

"Only one to baptize in the creek is Reverend Dodge," Lona drew out.

"Then we should do it while Brother Carver is still here," Ruby said and the whole room turned toward her. "It's the best time. When?"

"I'm ready right now."

"Now?" Ruby asked him in a small voice.

"Now." Adam faced her. "I need you to come with me to wash all of my sins away, will you? Help me?"

The room was silent. And the first brightness appeared on her face. "I will. I will help."

"Let's go then!" Delie shouted and the room became a whirl as breakfast dishes were cleared away. "We going to the creek for a baptism party! Praise God!"

The entire room laughed, but Adam watched Ruby's face, willing her brightness to stay there with him, present and strong.

Chapter Twenty-Three

The group went into the small woods and creek behind the Bledsoe farm. They were all happy and celebrating. Ruby knew she should have gladness in her heart, but the sight of David in the woods made her want to grip something and hold it tight. Instead, she carried Solomon and kept kissing his forehead, while he happily babbled on her shoulder. The gladness bubbled inside her at seeing Adam, looking satisfied despite his prison gear that was too tight and small, and showing off his bulging muscles to a great advantage.

Her sponsor him? How was it possible?

The Bledsoes and Sister Jane lined up on the side of the small creek while Brother Carver and Adam waded in, only thigh deep for Adam. Ruby watched while kissing Solomon and holding him tightly, her hands clammy and cold.

"Ruby Jean? You got to come in."

Lona reached for Solomon and tried to take him but Ruby held on.

"I don't think I'm the right sponsor. What about Daddy?"

"He didn't ask for me, Ruby. He asked for you." John Bledsoe shook his head.

"It's chilly. I might catch cold in that creek and pass it on to the baby."

The celebratory chatter stopped and everyone looked at Ruby. She knew why. For her to say that she didn't want to be in the creek? Something was wrong.

Adam held his hand out. "Please. Come."

The kindness on his handsome features was so welcoming, Ruby nearly believed that she could be clean in that creek water. "Come on, Sister Ruby. In the creek with you."

Sister Jane took Solomon up into her sure arms. "Go on, honey."

Ruby stepped forward slowly with the small pebbles in the creek stabbing at her feet until she stood next to Adam.

"Brother Adam. Do you take up God's promise to man that to be baptized is to be washed clean in his word?"

"Say, I do," Ruby cued him.

"I do." Adam reached over and palmed her hand in his big one.

"Then in the word of God, you are born again, and are clean. Come over and be baptized anew," Brother Carver boomed out and Adam kneeled down to receive the water on his forehead, but Brother took him over backwards and he laid out in the small creek. Adam sprang up wet from head to toe, glasses still firmly in place, but laughing joyfully.

The entire bank of Bledsoes laughed and cheered at the sight. Even Ruby smiled at the creek water dripping down off of the tall doctor. He stepped over to her. "Doesn't the sponsor give a kiss at the baptism?"

"Yes," Ruby shook a little.

He reached down, quite a task for the tall doctor and kissed her on the cheek with a chaste protectiveness.

"That wasn't no real kiss!" Sister Jane shouted out and Solomon gurgled, as if he agreed with her.

"It was a sponsor kiss," Ruby shouted back, catching some of their gladness.

"And what about you?" Adam spoke into her ear.

"What do you mean?"

"You should be clean too."

"I was only here to watch you. I'm not trying to be wet." Ruby started to make her way out of the creek to the baby and Adam grabbed her by her wrist, pulling her back. She was jerked off her feet and in the creek before she knew it. The water surrounded her and she began to breathe as she knew to, under the water, where everything was distorted and felt so clear and clean.

Clean.

She popped up out of the water and cleared it from her face. "What? What was that?"

Adam's face was serious and grim. "You're washed clean too, before God, Ruby. I'm washed of my sins. So are you."

He reached down and gave her a real kiss on her lips and his sudden actions and the stones in the creek cutting at her feet threatened to sweep her away.

"What is going on here?" The sound of a different male voice broke them apart. Dodge.

"We having a baptizing party," Delie's little voice piped up in the warm July air.

"Only one to be having any baptizing parties is me. I'm the ordained minister at First Water. I does this. Not no traveling preacher men."

"Beg pardon, Brother Dodge. I been doing this before you was born, I believe," Brother Carver said with the genuine insult in his voice. It hurt Ruby to hear his hurt feelings.

"And I asked him to do it." Adam faced Dodge and put Ruby firmly next to him.

"Well, then. I don't mind telling you that it didn't take. You still a sinner in God's eyes. Even if you're clean of the dirt of the chain gang."

"Well now. It isn't for you to say who is a sinner in God's eyes," Adam shouted.

"I don't agree with you, Doctor. I am what I say. And to dip her in that old creek water. Well now. She's the one who is unclean in God's eyes."

John Bledsoe was about to speak, in a not nice way, but Lona put a hand on him. "Is there something we can help you with, Reverend? We just having a picnic on this beautiful day."

"I come by to make sure everything fine since the doctor got on the gang, but I see he got off again. Slippery fellow, isn't he?"

"You see I'm here. You can go now."

"And that's what I come to tell you all. I'm leaving. Going back to Tennessee. Where I come from."

"Good," Adam said. "Tell all the home folks I said hello, 'cause I'm never going back there."

"Not so sure you be welcome."

"I wouldn't want the woman who is to be my new wife," Adam put an arm around her shoulders, "to be uncomfortable in such a place. I've shed Tennessee for good. God's traveling mercies on you to go back there."

Brother Carver made his way back to the creek bank. "Amen to that."

Their nonchalant attitude at his leaving seemed to make Dodge even angrier. He was such a sad person, Ruby resolved as Dodge walked to his horse in a huff. Being in Adam's arms, the dip in the creek, seeing Dodge ride away, should have lifted everything from her, but it did not. As Adam helped her from the creek, she wondered—what would?

Adam knew Ruby was still thinking of the attack and how it made her unsuitable to be his wife. There was nothing he could say or do to make it right for her. He could tell her all day long about how wonderful and virtuous she was to him, and she still would feel as if she was less than deserving.

He resolved just to stay by her side in whatever way possible for strength. It was all he could do, he realized as they all sat down. Everyone laughed and smiled, but they could still see Ruby wore her shame like a garment she refused to shed. Could Lona tell her something to make her understand? Sister Jane? He didn't know. Shame was a jail. He had found his way free of it, and he could only hope she would as well.

He would never have thought it possible a month ago, but he felt better to go to revival later. He and Ruby held hands as they drove to the tent together and sat in the uplifting service. It was truly a miracle, how much these people found joy in their faith, even as they lived hard lives. Their joy in living made him feel ashamed as to how long he carried his own shame around.

At the revival that night, people were especially joyous at his return. As Brother Carver and Sister Jane took down the tempo from one joyous hymn, a shuffle stirred in the back of the tent.

He turned around and David Winslow came down the aisle. The sheen of sweat he had seen on him that morning was thicker and more pronounced. Adam longed to go to the man to help him. David staggered to the front. People might have thought he had been drinking, but Adam knew better. David was ill. He stood up and watched his brother and, as loud and joyous as the tent had been, it was quiet now.

"Brother, I—" David tripped up the aisle and stood in front of Brother Carver. "I used to come in here when I was little."

"I remembers you, sir," Brother Carver said in a sympathetic way.

"I've sinned."

"We have all sinned. That's why we are here."

Ruby's hand was on her mouth with tears streaming down her face. Adam put a hand on her shoulder to comfort her.

"Please, Brother, you don't understand."

"I understands you. You looking for God's forgiveness."

"I did wrong. I did wrong in his eyes, and I want him to know."

"He knows. He knows and forgives you." Brother Carver pressed a hand to David's shoulder, something as a Negro, he wouldn't have dared to do anywhere else. Here, in the revival tent, Brother Carver's power came from a higher source.

David fell to his knees under Brother Carver's touch. "Please, help me. I need for God to know, I'm sorry."

"Amen," Adam heard Lona say.

A wail right next to him made his spine tingle. Adam hadn't realized it, but it was Ruby. She stood next to him and wailed from right under his arm.

David wailed too, and his body folded in front of Brother Carver, who uttered words of forgiveness over and over again, blessing David. Adam folded Ruby into his arms even deeper and held her as she wept loudly and copiously. All of his attention was on comforting Ruby until Sister Jane's voice came, sharp and loud, "Something's wrong. Doctor, quick."

He handed the sobbing Ruby to her mother, where they both began sobbing together. He went to where Sister's voice had stirred him, over to David. David had folded over in supplication before, but now his body was stick straight, his eyes glassy, almost as if he were having a fit. "I need my ba—" Adam gestured over his shoulder and he imagined Delie or one of the Bledsoe sisters would bring it to him. One of them did, but it was Ruby.

"What is the matter with him?"

"He looks as if he's having a fit." Adam snapped his eyes up. "I need to get him into an open place. He needs some air."

Bob stood up. "We can take him on up to the house. Something wrong with Mr. David, Miss Mary be wanting him at home."

Bob lifted David's thin body into his arms and Adam followed him. Ruby hovered at his elbow. "You go on. I'll help treat him."

"I'll come with you," Ruby said quietly.

"Are you sure?"

"Whither you goest, I will go," Ruby quoted, so determined.

Gladness rose in his chest, but he didn't want her to feel worse about herself. "It may take a while."

"That is what a wife does, when she helps her husband." Ruby fitted her hand in the crook of his arm. "Let's go."

Had Ruby just accepted his proposal?

As he brought Ruby forward to the car, he walked with a lighter step and flexed his hands as he focused on doing what he had to do to help David.

He had a home. What a treasure it was to be able to have a home. Even in his doctor's mindset, his heart and his life had changed.

Thank you. Please be with me as I help this man—my brother.

Chapter Twenty-Four

Ruby sat up front in the car with Bob while Adam tended to David in the back. She asked in a loud voice, "What do you think is wrong with him?"

"He might have tuberculosis."

"The galloping consumption?" Ruby asked and Bob blinked his eyelids more quickly and drove up the road a little faster.

"Lawd a mercy, I can't get no TB and take it home to Agnes and the girls."

"And the baby," Ruby said to him.

"What about your baby?"

"Solomon will be fine. I got to help Adam."

"The consumption's catchy."

"I know. My place is with him now." Ruby patted Bob's arm. "It's going to be okay."

They encountered the front of the Winslow house first, but Bob, as dutiful as ever, drove around the back and prepared to carry David into the back door.

"What's wrong with him?" one of the cooks called out.

Bob called back, "Get Miss Mary and tell her Mr. David fell out at the revival."

"Praise, God. He got saved?"

"He got saved, but this is after. He sick."

They went through the kitchen into the front of the house and Bob prepared to climb the stairs with David in his arms. As Ruby came through the kitchen carrying some supplies Adam needed from his car, Mrs. Winslow screamed. She went into the parlor where Mary Winslow was and Bob had her son in his arms.

"Let them take him to his room," Ruby put a hand on Mrs. Winslow's lace-covered thin arm to stop her. As she touched the papery skin under the lace, Ruby realized it was the first time she had ever touched this important woman.

"What's going on? What're you all doing here?"

"David came to the revival tent, and he fell out. He has lost consciousness," Ruby said.

"I didn't even know he had left the house. What's wrong with him?"

"Take him upstairs," Adam directed Bob.

Mrs. Winslow sat down in Paul Winslow's big overstuffed chair.

"He hasn't gone to revival since he was little. Why did he go? He's probably caught some dreadful disease from you people."

Ruby breathed, unable to take in this woman's irrational hatred. She calmed herself and tried to think about it from Mary Winslow's perspective. What if it were Solomon?

A short time ago, it had been Solomon.

She took a breath. "Dr. Morson thinks it may be TB, the galloping consumption." Ruby nodded her head at him and he disappeared up the stairs, following Bob.

"Then he got some dread disease from going around to those camps looking for the doctor. Now he's sick. How can this happen?"

"I'm sorry, ma'am. I came with Adam to see how I could help."

Mary Winslow looked at her and gave a laugh. "You're just an ignorant colored girl. What can you do to help?"

"I can nurse him."

Mary Winslow stood up. "I'll nurse my son. And I'll send to get a real doctor in town." She gathered her skirts to prepare to go up the stairs.

Ruby stood up and matched her, toe to toe. "You can do whatever you want. The doctor can help until the other doctor gets here. And I intend to help him."

"Get out of my way. You're nothing but trouble, and have always been nothing but trouble. Get out of this house and get out of my parlor." Mrs. Winslow swept past her and went up the stairs.

Ruby sank down in the chair. She should leave as she had been told, because she did not want to cause any trouble, but she could not abandon Adam. She *would* not abandon Adam. She got on her knees and prayed.

Bob came downstairs and spoke to her in a shaky, soft halting voice at seeing her on bended knee in the parlor, like she was invited company. "Miss Mary wants me to fetch a doctor."

"Do what she say."

"Don't she see Dr. Adam is up there, working hard? He done given him something to help him wake up. He talking now."

Thank you, God.

"I guess she's concerned about her son."

Bob gave a snort. "She concerned about herself is all. I'll go send a telegram for Mr. Paul and get the doctor." He stopped and turned on his heel. "He been saying your name, over and over."

Ruby stood up. "Adam?"

Bob shook his head. "No, Mr. David. He asking for you."

Her place was next to Adam, but she hesitated, remembering Mary Winslow's words telling her to leave. Just then, Mrs. Winslow came down the steps, wringing her handkerchief. She stood over kneeling Ruby. Her breaths seemed to catch and Ruby wanted to make sure she was okay. She stood. "He wants to see you. He asked for you. Not me."

"I didn't know if I should go or not."

"By all means." Mary Winslow gestured up the stairs. "He wants you."

"I'll go, but only because he asked. I don't want to interfere."

Mrs. Winslow sat down on the davenport. "How could I deny my only son his dying wish?"

Ruby's heart beat faster, and she eased herself onto the davenport next to the woman. "You think he's dying?"

"He told me so. Just now," Mrs. Winslow voice was steady and calm.

"Have you prayed, ma'am?"

"Prayer? What for?"

"To help him." Ruby took her hands in hers, touching her for a second time. "To help you. Let's pray together. God, please, look out for David. Please, help him to be well. Help him to receive your healing power."

"And, if he cannot be well, take him into your loving arms," Mary Winslow choked out. "Go to him, Ruby."

Ruby rose and went upstairs, turned right and went down the hall. She had known where to go because of all of those Saturdays when she would help Lona bring the clean laundry back to the Winslows and put fresh sheets on David's bed.

When she stood in the doorway of his room, the room looked the same as when he was young, except all of David's spinning tops were gone, replaced with tennis rackets. He must really like tennis. Adam and David turned towards her as she emerged in the doorway. "Ruby." David reached out his hand. "Come here."

His voice was strong. Mary Winslow had been mistaken. Even so, her heart raced, and threatened to explode inside of her.

Please, God, give me courage. Ruby moved closer to the bed where he was resting. "I can leave." Adam's mouth pressed into a thin line.

"No, I want you to hear. It's about you too." David took in a labored and ragged breath.

Adam's mouth relaxed a bit and she was glad to see it. He said, "Fine, but don't expend all of your energy."

"I don't have much time," David insisted, "and I have to tell her." He turned to Ruby. "I'm so very sorry. That's what I want to say to you. I'm sorry for what I did. My life has been made empty, meaningless, over this year because of it."

Ruby closed her eyes and moaned. What was he saying? Why was he telling her this now? "I don't understand."

"I wronged you."

Ruby opened her eyes and looked over at Adam. His handsome features reflected strong disapproval of David, or his confession, she didn't know which. "I don't know what you mean."

"You do. I took terrible advantage of you. Ever since it happened, my heart. I mean who I am. I've been lost. And I stayed up here in the house, not wanting to listen to what the cooks said in the kitchen about you, that you were having a baby. Or when I first came and the baby was here. I wanted to come and say something to you, to help. I just didn't know how. Forgive me."

"Forgive you?" Ruby croaked out. She had not expected him to ask for forgiveness.

"Yes." David laid his hand on his chest. Ruby glanced over at Adam and the thin line of tension in his beautiful lips was still there.

"I'm so sorry. That's what I wanted to say." David Winslow's eyes were fixed on her, waiting.

What she wanted to hear. The words seemed so small and piddling, yet, the weight of them was heavy on her shoulders. She was overwhelmed by them. He had put it all on her, in this moment, to let it all go and be free of it. She didn't know what to say.

"I can't. I don't know," Ruby whispered her uncertainty. What was the matter with her? Why couldn't she say it? Here he was, her childhood best friend, the one she splashed into the creek with, played in the mud with, played house with, and ultimately had a beautiful little boy with. David was sorry. He tried to fix it by helping with Solomon and helping Adam. Now he was dying. She would never see him again, and never talk to him again. Solomon would not know his father. Ever. The thought melted the hard icicle in her heart.

"Please think about it, Ruby. Please."

"Ok."

David fixed his empty eyes on both of them. "Please, take care of each other. And Solomon."

It was the first time the name of their son had come from his lips. David struggled to reach his hand toward his nightstand. "Save your energy," Adam admonished him.

"There's something," David's speech came halting.

"Yes?" Ruby said.

"Here in the drawer." David pointed with a weak hand. "There's a letter about his future. I wrote it a while ago. He'll want for nothing. I want you to use everything I would have gotten to help him. If it means sending him away to a school where they don't know who he is, there'll be money for him."

Adam squeezed Ruby to him and said in a firm voice that caused her to turn around and look up at him. "We'll help him to be proud of who he is. Thank you."

When had Adam become Frederick Douglass? A rush of warmth stirred in her limbs. *Thank you, God.*

"I'm tired." David closed his eyes.

"Rest then," Adam directed. "Your mother's doctor will be here soon."

"I don't want another doctor. I don't want to be here anymore," David's eyes slid away into the back of his head.

"Life is a gift, David." Ruby insisted. "A precious gift from God. Don't throw it away."

David opened his eyes to look at her. "I have already thrown away so much. It seems foolish to hope you would overlook my sins."

"Don't worry about what I say. God forgives. You just have to ask him."

"I know I'll pay for what I've done."

Adam squeezed her shoulders and they stepped away from the bed together. They moved to the small loveseat couch in the first part of David's large bedroom. "Let's rest here. We can stay with him while he sleeps."

"Yes, you and me." Ruby rested her head on his shoulder and they sat on the couch together to watch over David as he rested in the bed, with the possibility of forgiveness in the air. It was all on her to let it go.

The town doctor insisted nothing else could be done for David. "He doesn't want to be here," he told Mary Winslow in a no-nonsense way. "The best to be done for him has already been done. He's comfortable. He may hold on until his father gets here—he may not." He put a hand on her arm. "I'm sorry, Mrs. Winslow."

He ushered Mary Winslow out of the room and Ruby and Adam kept watch. Ruby napped on and off throughout the night. At some point, Adam rose and went to the bed. She shook the sleep from her eyes and moved to join him with jerky movements.

"Ruby, please," David rasped out grabbing her fingers with a familiar fierce strength. A trickle of sweat slid down her neck.

She swallowed. "God bless you, David."

"Say the words, Ruby, please. I am so so sorry." Tears bathed his face.

"I can't forget what you did. Solomon is there every day of my life."

"I know, but, just please...."

Just to keep him quiet. She would say the words. "I forgive you."

At the three little words, a light went out of his face. Ruby covered her mouth with her fingertips, cutting off a startled cry.

By speaking the words, she was free. Painful tears pricked from behind her eyes and rolled down her face. Adam came around the side of the bed and held her to him. His warmth and closeness were next to her heart because the weight was gone from her shoulders.

Adam listened for his breathing and touched David's face. The July sun shone through the curtains in the room with an extra fierce intensity. "He's gone." Adam pulled the bed sheet over his face.

"Just a second." Ruby stayed his hand. Her former childhood playmate. Her former best friend. Her attacker. Solomon's father. Adam grasped her hand and their fingers interlaced.

"You are free to live your life as you want to."

"With you."

"Always."

"Thank you." Ruby had never felt such gratitude.

Adam kissed her on the forehead. Then, together, they moved the sheet over David's face.

"I have to go tell Mrs. Winslow," Ruby said, hurt. What if Solomon had died? It seemed hard to imagine moving her lips to tell another woman her son was dead.

"I'm the doctor of record," Adam said. "We'll go together."

"Together." Ruby repeated and they walked to the doorway, hand in hand. Suddenly, the front door slammed and loud steps echoed up the stairs.

"Mr. Winslow is here," Ruby said.

Adam stepped ahead of her to the stairs, ready to tell his father that his son, his youngest son, was dead.

Everyone had always known the Winslows had no feelings. This had been a bonding principle between she and David when they were younger. He liked to come over to the Bledsoes because at least there was love in the house. He said the food tasted better too. Of course, the Bledsoes knew Claudia, the woman who was then head cook at the Winslows, would be offended but they resolved never to tell her. Lona would just smile and take in the praise of young David. Only when David was gone, only when he had departed the earth was when the Winslows could finally show emotion and feelings about their loss.

But when Adam drove her back to the farm, she never thought she would get the sound of Mary Winslow's keening out of her mind. Then she cried, only feeling genuine sorrow at the death of Solomon's father and genuine empathy for Mary Winslow.

As she came down the stairs with Adam, she wanted nothing more than to hold Solomon in her arms. It was hard to sit there in the parlor, while Adam did his job as a physician, finishing up some paper work and beginning the process of issuing David's death certificate. He would finish it up later when he had an opportunity to further question the Winslows.

Adam's eyes gazed on the Winslow family Bible on the Bible stand and opened it. He carefully wrote in the date of death for David and closed it. All that was left of the Winslow line to go forward, after Adam was Solomon.

Adam opened the Bible again and wrote in Ruby's name and her birthday. September 1, 1896. "What's Solomon's birthday?"

"January 16, 1915."

Adam wrote it in. He closed the book again. He cut his eyes upstairs. Then, he opened the book again. "What are you doing now?" Ruby dabbed at her eyes with a handkerchief.

Adam set his jaw. "I'm putting myself in this Bible. I belong here."

Now, he was his father's only son. This was the Winslow Bible and he belonged in it. Ruby stood and came next to him, her thoughts fuzzy. "Goodness."

"I have to own all parts of who I am. If I own the Negro part of me, I have to own the white Winslow part too, and not be ashamed of it."

Ruby nodded. "I understand."

He squeezed her hand on his shoulder and she watched as he wrote in, on another line, his mother's name: Matilda Anne Morson.

"Her name was Matilda?"

Adam nodded and Ruby said, "I like that. For a little girl."

Adam gave her hand another squeeze as he wrote in, "Adam Johnson Morson, born May 14, 1890." He closed the Bible and put it back on the special stand where it stayed. "Let's go." He held out a hand to her as they walked out of the parlor then out of the front door together, arm in arm, to leave the Winslows to grieve on their own.

Chapter Twenty-Five

"Once you get the paper, you can get married as soon as you want," Brother Carver told them. So the next morning was a bustle of activity. Adam and Ruby went to the courthouse to get a marriage license so they could marry before the Carvers left town.

Lona bemoaned the fact they could not have a real ceremony. Ruby wanted to laugh at Lona for caring so much—her mother had wanted to see her married off for so long, now it had to be done with ceremony. "I don't really care," Ruby said. "I just want to be married here at home with family. No one else really matters. Now that Dodge is gone from First Water I don't have a minister. When we go to our new home, we'll find a church home to nurture us. I'm happy the Carvers are here. They've known me since I was a little girl, and that's who I want."

"Bless you, child, we're glad to be here." Sister Jane beamed.

"And," Brother pushed away from the table. "We got to get ready now if we are going to marry these children this afternoon."

"We got lots of decorating to do," Delie said. Ruby gave Solomon another kiss on his forehead and handed him to John. "We'll be back as soon as we can."

Adam put an arm around Ruby's shoulder. "I don't expect there will much trouble. Once we tell them we're leaving town, they will be happy to see us married. We'll go past the Winslows to finish some of the details on the death certificate and we'll be back."

When they arrived at the courthouse, the clerk gave them suspicious glances. However, the clerk made mention of Adam's connection with Paul

Winslow, and he gave his condolences. Even though the offices were in the same building, they did not see the sheriff and wanted to depart as fast as possible once they had the license in hand. When they pulled up in front of the Winslow house, it looked quiet and abandoned. "Want to come in with me?"

Ruby didn't want to. She didn't want this house of death to intrude on her wedding day. She shook her head. "He'll be in the parlor."

"All the more reason to get it over with."

Ruby came out of the car. They climbed the steps together and knocked on the door. The front door. Lavinia, the head maid, opened the door and let them in. She embraced Ruby. "I wish you joy. Be happy. You deserve it."

"Thank you. How are they?"

"They taking it real hard." Lavinia walked with them into the parlor where the casket was set up. "They haven't gone to sleep. They upstairs now. It's real hard."

"When will they bury him?"

"Day after tomorrow. Some of Mr. Paul's people is coming in from Tennessee." She looked at Adam. "You aren't staying?"

Adam squeezed Ruby's hand and spoke, "We hope to leave tomorrow. It's for the best."

"You all are all he have left. Colored, white, whatever, you're it. I don't know."

Ruby patted her arm as she looked down at David, appearing small and forlorn in his casket. "We just don't want to cause any more trouble." The Winslow family Bible was gone from the stand. Adam moved some papers on the desk and saw the death certificate. "He has filled in more of what I needed, so it's good."

Adam came and stood next to her then looked down at his brother. "He looks peaceful," Ruby said.

"It's hard for me as a doctor to come and see my patients deceased—we work so hard to keep them alive. It's really hard. However, he was more than my patient. He was my liberator, and my brother. I have to pay my respects."

There was a slight movement in the doorway and Paul Winslow stood there. He had aged fifteen years in the past day. Ruby did not think it was possible to appear so burdened and crushed in such a short amount of time, but he did. Then again, if she had lost Solomon, she could see how overwhelming his loss would be to her, even though he was born under difficult circumstances. Her son was her heart. What would it feel like if your heart was gone all of a sudden?

Ruby stepped over to him. "I'm so sorry for your loss, sir, if I didn't say it yesterday."

"Thank you."

Adam came and stood next to her. "I also want to extend my condolences."

"I hear you all are getting married."

"Yes, sir."

"When?"

"Today." Adam put an arm around Ruby's waist.

"Goodness."

"Her speed cannot surprise you, Paul. This one is a fast worker." They heard Mary Winslow talking and she stepped forward from the shadows. Her grey hair cascaded down around her shoulders and she clutched the big, heavy family Bible to her chest. "She's probably the one who desecrated our family Bible by putting all of their colored names in it."

"Ma'am." Ruby put her arm in the crook of Adam's elbow. She liked her hand there. "I didn't."

"I did it," Adam said quickly, over her. "I just thought it felt right to include at a time of such incredible loss."

"You." Mary pointed a finger out to Adam. "Are not my son. You're my husband's by blow with some harlot maid, and I don't have to have you in the Bible. I cannot tear these pages from God's word, but by his holy name, I'll figure out some way to get your name out of there."

Adam stepped back a bit, clearly shocked at Mrs. Winslow's words and Ruby put her hand on his arm. "We didn't mean to cause trouble. Adam wanted to finish some paper work and now he's done, we'll leave."

"Yes, get out. I would throw this Bible after you if it weren't the holy word of God, not that you godless people know anything about it."

Paul Winslow took them toward the front door. "Thank you for coming by."

Almost instantly, they found themselves outside with the door shut behind them. "I think she's been drinking some," Ruby put in when she realized they'd been let out the front door.

"Yes, I smelled it on her breath." Adam adjusted his hat on his head and offered Ruby his arm. "I'll not condemn her."

"Let's go."

"To our wedding." Adam smiled down at her and squeezed her hand.

That afternoon the family gathered in the big front room to witness Brother Carver marry Ruby and Adam. In an amazingly short amount of time, Ruby became Ruby Morson. After Brother Carver pronounced them man and wife, Adam leaned down to kiss her. As he kissed her with all of his heart and soul, the bond between them melded. Finally, he'd gotten what he had come to Winslow for.

A family. What a wonderful thing it was, to finally be on the receiving end of the very thing he had always wanted.

Lona set up a wonderful picnic outside and they all feasted on chicken, vegetables, fresh peaches, bread and cake. He and Ruby fed one another pieces of cake. They sat on a blanket, laughing at some of Ruby's sisters playing tag through the orchard when, off to the side, a Winslow car pulled up.

"It's Paul Winslow." Adam stood and rolled his sleeves down his arms. "I'll go see what he wants."

"Do you want me to come?" Ruby held his hand.

Adam squeezed her dainty steel-strong hand and let go. "No, my love. You stay here. If he needs medical help, I'll be back soon."

"Okay."

Adam clipped his sleeves together at his wrists for a more formal appearance. "Sir." He walked to his father who stood at the Bledsoe's front gate. "Is there something I can help you with? Is Mrs. Winslow all right?"

Paul Winslow waved a hand. "She's resting now. I know she's sorry for what she said earlier, but she's not in her right mind, you know."

"I understand."

"You all married?"

"Yes, sir. About an hour ago."

Paul Winslow looked down at the ground. "Congratulations. I'm sorry I couldn't make it."

The callowness of his thoughtlessness hit him full on. Adam should have invited him. Paul Winslow was his father. He would never have a chance to see a child of his marry, ever again.

"It all happened pretty fast. Ruby wanted Brother Carver to perform the ceremony before they left today," he rambled on, but he did not know what else to say.

"I understand."

Adam stopped talking. Paul Winslow apologized for so much in those two words.

"Where are you all staying for the night?" he asked Adam.

"Since the Carvers are leaving today, the guest room in the back will be vacant again, so we'll stay there until we leave."

"Leaving for the north?"

"Yes, sir. I've taken a job up there as a doctor in one of the steel mills in Pittsburgh. We leave tomorrow morning. I'm going to take Ruby and Solomon where they can get a new start in life."

Silence fell between them.

"Before I got here I went to Bouganse up in town. Got the honeymoon suite for you if you like. They won't give you any trouble if you go there."

"Are you sure, sir?"

"You can't spend your wedding night with her parents." Paul Winslow gave a sad little smile.

Adam smiled back at him, touched by this singular gesture of thoughtfulness. "Thank you."

"You're welcome. I came to give you a wedding present." He opened his jacket and retrieved an envelope in the fold. "For you. And Solomon. He'll want for nothing his life long. I just made the adjustments to my will. And for you. A start. I want to provide for Solomon so he won't have to suffer the slings and arrows of his race."

"I appreciate it, sir, and I'll tell Ruby. But, from my perspective, a little bit of suffering has helped me to come to an understanding. I know who I am. I'll hope the same for him, and he'll be proud of who he is."

Paul Winslow pressed the envelope on him. "All well and good. But money always helps."

Adam took the envelope into his hand. Such an empty gesture. But it was all Paul Winslow had to give. When they got to Pittsburgh, he would make sure Solomon had an account for his education.

"Thank you," Adam said.

Another silence. Was there more? What could it be? Finally, his father cleared his throat and spoke.

"Are you sure you don't want to stay and attend the funeral? Some more Winslows—my sister and her family are coming," He cleared his throat again. "She knew Mattie and would probably like to meet you."

The mention of his mother's name tugged at his heart, but not nearly in the same way it used to. When he had first come to Georgia, he was searching, yearning for just this type of connection. An aunt who had known his mother, someone who could fill in the details of who his mother was.

But that was a couple of weeks ago. He had changed.

Intrigued, but now more intrigued with the future God had provided him with Ruby. His life had a bigger scope and more focus. He belonged on the train with Ruby and Solomon, starting their new lives together.

Strange, but the yearning that had been in him when he first arrived was in Paul Winslow's eyes now. Knowing how the yearning felt, Adam registered a pain in his heart for his father and he wanted to let this man down, easily. "I'll talk to Ruby about it and see what she thinks. But it would be awkward to have her come, given how Mrs. Winslow feels about her."

"Oh no, no, I'll take care of it. Ruby'll be treated just fine. Please."

"I haven't been married long, sir, but the sense I get about the situation is the wife must be happy. If Mrs. Winslow isn't happy with Ruby being there, I don't know if you or anyone else can say anything to make her happy."

The yearning light went out of Paul Winslow's eyes, and the aged look came onto his face again. "You're right. I probably should do what I can to make her happy now."

"Yes, sir. We'll be fine."

Paul Winslow's gray eyes edged in red and were full of sorrow. "Maybe you all can write sometime. Take yourselves to a picture studio and have a picture made and send it down. If you need anymore money for a portrait." He reached into the fold of his jacket again, but a hand in the air from Adam stopped him.

"I'm sure you have been generous enough, sir." He held up the envelope.

"Well, I better get on home." Paul Winslow stuck out a hand and Adam shook it for the first, and probably the last time.

"You all take care, now."

"We will, sir. And thank you."

Adam watched him depart in the car, driven by the loyal and faithful Bob. He closed his eyes in reassurance as Ruby's presence lighted next to him. She slid her hand in the crook of his elbow and he grasped it. There was strength. And love. And a home. "I sensed you needed some time alone with him."

"And your feeling was perfect. Thank you, my love." He bent down to kiss her soft lips, relishing the way they melded with his. He was reminded of the generosity of Paul Winslow's gift. "He wanted to give us a wedding gift."

"He did?" Ruby's brown eyes were wide.

"We're going to the hotel tonight."

"The Bouganse? Where I stopped you from going?"

"The very one. He arranged it. We'll drop the Carvers off at the train station and then go there for our wedding night. We'll be the first Negroes to stay there, no stories."

His new wife's mouth was slightly parted. "Don't you believe him?"

Ruby shook her head. "Yes. One thing you learn growing up in Winslow is Paul Winslow's word is bond. I believe him. I'm just stunned. So thoughtful. I had wondered about how comfortable we would be in the guest room together, having to keep Solomon out front with his aunties. He came up with the perfect solution."

"He also let me know he wants to provide for Solomon. And me. He made changes to his will. He had just come from town seeing his attorney."

"I just didn't think he would be so thoughtful. The hotel, well, that was enough. I didn't really want his money for Solomon. But that was what David's letter said."

"I know." Adam turned her around to walk her back to her family. "We'll talk about it. And the way to think of it may be the amount might be better used in the form of a restitution to you."

"Restitution?"

"Yes. Paul Winslow has, in effect, paid you for what he did to you, through David."

"I wouldn't want his money."

"You want to finish school, and go to nursing school. In order for you to do those things, we would want to make sure we had a nice house, maybe some help. I've been in touch with the main Negro church in Pittsburgh where they can let us know where to live and who to hire. The money could pay for those things. To make your life easier."

His words were getting through to her. "My, I never thought I would end up with those things—an education, help? Me?"

She stopped walking and turned to him. "All I needed was love."

Adam spanned his hands on her small waist and bent down to kiss her. "And you have love, Mrs. Morson."

"And I thank God for it. Every day." Ruby reached up and wrapped her arms around his neck and they really did kiss this time. The happy cheers and applause of their family sounded in the distance.

Leaving his life in God's hands had led him to his heart's desire. When he touched the soft black hair of his Ruby, it was hard to imagine anything better than the here and now with Ruby and their beautiful son.

Maybe there would be other children, and the notion thrilled him all over again. There was always more room for love. God made love possible, and it delighted him so much to know all about it.

Author's Note

The infamous movie, *The Birth of a Nation*, is now one hundred years old. Still it usually took a longer time for such an eventful cinematic movie to be shown in a small town. It wouldn't have shown in Calhoun until later, as in 1916. *The Birth of a Nation* was quite an event, but I needed that movie so that Adam could see Ruby's frustration at the racial portrayals in it. I appreciate your indulgence.

Several texts inspired me to write this story. I had always wondered what would happen if Thomas Hardy's *Tess of the D'Urbervilles* met up with James Weldon Johnson's *The Autobiography of an Ex-Colored Man*. In the pages of *A Virtuous Ruby*, it was fun and satisfying for me to imagine a happier ending for my characters than Hardy or Johnson did.

Some of the books that helped me were:

One Drop by Bliss Broyard

Plum Bun by Jessie Fauset

A Chosen Exile by Allyson Hobbes

At the Dark End of the Street by Danielle McGuire

Passing Strange by Martha Sandweiss

The Warmth of Other Suns by Isabelle Wilkerson

About the Author

Piper G Huguley, named the 2015 Debut Author of the year by Romance Slam Jam, is a two-time Golden Heart® finalist and the author of "Migrations of the Heart," a five-book series of inspirational historical romances set in the early 20th century featuring African American characters. Book one in the series, *A Virtuous Ruby*, won the Golden Rose contest in Historical Romance in 2013 and was a Golden Heart® finalist in 2014. Book four, *A Champion's Heart*, was a Golden Heart® finalist in 2013. Huguley is also the author of the "Home to Milford College" series. The series follows the building of a college from its founding in 1866. On release, the prequel novella to the "Home to Milford College" series, *The Lawyer's Luck*, reached #1 Amazon Bestseller status on the African American Christian Fiction charts.

Piper blogs about the history behind her novels at www.piperhuguley.com. She lives in Atlanta, Georgia with her husband and son.

It's all about the story...

Romance

HORROR

www.samhainpublishing.com

CPSIA information can be obtained at www.ICGtesting.com
Printed in the USA
BVOW08s0459160715

408900BV00002B/62/P